On Bur Oak Ridge

Sheltering Trees: Book Three

Jenny Knipfer

Other books by Jenny

BY THE LIGHT OF THE MOON SERIES:
Ruby Moon
Blue Moon
Silver Moon
Harvest Moon

SHELTERING TREES SERIES:
In a Grove of Maples
Under the Weeping Willow
Coming in 2022
By Broken Birch Bay

BOTANICAL SEASONS NOVELLA SERIES:
Holly's Homecoming
Violet's Vow
Coming in late 2022 – early 2023
Daisy's Determination
Marigold's Muse

Praise for the
By the Light of the Moon series

Ruby Moon

"This novel is filled with drama and a writing style that is insightful. From the beginning, the author creates a sense of mystery, capturing sensations in a style that defies perception." Readers' Favorite, five-star review

"Knipfer's characterization is stellar in this novel, and she skillfully ties in the themes of faith, forgiveness, and trust." Wisconsin Writers Association

"Ruby Moon is the type of book that hooks you from page one… and has you quickly turning the pages to discover more." Ya It's Lit Blog

"The prose is just beautiful with a lyricism that ebbs and flows perfectly. I love a story that sounds to me like a song." Jypsy Lynn

"Jenny is a talented wordsmith who knows how to be creative and brazen with her thoughts and think outside of the box. I adore how Jenny took risks with Ruby Moon *and decided to put a twist on a much-loved genre…"* The Red Headed Book Lover

"It does not always happen but when it does it feels miraculous. I'm talking about when you read a book and you are immersed in it. I started to read the first page… and when I got to the last page, I closed the book and held it to my heart." Linda McCutcheon, book blogger and reviewer

Blue Moon

"Knipfer creates a strong sense of place, and she draws on her own experience with MS to depict the course of Valerie's illness with great sensitivity." Wisconsin Writers Association

"Blue Moon continues a well-written and highly engaging saga of family ties, betrayals, and heartaches. A must-read for historical drama fans everywhere." Readers' Favorite, five-star review

"In Blue Moon, *the author tells a breathtaking story of twins Vanessa and Valerie. Page after page, the author masterfully weaves other exciting characters into the story..."* Ksenia Sein, author of *Agape & Ares*

"Knipfer continues to welcome her readers into Webaashi Bay... back into the town and characters we fell in love with... For in this book, Knipfer has woven an entrancing tale we all need to hear." Amazon reviewer

Silver Moon

"Silver Moon is a highly recommended read for fans of historical wartime fiction, powerful emotive drama, and excellent atmospheric writing." Readers' Favorite, five-star review

"I am stunned by the amount of detail the author gave in this single story. On one hand, we have powerful characters... and on the other, we have a plot that demands all our attention. Jenny Knipfer pulls no punches and holds nothing back." Readers' Favorite, five-star review

"This story felt comfortable for a first-time reader to the author, more like being welcomed by new friends. The setting, a time of need, camaraderie and survival, brings the large cast and reader together. Ultimately, Silver Moon *is a story of forgiveness, second chances, prayer and patience."* Wisconsin Writers Association

*"*Silver Moon *is very highly recommended for readers who want a compelling inspection of love, duty, and battle based on historical fact, but flavored with the struggles of very different characters intent on not just surviving but creating a better future for themselves."* D. Donovan, Midwest Book Review

"Taking an original angle on a tumultuous time in history, Silver Moon *by Jenny Knipfer is a sparkling slice of historical fiction. Rather than focusing solely on the violence of this tragic conflict, Knipfer fleshes out the complexity of wartime… a thought-provoking and surprising work of historical escapism."* Self-Publishing Review

"Not a light-hearted read, this book will engulf your senses, evoking the deepest and highest of emotions as you cheer and cry for the survival of dearly loved characters." Kathryn V. Goodreads review

Harvest Moon

"As in her prior books, Jenny Knipfer does an outstanding job of cementing place, time, and culture against the backdrop of evolving relationships. These approaches lend a solid feel of authenticity and attraction to her plot to keep readers both educated and engrossed, as spiritual and social matters evolve." D. Donovan, Midwest Book Review

"Wielding descriptive language and unexpected imagery, this narrative transports a reader with ease. Harvest Moon *is a moving, authentic, and original work of historical fiction, while this series is a testament to Knipfer's skilled and versatile storytelling."* Self-Publishing Review

*"*Harvest Moon *by Jenny Knipfer is one of the best books I have read in 2020. In fact, it is probably one of the best historical fiction novels I have ever read. I have come away deep in thought, feeling somewhat like I've had a mystical experience and one I will never forget."* Viga Boland, Readers' Favorite, five-star review

"The author created the perfect atmosphere for her story to truly bloom and progress. I would highly recommend this historical fiction novel to anyone who loves reading stories with intricate plots and powerful characters." Rabina Tanveer, Readers' Favorite, five-star review

"Knipfer creates her characters with so much emotion and physical presence that they become almost real in the imagination. A captivating and evocative novel of the importance of family, faith, and forgiveness and how, together, those things help heal a broken heart." Gloria Bartel, Wisconsin Writers Association

Praise for the *Sheltering Trees* series

In a Grove of Maples

"A heartfelt tale of the struggles of married life on a nineteenth-century farm. Edward and Beryl are both relatable and sympathetic. Knipfer expertly captures the emotion and stress of their lives and relationship. It's a touching and realistic portrayal of love, loss, and friendship." Heather Stockard, Readers' Favorite, five-star review

"Dramatic character development and lavish descriptive language make Knipfer's prose shine and carry this emotionally stirring plot from start to finish. The storytelling is casual but unmistakably aged, and the research into this particular time period is remarkable, while the variation in narrative format keeps the story engaging throughout." Self-Publishing Review

"An engrossing story of 19th century rural life that examines matters of heart, ethics, morality, and belief as Beryl faces a new world with few resources other than her faith and love. It concludes with an unexpected twist that comes full circle to leave the door open for more." D. Donavon, Midwest Book Review

Under the Weeping Willow

"*This time-split novel captured my heart and didn't release it until the final page. Beautiful and haunting, Robin and Enid's story swept me to another era. These characters lived, and I loved watching them find their way to each other. Keep the tissues handy. You don't want to miss this story!*" Candace West, Selah award finalist and author of the *Valley Creek Redemption* series

"*A gorgeous storyteller, Jenny Knipfer has the gift of blending strong imagery with vivid emotions to capture readers' hearts in this spellbinding story.*" Christian Sia, Readers' Favorite, five-star review

"*Fans of Christian literature and women's fiction will adore Knipfer's work. It is passionate, steadily paced, and filled with intense, emotional moments. The prose is exquisite; the descriptions are terrific; the setting well-written to feel like part of the reader's world.*" Divine Zape, Readers' Favorite, five-star review

"*A sensitive and well-crafted drama unpacking issues of mental health, layers of grief, societal expectations, and the instability of memory, this novel is touching on the surface, but subtly and profoundly layered with meaning.*" Self-Publishing Review, five-star review

"*You don't have to be a fan of Christian historical fiction or family dramas to like this novel. Knipfer has created a story that crosses many genres and will appeal to those who love poignant epics about complex characters, engrossing plots, relatable situations, and a satisfying ending.*" Tammy Ruggles, Readers' Favorite, five-star review

Praise for the *Botanical Seasons* novella series

Holly's Homecoming

"*Knipfer weaves a historical novella that offers twists and turns you'll never see coming, only to tie up this lovely holiday tale with a bright red bow. As always, the prose is nearly poetic —Knipfer's great skill, and it makes reading a delight. The characters are well thought out and not simple cut-outs — a difficult feat considering this is a novella and not a full-length historical.*" Jenny Cary, author of the inspirational series: *Relentless, The Crockett Chronicles*, and *The Weather Girls*

"*A perfect short historical read for the busy season. Author Jenny Knipfer delivers a warm and festive story with a twist of mystery. I adored the ambience! Readers looking for their next favorite holiday novella will not want to miss* Holly's Homecoming.*"* Naomi Musch, author of fifteen novels including Selah and Book-of-the-Year finalist *Mist O'er the Voyageur*, the sequel *Song for the Hunter*, and the *Lumberjacks and Ladies* novella collection.

Violet's Vow

"*Author Jenny Knipfer made the 1890s come alive; the characters all seem real and the plot so believable. It is a must-read for all romantics, Victorian-era historical fiction lovers, and anyone who just enjoys a good book!*" five-star review, by Trudi LoPreto for Readers' Favorite

A voice said, 'Look me in the stars and tell me truly, men of earth,
'If all the soul and body scars were not too much to pay for birth.'

Robert Frost

For all those who have lived with scars.

From the song "The Rosary"
by Robert Cameron Rogers

CHAPTER ONE

Molly

September 1919

We're better at looking back than forward. Since such is the case, our eyes would be better placed at the base of our heads. I see nothing when I gaze into the future. It appears like the purple haze of the distant hills—without definition, lacking firm, clean, and distinctive lines. In a word—smudged.

The ironic truth is that "smudged" could explain my appearance. Life has taken an eraser to the right side of my face. Melted, waxy patches of pink skin shine in the lamplight from my temple to my neck. The skin around my right eye hides the small world of greenish-blue color—the window to my soul.

I know what people see through this broken window—a monster. I tilt my head and run the tips of my fingers over the corded texture of my skin. From this viewpoint, I could play the part of Dr. Frankenstein's creation. My fingers explore lower until they reach the hollow of my neck, where the music once lived. But no longer. The notes have died. I sigh, reliving a memory of grief for what I've lost.

My hand falls. With the stare of the dead, I look back at myself in the cracked bureau mirror. A crack in the glass runs diagonally across my face from temple to jaw, bringing a visual division to my deformity. I puff out air from my nostrils with a resignation I am getting used to. Bit by bit I've buried who I used to be. That grave leaves me uncertain of who I will become.

What is left for me? Next to nothing. I have the flowers and little else.

You've made friends, my conscience tells me. Yes, I have. I should be grateful instead of mourning the past.

For the first time in years, I will leave behind the walls of my strange shelter: the asylum. Tomorrow I board a train to visit Mabel, my friend. I'll wear a mourning veil in public, so people won't gawk or reel back in revulsion at the naked sight of my face. I grieve the worst when the children cry; then I become a nightmare to some poor little soul. I hate that: adding to another's fear. We all bear enough.

My lungs command a deep breath, and I reach to turn down the lamp. The future comes tomorrow whether I am ready or not.

"Ready or not!" The words stab me in the throat, and I feel as if I'm being basted with a sharp needle. Those were Lonny's last words. My eyes roll shut, and I see the flash of white, the brown, curly head, the grin before he turned, the crash of the poles, like the blast of a mighty horn. I wanted to scream, but my voice caught in my throat, choking me. My mouth hung open, but all that came out was silence.

I breathe, in and out slowly, like the doctor taught me. The visions recede.

My eyes open. The room has been thrown under a dark caul, and I realize I must have turned down the wick of the kerosene lamp. Now my face looks ghostly in the slightly spotted, silver-backed glass. I move to the bed, jump in, and tuck the covers up to my chin, praying I won't dream of Lonny.

Please, God. Not tonight.

The next evening
Pleasant View, Minnesota

I draw back the edge of the muslin curtains at the kitchen window of the Nelson farm, peering out at the barn, trying to catch a glimpse of the tall, lanky man Mabel and Lincoln have employed as a farmhand—a Mr. Woodson, Mabel told me.

"Does your hired help usually eat with you?" I ask Mabel.

I hope not.

I let the curtain drop and turn to the young woman who has fast become my friend. Our initial connection was her sister, Robin, whom I met at the asylum and became close to.

Mabel spills out a giggle. "Of course, Samuel eats with us. He can't very well cook his supper in the hayloft, now, can he, Molly?" She flashes her dark eyes at me. "Here. You put the silverware on."

She hands me a clutch of forks, spoons, and knives.

I accept them. "Very well."

Placing the utensils on the napkins by the Blue-Willow-patterned plates, I round the table, pondering my good fortune. It gladdens my heart to be here with Mabel. Thankfully, the journey here went better than expected: no gawkers, screamers, or fainters.

Despite Mabel's reassurance about how her husband would react to my disfigurement, I worried, but I needn't have. Lincoln Nelson, a man of average height and build but above average character, did not appear fazed at all. When Mabel introduced us, he held my gaze directly; his green eyes didn't roam around my scarred facial features at a loss for where to settle. I liked him immediately.

However, the thought of yet another person to sit across the table from—and an attractive man my own age, at that—makes the moths in my stomach flutter to get out. My mother always said that the term "having butterflies in your stomach" was wrong. *"Butterflies are too beautiful a creature to be flapping around on the inside of you. Now moths, on the other hand, I can see."*

It's been years since I've seen Jacob, my husband. The rascal abandoned me after the accident. Whether he's alive or dead, I do not know. Nor do I care. To me he is dead, and that's what I've told people, those who've gotten close enough to me to ask. The things I once missed about him—his laugh, rakish good looks, and good-natured teasing—I pine for no longer. The memory of his arms around me once whispered to me, but I am almost deaf to it now.

Fortune shines on Mabel to have the care of a trustworthy man like Lincoln. I watch as she puts cranberry-colored glasses at each place setting; they seem a little too fancy for a country dinner and sparkle under the simple, lit, candle chandelier. The shade of the glass matches her drop-waist, poplin dress. Pleats at the bottom fan out as she moves around the oak dining table and matching chairs with oak-leaf carvings on the backrest. She wears her dark, wavy hair tucked up in a loose roll at the base of her head. Ringlets fringe and curl around her smooth, China-doll face. If Mabel wasn't such a sweet person, I'd be jealous of her lovely features. But I can't be, for I could never match her inward beauty. I'm far too strong-willed.

She winks at me as she sets the last glass down and says with a smirk, "He doesn't bite, you know. In fact, he's almost as shy as you."

I can hardly imagine.

"It will be a quiet meal then."

I smile to soften my little jab; the skin on my face tightens. Smiling never used to be painful, but now it is, even after five years. I can hardly believe it's been that long since the accident.

Mabel places her hand lightly on my forearm. "And that will be perfectly fine."

We share a smile.

"Thank you again for inviting me," I tell her.

"Honestly, I didn't think you would come, but I'm so glad that you have."

Mabel resorts to an embrace to show me how she feels. Being demonstrative is part of who she is, so I don't cringe but welcome her show of affection, which I've rather been starved of these last few years.

I lean back, hoping she'll release me; she gets my hint and slowly drops her arms from around my shoulders.

"Yes. Me too," I tell her.

With a low creak the front door opens, and the men walk in. I turn my back to them and move to place the boiled dinner Mabel and I made in the middle of the table. Rashly, I lift up the handle of the cast-iron pot, forgetting it's hot. I drop the handle and it clunks against the side of the pot.

"Yow!" I can't help uttering.

I shake my hand, trying to flap away the pain, red marks blooming on the underside of my middle fingers.

Mr. Woodson steps forward and grabs a tea towel to lift the pot to the table.

"Let me," his low voice rumbles out.

I keep my eyes lowered as I offer him a "Thank you."

I don't need to say more.

Mabel holds her hand out to me, motioning with her fingers, demanding my burning hand. "Oh dear. Let me see."

I don't resist and place my hand, palm-up, in hers.

"Oooh, that might leave a welt." Mabel drops my hand and steps toward the icebox. "I'll chip off some ice to place on it. Sit down at the table."

I obey. Lincoln steps closer to his wife.

"Should we do the same, Mae? Is supper ready?" he asks, using his pet name for Mabel, concern present in his tone.

"Surely. Take your seats. This won't take but a minute, and then you can say the blessing," Mabel says with confidence.

While she chips at some ice with an ice pick, we all sit, looking a bit uncomfortable. Lincoln watches me with what I imagine is genuine care.

Mr. Woodson, Samuel, folds and unfolds his fingers over the top of his plate and clears his throat several times, yet retains his thoughts and his gaze. It gives me the opportunity to study him. He wears his ash-blond hair long, but his face sports no facial hair. His eyes are wide and well-set but not shrunken. Because of his downcast gaze or the candlelight, I cannot decipher what shade they are. The oval shape of his face puts me in mind of more feminine features, but his strong brow and prominent jaw are decisively masculine. Altogether, he presents a pleasing figure.

Mr. Woodson suddenly glances up, as if he can read my thoughts.

I instantly drop my inspection of him and turn my face, so my good side is to him. My neck begins to prick and itch, and I look at Mabel, begging her to hurry up. She gathers the ice shards in a flour-sack towel, folds it several times, and hands it to me.

"There. You rest your hand on that; it should start to feel better soon. After dinner, I can put some balsam of myrrh on the burn."

I gulp, swallowing the word "burn."

I know about burns. I've lived through them. Almost died from them.

Mabel's eyes widen, and she holds perfectly still, a fly caught in a word-web. "I'm…I'm sorry. I didn't think…"

Her eyes glisten with the brown, gold-flecked sheen of sand-polished ironstone.

"It's…"

I want to reassure my friend that I've put the past behind me and that it no longer has the power to scar me. But I'm unsure. Perhaps it still does.

Lincoln rescues me, closing his eyes. "Ahem, let me say grace."

I watch him.

He prays with heartfelt inflection. "Lord, thank You for all gathered around this table; make us truly grateful for what we are about to receive. Amen."

That wasn't long enough. Not long enough for me to hide my embarrassment over my reaction and what I feel is a deeper-than-usual flushed face.

"Thank you, dear," Mabel comments.

She urges us to eat up, serving out portions to the three of us in turn.

Mabel fills my plate with chunks of ham, potatoes, carrots, and rutabaga, and I utter, "Thank you."

Mabel nods and turns her modest lips up in a slow smile.

Lincoln addresses Mabel. "We start the corn harvest tomorrow."

Mabel dishes up Mr. Woodson's food, asking, "Do you have extra help coming?"

Lincoln forks some potatoes into his open mouth and talks while he chews. "Yep. They'll be here at the break of day."

Giving me a put-out expression, Mabel smirks sideways, tilts her head, and flicks her eyes up. "I suppose I'll have to sacrifice another ham."

With a shrug of his shoulders, Lincoln comments, "Whatever you think best."

He continues eating, and Mabel turns quiet as she serves herself last and sits down. The screech of the chair legs on the floor makes me jerk.

As we eat an uncomfortableness settles on us. Some unspoken tightness between Mabel and Lincoln has pulled up a chair and sat down to supper too. I don't know what to say, so I resort to my usual quiet. I venture another glance at Mr. Woodson. He surprises me.

He flicks his gaze up at me, and I see a blue-green glimmer before he focuses on his plate again. "Mrs. Nelson says you're from Wisconsin, Mrs. Lund."

His fork scrapes against the egg-colored stoneware, causing me an involuntary cringe.

I clear my throat and meet his eyes to be polite. "Yes. I'm originally from Land O' Lakes, Wisconsin, but...I've lived in Menomonie for the last few years."

He nods, and I hope to God that he doesn't ask further questions about why I moved.

Thankfully, Mabel picks up the thread. "Molly is a gardener. She kept the grounds of an institution where she worked."

"You and Mabel will have plenty in common. She's a hard task-master when it comes to weeding out the vegetable patch," Lincoln points out, wearing a grin.

He jabs his table-knife in the air at me. The tension between the newlyweds has lessened.

"Thanks to my father I can grow vegetables," Mabel replies with some sarcasm in her tone, "but Molly specializes in flowers," she informs the men.

Mr. Woodson looks at me with some shyness in the quick flash of his eyes. "Do…you have a favorite?"

I set my fork down and try to hide my facial scars with my hand by fussing with my hair. I turn my unhooked eye on him. "Hollyhocks and daisies." I think for a few seconds. "And dahlias."

He holds his fork in mid-air and focuses on a far-off point. The potato skewered on its tine falls off; he doesn't notice and seems lost in a memory.

"My mother grew flowers," he says, then he jerks and continues eating, as if he hadn't paused awkwardly for some seconds. Between bites he says, "Red geraniums were her favorite."

Were? Perhaps his mother no longer lives. He appears to be in his late twenties, as I am, so his mother can't be elderly.

We all continue eating. Mabel and Lincoln chat about the harvest, and Mr. Woodson and I keep quiet.

Lincoln pats his middle. "Well, time to let this digest."

I don't know how he's eaten so fast. I've barely taken a few bites, and he's cleaned his plate.

"I'm off to lounge on the settee for a mite." He stands and

kisses Mabel on the cheek. "Thanks for the meal."

Mabel doesn't say anything but simply smiles.

Lincoln nods my way. "Mrs. Lund." He turns to Mr. Woodson. "Samuel, join me if you like."

He pushes his chair in and waits for Samuel's response.

"Oh, no." Mr. Woodson makes quick work of his remaining meal, telling Lincoln, "Think I'll finish bedding down the cows then hit the hay myself." He nods and smiles slightly. "Good evening to you," he says, before pushing the last of his food into his mouth with his fork, chewing with vigor, and standing as well.

"Get some rest, Sam. We've lots to do tomorrow," Lincoln responds before he walks to the sitting room.

Mr. Woodson nods. "Right."

Lincoln walks a few paces before settling on the stuffed seat about twenty feet away in the next room.

Mr. Woodson acknowledges Mabel, saying, "Thank you kindly for supper, ma'am."

All sweetness, Mabel smiles. "You're welcome, and call me Mabel."

"As you wish, ma'am…ah, Mabel." He turns to me. "Mrs. Lund."

He holds my gaze for a moment.

I offer a slight smile and watch his eyes pass over my face, but he doesn't grimace. The thought of allowing him to call me Molly doesn't agree with me, so I don't correct the formal address.

"Pleasant dreams," he utters quietly, and he slips out the door, closing it carefully behind him like a shadow.

He's like me, unassuming, blending into his surroundings with little to comment on. I have to wonder, what is he hiding?

Strangely, I look forward to finding out.

Love is my sin, and thy dear virtue hate,
Hate of my sin, grounded on sinful loving.

From *Sonnet 142*
by William Shakespeare

CHAPTER TWO

Samuel

That night

My hate can kill a man. And it has.

To look at me, you wouldn't think it. You couldn't tell that a brief fire as evil as hell burned within me, eating me up until I was nothing more than a plan of destruction with legs. I'm nothing: tall, slim, and dull. I'm just a skinny reject who's lost everything, but it's my own fault and perhaps, partially, Mother's, fool that she was.

I can't even write his name—her man, that wolf in sheep's clothing. It regurgitates in my gullet like acid, causing my chest to burn with the weight of it. There's that word again—burn.

Strange that Mrs. Lund seemed so affected by the word too. When Mrs. Nelson, Mabel—I have to get used to calling her that—bandaged Mrs. Lund's burn on her hand before supper, she spoke the word. At the time it didn't hit me as odd how Mrs. Lund cringed and went pale.

Mrs. Lund hides about as much as I do from others. I recognize

11

a secret keeper when I see one. I wonder what secret lurks in her heart. I can't imagine it's something as sinister as mine. Her face tells me that she has endured pain. Both the physical evidence of scars and an inner grief—I can only imagine—highlight her features. I see loss in her. But what has she lost? Has she lost as much as me? Perhaps more.

It's time to put my thoughts to rest, so I'll lay down my pen. Tomorrow comes, and along with the new day, work waits to be done. I don't mind. Working hard helps me forget.

I dread the night when visions of Mother and that man cloud my mind in a mixed-up order. Falling asleep every night dips me into the depths of regret, remorse, and restitution. I relive that fateful day all over again. How many days must pass before I can lay my head down in peace? To be truthful, I'm not even sure that's possible anymore.

I cap my inkwell, rest my pen in its brass holder, and blow on my written words so they dry before I close my walnut-colored, leather journal. Walking to the small, potbellied stove, I pluck two more split chunks of oak from the stack against the loft's wall. I flick open the handle, stoke the coals with a steel poker, and set the wood in the stove. I watch as a flame rises up and embraces its food, rather envious at the ease of it. I shut the door and let the handle fall in place with a clink.

Fire. I need it for warmth on this chilly autumn night up in the Nelson's loft in the barn, where I've made a room for myself. But such a small spark can set a piece of wood to burning and a life ablaze, like the potential power of one lie. I rub my hands together, my rough skin chafing as I warm them overtop the stove. A few more minutes then I'll try to sleep. I don't want to, but I must.

Eventually, I walk the few feet to my bed, remove my outer clothes, button my long johns up all the way, peel the patchwork quilt back, and lie down, covering myself up to my chin. I blow out the candle on the side table. A single plea rings in my heart.

Let the morning come soon.

The next day

The noise of activity wakes me, and I realize that I've slept too late.

What must Lincoln think?

I shake my head, throw back the covers, and hop out of bed, rushing through my morning administrations as quickly as I can. I plunge my stockinged feet into my boots and cram my green, wool cap on my head before running down the loft steps and out the barn, tying my neckerchief on as I go.

In the middle of the drive, rosy-cheeked lads and a few older men mill around a corn picker and binder hitched up to several horses. The extra manpower will help set up the bundles of corn in shocks to dry.

Lincoln walks over from around the other side of the machinery and gives me a pointed look. "Decided to join us, did you?"

I owe him much and dislike that I may be falling behind in my duties. "Ah…yes, sorry. Won't happen again."

I sniff, rub my finger under my nose, and focus on my boots. I could trust my old friend and tell him why I can't sleep, but I don't.

Won't.

He's not asked any questions, which I'm grateful for, and I don't want him to start.

Lincoln tucks his thumb in a belt loop and pats the rump of one of the horses. "We missed you at breakfast. Mabel made her ma's cinnamon rolls, but if you're lucky, you might nab one before we head out to the fields." Lincoln yanks his thumb back toward the house and grins. "Better hurry."

I nod and tap my cap in thanks, turning to do as he suggests. I stride up the hill to the house, sitting directly across the yard from the barn and the brick silo. The Nelsons' home perches like a demure country queen, painted in cream with burgundy and forest-green accents on the spindles meeting in the corners of the two-story, Victorian-style house and on the railings of the three porches, facing the north, east, and south. Decorative fish-scaling covers the outer surface of the upper story.

Four lovely maple trees, several pines, and a small smattering of lilac bushes and flowerbeds skirt the house and lawn, adding life to the setting. An apple orchard displays round, red and gold apples, ripening in the crisp weather. A summer kitchen and woodhouse sit on the west side of the house, near a brick-lined well. About sixty yards opposite, a chicken coop and penned-in yard stand. Attached to a cistern springing from a higher portion of the ridge, a tall windmill marks the farm, even from way off. Scraggly bur oak trees toward the north cover the ridge—the reason the Nelsons have dubbed their place Bur Oak Ridge. Cresting the hill, one can see for miles. This time of year, autumn colors dot the far-off hills. Fields of corn and wheat can be seen in almost every direction. It's a beautiful spot for a farm. Lincoln has a small dairy herd and sells his excess crops for cash.

I finish glancing around and focus on my feet as I near the house.

"Oh! Sorry…" a voice rasps out in shock.

I gasp and feel the heat before I ascertain what has happened. Hot coffee has sloshed down the front of my thick, twill shirt. I use a couple of fingers to pull the wet fabric away from my chest. A waft of roasted brew rises to my nostrils. I've always liked the smell of coffee but not the bitter taste. I prefer tea.

Mrs. Lund stands inches from my chest with a tray of mugs, her mouth agape. We briefly look at each other, full in the face, before she bows her head to the side, hiding her scars. Her lovely, dark hair drapes over the smooth side of her face. The pink shade of her lips reminds me of the wild roses that grow in the ditch. Smooth, unblemished, ivory skin covers the pleasing planes of her face. Her fetching image puts me in mind of a harpy from the sea. Mother told me stories of such creatures when I was a child. I doubt Mrs. Lund knows how beautiful she is. It saddens me to take in the other half of her face. I hate to think of the pain she endured to have such scars. Burns, I now surmise.

"Again, I apologize. Mabel sent me out with coffee for the crew before things swing into action."

She says the words without looking up; they exit from her mouth rough, strained. I wonder what makes her sound as if she's smoked too many cigarettes. I wouldn't guess her to indulge in what Mother would call *"the sin of smoking."*

With a hint of the sarcasm I feel, I tell her, "Linc did send me to get some coffee, but I didn't think I'd be wearing it."

Why am I talking so much?

I feel a need to engage this woman in conversation, to pull her out of her shell, but ironically, I usually act the same way she does—reserved.

Her clear eye—green-colored with bits of brown and blue—tilts up at me at a strange angle, in question. "Linc?"

I let my childhood name for Lincoln slip, but she was bound

to find out eventually. "Yes. Lincoln and I are…old friends. Schoolmates. I called him Linc in our younger days."

I shrug, release my shirt, and wipe my wet fingers on my thigh. Again, I'm revealing too much. She nods and looks back down at the mown lawn, making as if to return to the house.

"Wait." I stop her and place my hands on either side of the wooden tray. "There's no harm done, except I'm a little damp. Still plenty here to drink. I'll carry it out to the men for you."

I pull the tray, but she holds firm. She's stronger than she appears.

She points her chin to my chest. "You'll need to change."

"It'll dry in no time, I reckon."

"But it's chilly. You'll…" she gives me a one-eyed gaze, "be cold."

I gently pull the tray again. "I've faced worse."

She relinquishes it with a quiet sigh.

"Much obliged," she utters, and she drops her hands, brushing them on her blue, gingham apron.

"My pleasure," I say and inwardly kick myself. I sound like a salesclerk.

She pauses before she turns. I decide to skip asking for a cinnamon roll. But something else eats at me besides hunger. Some need to connect with another who obviously knows what pain is gives me the courage to ask.

"What…is it that you grieve?"

I surprise myself with my raw boldness. She stops, her hand on the knob of the door to the house and her back to me. Her head droops farther south.

Her voice sounds hollow, tinny. "You mean who?"

I swallow at my audacity and tighten my grip on the tray. "I suppose so. Who, then?"

Mrs. Lund turns partially back, captured in a perfect silhouette, backlit by the slanted morning light.

"My son," she tells me, and she slips into the house without so much as a creak of the door.

The words sound like they hurt in more ways than one.

Family—deep love and deep heartache.

I shake my head of thoughts that will weigh me down, turn, and walk to the men and their machine to serve up some half-empty mugs of coffee on a drenched tray.

I'm curious about Mrs. Lund's story, and if I ask her more questions, she may answer. But then she'll want to ask me some, and I am not ready to confess my sins to her. For some reason that I can't name, it's important to me for her to think well of me.

Why, I do not know.

From the poem *The Mystery of Pain*
by Emily Dickinson

CHAPTER THREE

Molly

A while later

Mabel and I are entrenched in the kitchen preparing for the noon meal. While Mabel adds some chickens to a large stew pot, I knead a round of dough. I work it a bit, then cut it in half, quarters, and halve those portions to make buns, rolling out the rounds and placing them on a buttered sheet pan. As my hands work, my mind wonders about Mr. Woodson; I can't help myself.

I ask Mabel, "Are Lincoln and Samuel friends? I mean…Mr. Woodson."

I already know the answer to that, but I hope Mabel will elaborate on their relationship.

Mabel slices up some raw carrots on a cutting board. "I think he'd be fine with you calling him Samuel." Mabel gives me a sideways smile, which suggests mischief. "Yes. They were schoolmates. Buddies. He would have been the best man at our wedding, but…he had a family emergency."

"Oh?"

I fish for more, rolling the last bun and placing it on the pan, wiping my hands on my apron.

Mabel lifts the cutting board and scrapes the cut carrots into a bowl. "Yes. His pa died. He'd been ill for some time, but I don't recall what with." She starts slicing another washed and peeled carrot. The antler-handled knife rings against the board as she speaks. "He's a sweet and kind man. Never gives us any trouble. I don't rightly know how long he'll be staying with us, though. He lived with his folks before his pa passed, but for some reason he doesn't seem to want to return home. I can't imagine how his mother manages without him."

I cough into the crook of my arm, feeling a tickle in the back of my throat. Sometimes that happens when I talk more than usual, and we have been jabbering most of the morning.

I reach for the glass of water I always try to keep handy and take a sip before I ask, "What do you mean?"

Mabel puts the knife down and places both hands on her hips, leaning backward, stretching out her back. "He's Mr. and Mrs. Woodson's only child. Mrs. Woodson must grieve his absence, too, as she grieves for her husband."

I try to get a better picture of the man who's captured my attention with his questions. "How long ago did Mr. Woodson senior pass?"

Maybe he referenced his grief over his father when he asked me what I grieve.

Like recognizes like.

We may each be grieving someone, but that doesn't mean I am ready to reveal my secrets to a near perfect stranger. But he guessed, and I told him, in part, about my greatest loss. For some unexplained reason, he wisely sees what rests inside of me.

"Oh…" Mabel pauses and appears to be thinking. "About three months or so. He came here at Linc's invitation afterward."

She starts chunking up peeled potatoes. I nod, keeping the rest of my thoughts to myself. My throat pricks, and it feels as if a hand squeezes my neck, trying to choke me. I hate this feeling, even more than the raspy sounds my voice often brings forth.

When I think of the damage I've suffered and all that I've lost, it threatens to overwhelm me. Over the last few years, I've gotten better, able to push past those terrible feelings, but every once in a while, they come rushing back.

Sometimes in my dreams I sing, still, unencumbered by the pain and damage to my vocal cords. I touch my throat, fingering the familiar, marred skin, sensing the scorching, caustic water as if it were yesterday. The hot splash searing through my skin and down my throat. My vocal cords reaping the scourge of that moment. Instead of seeing the laundry kettle toppling, I see my vocal teacher, Mrs. Strenelli, sitting at the baby grand in her parlor…

"You must annunciate, Mrs. Lund. Annunciate!" she shouted at me, her words ripe with a heavy Italian accent.

Her fingers punched down on the keys, emphasizing each word.

"Yes, Mrs. Strenelli. I'm trying."

I worked at perfecting Ave Maria for an interview with the director of the Chicago opera. After a year of study with Mrs. Strenelli, she pressed me to apply for an opening at the theater.

"You must try harder! Again!" She punched out the words like a drill sergeant giving orders. Her forcefulness didn't startle me, as

this was her usual way of instruction. I knew she only wanted me to succeed. "Use your diaphragm."

She reminded me to breathe in and expel my air with the aid of my trunk muscles.

She rolled out an introduction to the aria, and I picked up at the appropriate spot, hitting the notes with perfect pitch, command, and what I hoped was clear diction. She nodded as she played, a large smile on her wide, thick lips. Her plump fingers, showcasing several rings with large stones, had no trouble in accompanying me as I sang with every ounce of passion and training that I'd acquired.

As the climax of the piece built, she encouraged me, reminding me to increase my volume. "Better! Forte!*"*

I felt so alive, so free, with my voice soaring with the music. We finished the final notes in a tapered way, funneling back to piano, *a soft timbre.*

She leaned back on the cherry piano bench, her teeth showing through her full smile, twinkles sparkling in her dark eyes, and her olive skin aglow with satisfaction.

"Bellissima!" Mrs. Strenelli exclaimed. She kissed the tips of her gathered fingers on her right hand, unfurling them back in an artful gesture. "Ah, well done. If the director does not select you for his vacant role, he is a fool."

I smiled, giddy and happy with the possibility of singing with the Chicago Opera. I imagined it: me, a small-town, backwater girl from the Northwoods of Wisconsin. It seemed a dream a year prior but now the possibility was within my grasp. All thanks to my teacher and coach, Mrs. Strenelli, a frequent guest at The Gateway hotel in Land O' Lakes, where I worked. One day she heard me singing while I stirred the laundry kettle and offered to give me lessons.

That seems like ages ago now. I was a different person back then, one not marred by life and its cruelties. The pain of not being able to sing and experience that joy and freedom hurts just as much or more than my melted skin did. Except it aches, over and over again. I bury the grief one day, thinking I've dealt with it, but it rises again and again—a living, dead hope.

"Molly? Did you hear me?" Mabel points at the stove, her forehead wearing a question mark of sorts. "Aren't you going to put the buns in? Pretty soon you'll have to punch them back down and start over."

I focus on the rising pieces of dough, approaching the size of an apple.

"Sorry. I was daydreaming, I guess," I offer as an explanation and quickly open the oven door and shove the tray of buns in.

Mabel shakes her head. "The men will be back soon."

A seed of terror rises in me. "Do I…must I…serve them?"

I shake my head, hoping she'll respond to my physical plea.

Empathy smooths her face back to its usual gracious expression. "Of course not." Mabel steps close to me and places a kind hand on my arm. "I invited you here to experience peace, not to cause you anxiety. You must do as you desire. Lincoln and I have no expectations of you."

She smiles, a calming, warm gleam in her eyes.

I reach for my friend's hand; we share a firm handclasp. "And I thank you for it. You've been most kind."

Mabel releases me and moves quietly to stir the stewed chicken, and I begin to set the table for seven. I'll fill a plate for myself before the crew sits down and eat in my room. I've resigned myself to a life of social exclusions.

From the poem *Emblems of Friendship*
by John Irmie

CHAPTER FOUR

Samuel
Days later

The sun shines golden on this Sunday afternoon. I've decided to take my journal and pen up to the ridge of bur oaks, sit a while, and write. Linc has mowed a rough trail through the tall grass. Mabel persuaded him to place a bench at the crest of the hill overlooking the rolling fields and distant hills to the north. It's peaceful here with nary but the birds and the breeze to lend some music. The north fields display shocks of cornstalks like a gathering of Indian teepees. The harvest has gone well so far, and Linc expects a good crop.

I turn my gaze to the expanse overhead. I believe only in autumn the sky spreads a special, deep, robin's-egg blue as today. Though it seems early, a flying "V" of geese honk and flap toward the south, I'm sure seeking warmer accommodations for the coming winter.

I shiver, wondering how to tolerate another winter in the drafty barn. The small stove helps, but the barn boards have too much space between them. I shoved old rags and rolled-up wads of straw in the cracks in the area of my room, but it did little good. I felt a constant chill until the finer weather came in April.

Mabel invited me to stay in the house. They have four bedrooms upstairs, but I declined. I need a space of my own. Now, I regret that decision. I'd like to broach the topic with Mabel and Linc again. I'm sure they would say yes, but it seems improper with Mrs. Lund—Molly—occupying one of the rooms. However, I may…

I pause in my writing, sensing something or someone. I look up from my journal into the eyes of Mrs. Lund. My cheeks blush warm; she has caught me writing and thinking about her. I quickly slap my journal closed.

Her good eye focuses on me. "I didn't mean to startle you."

I swallow, trying to settle my nerves. "Didn't expect anyone, that's for sure."

She looks over the scenery, a faint, rough edge to her tone. "A good day for a stroll."

"Yes." I look down and notice King, the Nelsons' pet blonde Labrador, at her heels. King, congenial to most people, has taken a special liking to Mrs. Lund. I remember my manners. "Care to sit?" I ask, and I move over on the slatted bench to make room.

Her hand flutters to her neck, wrapped in a colorful, crocheted scarf.

"I…suppose," she answers without much certainty behind her words.

She sits on the edge of the bench, leaving some space between our legs.

What do we talk about?

I regret asking her to sit. Presently, my mind doesn't dwell on conversing but on writing, and I can't very well talk with her about what I've written in my journal. *Or can I?*

She releases me of the initial duty. "Did you grow up on a farm?"

She gives me the briefest of looks and focuses back on the rolling hills to the north. King slumps at her feet, unperturbed by the interruption in their walk.

"Yes. A dairy." *How much should I tell her?* "You?" I ask.

She keeps her gaze straight ahead, but I notice how she nervously picks at the hemline of her blue, wool blazer. "No. My pa was a lumberjack and my ma a washerwoman. I took after my ma."

I sense there's more to her upbringing.

"Oh? How so?" I ask, hoping to draw her out.

I desire to know more about this mysterious woman with a past as veiled as her face.

She sighs heavily. "I married a man like my father and got hired on at the hotel where my mother worked."

"And…your husband did not move to Menomonie with you?" I inquire.

She intakes a sharp breath. Perhaps I shouldn't have asked.

"I'm sorry. I didn't mean to pry," I reassure her.

"No. I am sure you are curious about my…situation." She turns and slants a short-lived smile at me, looking almost mischievous. "I would be." She pauses and appears to be thinking. "To tell you the truth, I've not seen my husband for over five years. I believe that he's dead. Jacob left me after…" She doesn't continue but bows her head and clenches the fingers on her left hand into a fist. With her right she reaches for the scarred side of her face. "Well, after the accident."

I nod, not knowing whether to keep asking questions or not. Maybe if I offer something more personal, she might be more comfortable sharing those sorts of details about her life with me.

"I was…to take over the home farm after my father died. Even though in his will he left the place to Mother. Plans were that I would operate the farm. But, unexpectedly," I tilt my head and navigate how to proceed, "my mother remarried, and the farm is now in her husband's name."

I don't tell her that my mother's husband is dead and that it's my fault. That's too heavy. Too much.

She turns a sympathetic eye my way. "I'm sorry to hear that. It must be very difficult."

I nod and agree. "It was. *Is*." I switch the heat off myself. "But what about you? Why did you move from northern Wisconsin to Menomonie? And how did you and Mabel meet?"

"Ah, well. That's a long story." She smiles, slow and sad. "But I don't want to ruin this pleasant afternoon with my misfortunes."

"Well, it should be 'tit for tat.' We can share the unpleasantness."

On a whim I wink at her. She responds with a blooming blush on her smooth, ivory cheek.

"Let's just say ill-fortune led me to Menomonie, and I met Mabel through her sister, Robin, whom I…gardened with. And Mabel has been asking me to come visit for quite some time. I finally agreed."

Her voice sounds scratchier, and she coughs.

I offer my canteen of water to her, unscrewing the cap. "Here, take a drink."

She takes it, and our fingers brush; hers are icy cold. I'd like to wrap them in the shelter of mine, which, I'm sure, are many degrees warmer.

"Um, thank you," Mrs. Lund says.

She tips the canteen back, drinks, wipes her mouth, smiles, and hands it back to me. I take it, affixing the cap.

I search her good eye for the truth. "Are you glad you've come?"

She nods like a happy child. "Yes."

"Me too," I tell her, and we sit in silence for a few moments, watching a flock of blackbirds swoop and dive and land in the branches of a nearby oak.

Their cackle reaches an annoying decibel and severs the companionable link we share.

I stand, sling the canteen on my shoulder, tuck my journal in my large coat pocket, and offer my elbow to her. "Can I escort you back to the house, Mrs. Lund?"

A half-smile appears on her face. "I'd like that. Thank you. And you must call me Molly."

She stands, tucks her hand through the crook of my arm, and we walk. King jumps to his feet, happily wagging his tail, pleased to be on the move again. He gives a joyous bark and bounces ahead down the trail.

I give her the same permission in my best easy-going voice. "And please, call me Samuel or Sam. Whatever rolls off your tongue the best."

We walk. Her steps match mine, even our breathing aligns, and I can't help thinking we fit well together. I venture an intimate gaze. Her unblemished side is to me. Her eye slants back, and if I'm correct by her rosy cheek, the tilt of her lips, and the openness in her eye, she feels the same as I do—hopeful. For the first time in months, I think a fresh start just might be possible.

CHAPTER FIVE

Molly

Late September 1919

I see him, but I can't move. I stand rooted in place like a tree with my arms outstretched.

"Momma!" he giggles with glee, and he runs toward me, dangerously close to the vat of boiling water.

Water vapor rises from the vat and hangs suspended in the air in a slow, surreal way. Some soap bubbles float large and free, growing until they burst, appearing like a shimmer of glitter around the halo of Lonny's blond ringlets.

My frozen-in-place arms strain to rescue him, but they are immovable. I'm helpless to prevent what's coming next—what I've seen over and over and over again. The vat supports creak and groan, the mechanism tips, and Lonny is lost in a sea of boiling water and bedsheets. Next, I feel the hiss and pain. My hands fly to my face, where the burning-hot, carbolic water sears my skin.

My voice strains to scream, but no sound issues from my wide-open jaws…

"Molly? Molly!"

It takes me some seconds to realize that Mabel's form hovers over me, grooves edged on her face, set deeper in the faint glow of the candle she holds in one hand.

"You must have been dreaming," she says, somewhat breathlessly, and she sits on the side of the bed next to me.

I blink my eyes several times and try to make sense of her words.

Her eyes, flecked with questions, reflect the flame. "We heard you moaning."

She reaches out and smooths some hair away from my face.

I'm grateful she doesn't inquire about the origin of my dream. I push up on my elbows and raise myself into a sitting position, working to calm my breathing.

"I'm sorry I've disturbed you," I growl out, my throat dry.

She sets the candle on the nightstand. "There's no need to apologize." Turning back, she asks, "Do you want to tell me about it?"

How do I explain?

Swallowing, I begin, "I was dreaming about…my son."

One of her brows hunches lower. "It must not have been a pleasant dream."

She tilts her head, waiting. Patient as ever.

"No." I pause and search her eyes in the candlelight. "Did…Robin tell you about the accident?"

She nods. "Some. I know you got burned, but I didn't know your son was also involved." She shakes her head. "Well, I know you had a son, but Robin didn't say how he…" She lets her explanation hang and squints her eyes. "What did happen?"

I don't want to talk about it now. It's not that I don't trust Mabel, but I don't want to relive it again, not twice in one night.

"I think I need to rest. Do you mind if I tell you the whole story another time?" I plead.

She stands. "Of course. I…shouldn't have asked."

I intercept her hand as she reaches for the candle. "I want you to know the truth, Mabel, but I just can't bear thinking about it anymore tonight."

She nods and barely smiles.

Linc appears in the open doorway to my bedroom, his hair on end and his eyes droopy. "Is everything all right?"

Guilt pricks at me for interrupting my hosts' sleep.

Mabel steps close to her husband, a confident tone to her words. "Nothing we can't handle."

I value my friend's loyalty and protection so much.

"Nothing but a dream," I say and moisten my dry lips with my tongue.

But dreams have more substance than nothing. At times, they seem like my reality and the life I lead upon this Earth a woeful, fictional tale.

"Good, good." Linc runs a hand through his hair and yawns. "Tomorrow comes early. Let's get back to our rest."

Mabel steps through the doorway, offering a consoling lift of her lips to me before disappearing into the hallway. Linc nods once more, steps back, and closes the door behind him.

I lean my head on the metal bedframe, close my eyes, and breathe—*in…and…out.* Several bouts of this rhythm help quiet my yet pounding heart.

That particular type of dream hasn't manifested in some time; they sporadically reoccur. I tire of the burden and wish to have them as aptly erased as rubber erases lead off paper. But their stain remains, in my mind, on my body, and forever within my heart.

I lie back on my pillow in the darkness and pray quietly for peace.

"God, You've helped me again and again through my struggles. You never relinquished me to the darkness of my own thoughts or dreams but called me into the light. When my heart broke from grief, you comforted me with the thought that I will see my son again and that You are with him. I like to envision him picking daisies in a wide-open field with other small children while You watch. Your word says that Your eyes are ever on Your children.

"You saw me the day I picked up Pa's razor, intent on slicing the mutilated side of my face, but You stayed my hand. After much struggle and during the internment at the asylum, I had a strange dream. One I will remember always. I dreamt I met a man after a long walk. He sat on a big boulder, as if he waited for me. I stopped and rested near him and talked with him about my second grief and burden—my deformity. He replied with the words, 'Just live for His beauty.' Then his plain clothes fell away and raiment of glowing white covered him, and in a blink of an eye, he disappeared.

"I believe he was an angel sent to me with a message from You. I want to obey it and not be concerned about what I lost or how I look now, but my eyes tend to focus on the external. Help me to see past this temporal husk of skin and deeper into the lasting things. Things no one can burn or damage: hope, faith, and love.

"Amen."

I snuggle down in the covers, wiping the tears from my

cheeks, feeling better. Perhaps I am unburdened enough to fall back to sleep. I surely hope so, for Lincoln is right. *Tomorrow comes early.*

The next day

To me, the chitter-chatter sounds as welcoming as a nest of hornets. I've never been one for ladies' social functions, but since the accident even more so. Smoothing down the front of my navy-striped shirtwaist, I take the last step off the stairs and turn the corner into the kitchen. A trilling laugh grates at my ears as I get closer to the sitting room.

I lean awkwardly against the dark-stained, pine molding of the threshold. An empty spot next to Mabel beckons me. I sneak into the room in what I hope is an unassuming way. Mabel turns to me and smiles with encouragement.

She gestures to me with a graceful arc of her hand. "Ladies, I'd love to introduce you to my dear friend, Mrs. Molly Lund."

I can feel the heat of a blush on my face. *Good grief. I don't need to appear redder.* Keeping my face slightly turned, I try to avoid full-on shocking them with my scars. I've left my hair as loosely styled as possible to shade my temple and cheek.

"Mrs. Nelson has spoken highly of her friend from our neighboring state. How do you find Minnesota, Mrs. Lund?" a handsome, middle-aged woman with graying, dark hair and eyes of almost the same shade asks in a sincere voice.

She balances a teacup and saucer on one knee.

"Much the same," I answer and fiddle with my fingers, worrying the pad of my thumb with my forefinger.

"So I hear," the woman replies.

Mabel attempts a round of introductions, starting with the woman who questioned me, who turns out to be a Mrs. Bjorklund.

Mabel pauses when she reaches the young, plump woman on the sofa with chipmunk cheeks. Her brown and tan attire feeds the rodent affiliation in my mind.

When her beady eyes focus on me, she utters a slight gasp. "Good heavens. Your…face."

Her eyes widen, and her hand half covers her mouth. Her comment hangs in the room, an immediate dampener on the gathering.

A thin woman, who Mabel introduced as Mrs. Silvia Rusch, speaks up. "Sheila Brown, hold your tongue. When will you ever learn to think before you spew out tactless comments?"

Mrs. Rusch rolls her eyes and takes a loud slurp of tea from the cup she holds.

Miss Brown looks remorseful. She flicks her gaze my way and says, "I didn't mean…"

A deep posy-red blooms on her cheeks.

I tip my gaze down to my knees to avoid the pitiful looks I am sure the ladies are sending my way and run a fingernail over the decorative stitching on my skirt, waiting for the discomfort to dissipate.

Thankfully, Mabel comes to the rescue. I look up as she tucks a wisp of dark hair behind her left ear, announcing, "Well, now that we have introductions out of the way, let's move on to some business." Mabel turns and focuses on Mrs. Rusch. "Silvia, wasn't the topic of a book exchange on our agenda?"

Silvia Rusch fingers through a thin stack of papers on her lap. "Yes, indeed."

Her gaze follows her finger along the rows of neat handwriting on the top paper.

The group goes on to discuss the particulars of their book

exchange, and I focus on my lap, listening with one ear while the ladies chatter back and forth about how they will meet for tea and swap books. Hunching my back, I try to look as inconspicuous as possible. Minutes tick by on the wall clock, the steady sound my only anchor at this moment.

I glance up once in a while and offer a slight smile, so as not to be rude, but I'd rather be anywhere than here, even strapped to a bed at the asylum.

That only happened once, and I probably deserved to be restricted.

After weeks in the local hospital recovering from the burns of the accident, my mind moved into an angry stage. Blind with angst from my deep grief over Lonny's loss and my disfigurement, I attempted to harm myself and was committed by a doctor who'd been called in afterward by the Gateway Hotel manager, Mr. Morton, in consultation with my mother. However, I have no memory of being transferred hundreds of miles to Menomonie, Wisconsin.

Perhaps they sedated me.

Dr. Howington told me all this after I'd been at The Dunn County Asylum for the Chronic Insane for over a week. The first day there I remember waking up afraid, in a strange, white room, my hands tied with strips of cotton mesh and affixed to the bedframe.

I pulled and struggled. My heart fluttered in my chest like a trapped bird, and with a crackling voice I yelled—to my shame—every obscenity I'd ever heard.

"Now, Mrs. Lund! You must settle down," a woman with a nurse's white cap shouted back at me whilst forcefully pressing on my forearm with one firm hand.

"You have no right! You—" I choked out, the physical pain of the words fresh and raw. When my harsh words didn't bring about my release, I switched to begging and tears. "Have pity. Pl…ease." I spoke in a rusty whisper and clamped my gaze on the commanding, unflustered woman at my side, her pinched lips in an unmovable line of granite. "They're too tight."

I groaned and pleaded, jerking my arms in an effort to loosen my bonds. If I had loosened them, I'm not sure what I would have done.

"When you can show some sense and collect yourself, the bands will be removed." The nurse looked down her long nose and pinned me with icy cold, blue eyes. "Right now, you are considered a danger to yourself and others."

She spoke the words as if I were a child to be instructed and reprimanded when found lacking.

Finally, I gave up and went limp, plunging into a pool of drowned retribution. But who was there to blame? Me? Lonny? Jacob? God—that's who I settled on. A fire inside me flashed as hot as my burns.

But all fires fade, as mine eventually did.

Mabel touches me on the shoulder and jerks her head in the direction of the kitchen. "Molly? Will you help me in the kitchen?"

Her eyes widen, and her finely sculpted eyebrows peak upward.

I meet her gaze. "Oh…of course."

Inwardly, I shake myself of the memory of worse times. I stand and follow Mabel, glad for the opportunity to busy my hands and focus my mind on something happier than Miss Brown pointing out my horrid scars and memories of the asylum.

After Mabel and I reach the kitchen, she backs up against the sink, propping her hands on the basin for support.

A deep, frustrated growl escapes her throat. "Honestly, who does the woman think she is? Sheila Brown is far too outspoken for her own good. I don't know her well enough yet to determine if it's out of malice or just blubbering idiocy." Mabel's shoulders relax, and her eyes pool with sympathy I don't want. "I'm so sorry for her uncaring words." A slight smile angles her lips up at the corners. She stands up straight, letting go of the sink, and leans toward me. "You must not take anything she's said to heart."

I meet her eyes, challenging her to argue with me. "Well, it's true, isn't it?" I pause; she keeps quiet. "My face shocks people. It's hideous."

"None of the other ladies reacted thus. You must not lump everyone in with Miss Brown."

Mabel rolls her eyes and sighs, touching me on the forearm with her light, warm hand.

I study the pointed tips of my brown shoes, the hurting not as raw as in the past. "I suppose it is unfair of me, but you can't think the rest of your group weren't thinking the very same words. Miss Brown simply had the nerve to speak them."

On the one hand, unkind words prick; on the other, I realize I must move forward and not be forever stuck, living with the shadow of scarring. But it's so difficult to live with the physical evidence every day.

Mabel steps closer, her words strong as iron. "It's what we do that matters. And you must know—you are more than your scars."

I hear her; I do. And I nod.

My words come out slow, begrudgingly. "Yes…I know."

Mrs. Rusch enters the kitchen, a smile widening her thin lips. "My, what's holding you ladies up? The troops are getting restless." Kindness etches the corners of her eyes and feathers the tops of her cheeks, where no doubt many such smiles have left their mark. She comes closer to me, cradling the teapot in her arms. "Now, you must not heed Miss Brown's thoughtless remark." She shakes her head. "She's been that way since she was a child. None of her thoughts sift through her kind filter before being spoken. 'Sides, anyone with eyes in their head can see what a lovely woman you are."

Her words cause me some embarrassment. I really don't care to be the center of anyone's attention, complimentary or otherwise.

"Forgive me for my saying so, but I wanted to be sure Sheila hadn't caused you grief." She flashes one more smile my way and turns to Mabel. "How about a refill?"

She holds out the brownstone teapot.

"Surely," Mabel replies and moves to stoke the cook stove.

Wanting to transition from our discussion, I move forward to make myself useful, pick up the copper tea kettle, and pump water from the sink into it. I reason with myself. None of the other ladies looked at me as if I were a monster. A few raised eyebrows and strange smiles but not what I feared. Life is often not as grim as our fears.

For some reason I think of Samuel just now. I'd like to ask him what he fears. I'd only be paying him back, blunt question for blunt question. I wonder what he would say.

CHAPTER SIX

Samuel

That evening

I fear my heart will be forever tied to what I can't have. The word "home" once meant everything good to me: safety, warmth, love. Now, however, I have no home. It was ripped from me by the devious dealings of Mr. Alfred Skaggs. I wish I could put what that man did out of my mind. My conscience tells me I should write Mother, but hurt and anger still hold me back.

"She made her bed; let her lie in it."

The phrase rings in my mind like a warning bell whenever I think of her, but I know it's not charitable or forgiving. It keeps the door shut to my empathy and, dare I say, my love for her.

But reason tells me we are not meant to live with permanently closed doors between us and our family. Perhaps we need each other, but I can't make the first move. Not yet. I need more time to come to a place where I would be willing to set the past aside.

Maybe she doesn't want to see me.

The thought comes from behind me, shocking me with its

unexpected presence. But after all, I blame myself for separating her from her new husband. I think back to my outburst and the second worst day of my life.

"Still scribbling, I see," a familiar voice says.

I look up from my writing, startled. Lincoln stands on the steps, peering at me like he's caught me doing something naughty. I set my pen down and rise from the one armchair in the loft. I would invite Linc to join me, but there's nowhere for him to sit, except my bed.

I offer a weak smile and nod. "Yes. I write most every day. It's become a habit, I suppose." I scratch the back of my neck. "Want anything in particular?"

I stand in the middle of the room, awkward and wondering.

He takes the last few steps. Soon his eyes are level with mine. "Can't an old friend stop by for a visit?"

Shrugging, I snicker, "Shucks, I guess so." I turn and gesture toward my vacated chair. "Want to sit a spell?"

Linc makes a big show of looking around. "I see I need to wrangle up another chair for this place. Doesn't do to have nowhere for company to sit." He walks closer and points toward my unmade bed. "Reckon that's comfy enough for me. Sit yourself back down in your chair. I'll plant myself on the bed."

He moves to do so.

"Suit yourself," I say, again wondering what it is he has come for.

Lincoln isn't one for dropping in for social calls. And I'm still not sure how to navigate my role as the hired-help but also a friend. We sit and stare at each other for a few seconds then both start to speak at the same time.

I laugh. "You go ahead."

"Well, I was just wondering how your mother's doing." Linc's grinning face turns serious. "You know, with winter coming on and all. Has she written to you?"

A forked furrow lines the spot over the bridge of his long nose.

I brush the back of my hand over my forehead. "That'd be mighty hard for her to do since…she doesn't know I'm here."

I study the splintered wood of one of the boards beneath my feet in a kind of shame. It's gray and weathered like I feel.

"Sam," Linc says in a soft rebuke. He pauses, and I look up into his kind eyes. "You're gonna have to go back sometime. She's your ma."

His last words are a plea. He's right, but I don't want to. I can't face her yet.

"I know, but now's not the time." I breathe in through my nose and say firmly, "Don't press me, Linc. Let me get over this in my own way and time. I appreciate you giving me work, a place to stay, and a table to eat at, but I ask you to respect my wishes. I asked you not to talk about this."

Lincoln shakes his head and releases a hefty sigh. "Friends broach the hard subjects, Sam. Mabel and I care about you and can see you're hurting. We want what's best for you." He narrows his eyes. "At least get away from the farm now and then. The only time you leave is when I send you to town. Come to church with us. Socialize a bit."

He should know me better than that. I never was one for small talk. "I thank you kindly for concerning yourselves, but I'm managing just fine being here."

"I figured that's what you would say." A sly grin hikes Linc's lips up on his right side. It makes him look a little like a court jester. "Mabel wouldn't stop pestering me until I asked."

He shrugs, as if apologizing for following his wife's wishes. The man is in love and would clearly agree to almost anything Mabel asked of him, I'm sure.

Linc regards me with one eye, while he tilts his head back a little. "Saw you conversing with Mrs. Lund the other day." He waits, with an expectant look, like a hawk eyeing a mouse. "She's been a mighty fine friend to Mabel and Mabel to her. Had a hard life, I hear. Maybe you two have something in common, but…" He leaves his statement open-ended, and before I can respond, he stands and brushes his hands together. "Bit chilly up here, isn't it? You'd think your landlord would provide you with fuel for this drafty dump."

He winks.

I laugh. "Ya, if only I could find him to ask for some."

I stand as well. We grin at each other and share a chuckle.

"But seriously, you better haul some wood up and stoke your fire. And maybe shove a few more rags in the cracks."

We walk toward the stairs.

"If Mabel has an extra quilt in the house, I wouldn't mind if she borrowed me another."

"I'm sure she'd be more than happy to. I'll ask." Linc tips his head toward me. "Well, goodnight."

I nod and smile, glad for the distraction from my woes. "See you tomorrow."

Linc leaves as quietly as he came. I should go back to my chair and finish my journal entry, but I tire of rehashing the whole sordid affair over again in my mind. Instead, I do as Linc suggested, and I go down the stairs, light a lantern, take up a barrow, and walk to the woodshed to restock my supply of firewood. While I walk, I think about Molly. I'd like to know her better. She interests me, and Linc may be right: We have something in common; we share some deep wounds.

Days later

Molly chucks an old piece of wood, and it sails far out into the harvested cornfield.

"Fetch, King!" she shouts.

King chases after the wood. Watching him, I can see there's a happiness in his run that I find myself jealous of.

I step closer to Molly, and we are almost face to face. Perhaps too close, but I tell her, "Best beware; King'll likely play fetch until he falls over, or your arm falls off."

The warm vapor of breath from her lungs steams out and blends with mine in the chill October air, before it dissipates. But another cloud of our combined breath replaces it quickly.

She appears to cling to the moment as much as I do; we are a foot away from each other, starched in place and reluctant to move. Our eyes meet, and King is forgotten. We hold each other's appraisal a few more seconds, before Molly jerks her head to the side and slightly turns her body from me at an angle.

What will it take for her to be comfortable in my presence?

I hold back the sigh I sense rising in my chest and look out in the direction King ran. He's trotting back to us with something other than the wood Molly threw.

"Wonder what he's got there?" I think aloud.

Molly raises her arm to shade her eyes from the early afternoon sun. Her crocheted cap has no brim to do the job. "Can't quite tell, but it looks like he's dragging it."

She grates out her last few words and coughs, covering her mouth with her gloved hand. I wish I had a drink of water to offer her.

"Come on, boy," Molly calls and slaps her thighs to urge King on.

The smell meets us first.

"Land o' Goshen," I proclaim when King reaches us, and I see what he has dragged our way—a dead skunk.

Molly waves her hand in front of her nose, a sour, pinched expression on her face. "Oh my. Ooof…the stink."

She backs up, bending over coughing.

Pointing at King, I command, "Drop, boy!"

But his teeth are clamped tight around the critter's neck. I don't know how the dog can stand the smell. Granted, the reek is not as bad as an all-out spray from a live skunk, but close enough. Then I have an idea. I pick up a forgotten cob of dried corn, half eaten up by some critter, and throw it. Thankfully, King drops the skunk to chase the cob. A game of fetch trumps dead skunks, it seems.

Now, what to do with the skunk carcass?

"Any ideas how to keep him from running back to this…?" I ask Molly, pointing to the pile of pungent, bloody fur at our feet.

She puckers her lips then says, "Well, he loves to fetch so much. We could follow him and keep throwing things for him. Maybe we can distract him enough to circle back to the house, then I can take him and see what Mabel would like to do with him to get the stink out. While I'm dealing with King, you can come back and bury the skunk." She looks up at me. "What do you say?"

I can't believe she got through the explanation without coughing.

Smiling, I risk a wink. "Good plan. Although, I do wonder which one of us is getting the worst end of the stick."

We both laugh at my pun.

She smiles back, her scarred side still turned away from me. "That remains to be seen."

I gather up a few sticks, chunks of cornstalk stumps, and dried cobs and shove them in my coat pocket. "Let's get a move on." I point in the direction King went and offer my elbow, which she takes after a second or two of hesitation. We walk at the fastest pace we can manage over the bumpy, cornstalk-riddled ground. "This way, we'll have more time to talk."

I wait for her affirmation.

"Yes. I suppose."

I can't help but utter a brief laugh. "Not something you're necessarily looking forward to?"

"I didn't say that, Samuel."

Her words are relatively smooth. I like the way my name sounds on her tongue, thick, slow, and meaningful. I peek at her out the corner of my eye.

"Good. I'll try not to be too poor company," I tell her, and we walk steadily on.

She points at King. "Better get another ready."

He makes good time coming back to us, looking carefree and not like an animal bearing a cloud of acrid stench.

I pull a cob out of my pocket and wing it before he gets too close. "Yup. Here ya go, boy."

King drops the slobbered cob in his mouth, turns, and heads out after the new fetch toy.

Molly gazes after him. "How simple and happy the life of a dog is. Rather makes me jealous at times."

A wistfulness plays in her words, the way she holds onto the ending of her statements, clearly longing for something more.

"I know exactly what you mean," I agree.

We continue to step over crinkly, dry corn stalks and rocks, our steps out of alignment on the rough ground.

"Have you not been happy?" she asks, barring no barriers.

We seem to ask the most revealing questions of one another. I think back to happy days on the farm with my folks before Dad got ill.

"I was happy for a good many years…but life has a way of turning that state of mind on its head." I peer more intently at her. She gives nothing away. "Wouldn't you agree?" I ask, hoping for details, a hunger working up in me to hear her story.

Accompanied by a slight inclination of her head, she says, "I do, but I've also come to realize that there are different kinds of happiness."

"Hmm. Never thought about it like that. Can't say as I have experienced such a thing."

But I dwell on the notion as we walk in peace with one another for a few moments. I'm happy now—here with Molly. It's not the easy sense of life rolling along unencumbered, but how I feel at this moment goes deeper than that. I hit on what might be the reason: understanding.

"What do you think produces this other happiness?" I ask her, my mind delving into philosophical depths I've not fully explored.

I sense my mind and heart are safe with her.

Molly doesn't get the chance to answer, for King bounds back, tail wagging and ready for what's next.

Why can't I be as eager for life's changes?

I throw a cornstalk-root ball this time, only half as far as the previous, dried, shucked cob. King doesn't care, yaps, and bounds away to retrieve the mass.

Molly gazes over at me with the play of a smile about her

lips. "I'm still determining that, but perhaps we can decide together. I am fast realizing that you may be a man of wisdom."

I give a brief laugh. "I'd hardly proclaim to be wise. I'm more like the kid in school who needs the teacher to thump the textbooks over his head in order to remember the lessons."

We approach the end of the cornfield and the beginning of the yard.

"Maybe you should throw something for King one more time, then I'll tie a rope around his collar and lead him toward the house. I'll tie him by the clothesline," Molly tells me.

Nodding, I agree. "All right. Here goes nothin'." I toss another dry cob far into the yard, and just like every time before, King takes off. "Quick, I know where there's a length of rope in the barn." I grab Molly's hand in mine and urge her into a half-run. She doesn't protest but keeps up. We arrive barely winded. Running with her by my side, even for a short way, sits well with me. I fling open the barn door and grab the small coil of rope hanging on a hook inside. "Here we are."

I hand it to her. She looks at it as if it were a snake, but she swallows and picks it up.

Molly's bottom lip droops. "I hate to bring King's happiness to an end. He surely isn't going to like being washed with cold water and soap in this chilly air. Oh well." She sighs and shrugs. "Makes me sympathize with God, Him watching us wallow in our stench." She flicks her good eye up at me and half smiles. "Help me catch him?" she asks, looking me full in the face.

A twinge in my gut pricks as I glance over the uneven, waxy, red scars on the right side of her face. How I wish I could have spared her the pain.

"Of course." I offer a sincere smile. "Let's separate and get on either side of him when he comes back. After we get him tied to the clothesline post, you should ask Mabel for some tomato juice. I've heard it does wonders with alleviating a skunk odor."

With a wave of her hand, Molly shouts, "Here he comes! Get ready."

She widens her stance and reaches forward, the rope in her hands twisted into a loop. King trots toward us and stops between us. I lower my hands and catch him, while Molly slips the rope loop over his head.

"Phew," she utters with relief in her tone. "That was easier than I expected."

But she's spoken too soon. Despite the rope around his neck and Molly's hold on his lead, King takes off, like a rodent running from the blades of the hay mower.

I stupidly take in the fact that Molly still holds to the rope. She flounders along behind him for a few steps, before stumbling, falling, and subsequently getting dragged across the grass. After all, King's a big dog, and she's a small woman.

Finally, I come to my senses and holler, "Let go of the rope!"

She does, and King hurries away to the base of a maple tree by the house, barking furiously. Some rancorous chittering answers him. I run to help Molly, looking up and studying the tree boughs for the instigator of this latest fiasco; a red squirrel perches on the end of a branch, chittering nastily. I forget about the animals and turn to Molly.

She's rolled over onto her back, shaking. A giggle escapes her lips and becomes an outright chortle, accompanied by an unladylike snort. I bend down on one knee next to her. The backs of her hands cover her eyes.

My heart thumps extra hard, thinking she might be in danger. "Are you all right? You're not hurt, are you?"

In answer, she wipes at her eyes with her gloved fingers. "No. Good thing I had my wool coat on."

She lowers her hands and brushes off sticks, leaves, and dirt from the front of her coat. Our eyes meet. We both crack a smile and echo each other's mirth, as we break into laughter. I allow myself to fall back on the grass next to her, this silly moment bringing me more happiness than anything has in a long time.

When was the last time I laughed? Really laughed. I can't recall.

"Oh, that feels good," she says, turning her head toward me, her cheeks rosy and a deep smile lifting one side of her face.

I don't notice the scars; it's the joy I see reflected in her eyes that draws me.

I turn on my side, propping myself up on my elbow. A portion of her hair has fallen out of its entrapment of pins and curls around her neck. Reaching out a tentative finger, I brush the thick lock of hair. It's soft to the touch, and a faint fragrance of apple and chamomile arises when I stroke the curling strand. She sucks in a quick breath when my finger brushes her chin. I stop, gauging whether to proceed or not, but Molly doesn't protest. I see a surprised welcome in her eyes. The backs of my fingers stroke up her jawline to her cheek, on the soft, smooth side of her face.

All the sounds around us still; the birds quiet, King's yapping fades, and the breeze no longer whistles in my ear. All I can hear is the drum of my own heart. Her eyes widen, and she appears to be holding her breath, as I do mine. Of their own accord, my eyes focus on her lips, a perfect pair of petals in the midst of a half-ravaged flower. I dare to move closer; my lips hover inches above hers, the petals quiver, and our breath mingles once more.

"Dinner!"

A yell and a sharp *clang* of the bell from the back porch reverberates in the chilly air, and we jerk back from each other, the invisible net which gathered us together broken.

I suck in a deep breath, my lungs hungry for the air I've been holding. I sit back, and she rises to a sitting position and uses her hands to tuck her hair up under her hat.

I was so close.

Shaking off the disappointment, I rise to my feet and extend a hand to her.

"Shall we?" I ask in an unaffected voice, as if we hadn't almost kissed.

Molly coughs a few times, short and dry. "Yes, of course." She takes my hand and rises—all without looking me in the eye. "But what about King?"

She turns her head to where King lingers by the tree, sitting patiently beneath it.

"He can wait to get a bath until after we eat. His stench will still be the same in an hour. Besides, we might elicit more help by then."

I venture a wink, as she flashes her eyes up to mine. We share another smile.

She lets go of my hand. "Yes, I suppose so."

We tether King to the tree and stroll toward the house. I move with reluctance. I want to go back to the moment before the bell rang, when I almost fulfilled what I'd been thinking about doing for a while. But time moves on. We climb the steps. I hold the door open for Molly, and we go into the house. But something has changed. An attraction and an awareness rest between Molly and I that weren't there before today.

Oh, I had jolly well been interested and intrigued by her,

but as of that prior magic moment, I know now it's something deeper. I'm falling for her. But what troubles me is: I don't know much of anything about her. *What's her family like? How did she get burned? How has she survived? More importantly, what about her missing husband? Or is he dead?*

Those and other questions rise up in my heart. I pray I'll get another opportunity to ask her and that she'll be willing to share her past with me. I'm ready to tell her why I'm here. A confident peace about her makes me comfortable trusting her.

Hopefully, soon, we can uncover more of our souls to each other. I pray that she'll welcome and understand who I am and why I did what I did.

CHAPTER SEVEN

Molly

Early November

"The blue one, I think. Don't you?"

At Mabel's command, I hold a length of azure cotton fabric printed with a scattering of tiny birds and flowers against my chest. "It's nice."

I don't commit my favor either way. Mabel is determined to treat me to a new dress for an upcoming harvest dance, which I've told her that I'm not going to, but there's no arguing with her. Thus, we are here, at Driars' Women's Boutique—an old-fashioned millinery and dressmaker's store.

Mabel points at a bolt of brick-red fabric with brown dots. "Try the other one again."

I set the azure fabric aside and unroll the bolt of red fabric slightly before holding this one up to my front.

She backs up, leaning her head from shoulder to shoulder, thinking, and rolls her lips in. "Hmm, they're both nice."

I'm tired of playing dress-up. "I've always favored blue."

I hope this simple truth will prompt her to decide.

A sudden smile brightens her pensive face. "Really? Well, then we shall take the blue." With assurance, Mabel turns and demurely waves her hand in the air. "Miss Newsome," she calls. "We've made a choice."

A saleswoman—not old nor young, perhaps in her thirties—approaches us, outfitted in taffeta of the palest blue with indigo-colored trim. A tight smile, which appears to have been painted on by the color of her lips, a shocking, deep pink, is turned toward me. The closer she gets, the deeper the frown etches her rounded Scandinavian features into hard lines.

"Did you find something to your liking, ma'am?"

She directs the question in a smooth, slightly foreign-sounding voice to Mabel and ignores me. People usually respond one of three ways when meeting me for the first time: shock, revulsion, or non-recognition—simply put, I'm ignored. I hate being ignored; it makes me feel like I don't exist, like the world will go on turning perfectly fine without me. Like I don't matter one wit.

"Ah, yes." Mabel accentuates her words and first looks directly at Miss Newsome then turns to me. "*Mrs. Lund* would like enough yardage for a new dress."

"And will we be creating this dress for you, Mrs. Lund, or do you plan to piece and stitch it yourself?"

The woman actually looks at me this time, although with only a brief flick of her blue eyes, which are so bright against her pale skin and cropped, tightly curled head of white-blonde hair. Two pale pink spots highlight her rounded cheekbones, and her petite lips press together, as if she's swallowed something unsavory.

Apparently, that would be me.

Mabel answers her before I can. "Mrs. Lund will defer to your expertise, Miss Newsome, but I do want you to be aware that the dress is a gift from me."

Mabel spreads a wide grin my way.

"But Mabel…" I try to argue.

"Now, now. I won't listen to any opposition. It's from both Lincoln and I, to thank you for all you do."

I turn my head sideways, narrow my eyes, and lean close to Mabel, speaking through clenched teeth. "I think I should be the one thanking you with a gift."

Mabel rolls her eyes and lifts her chin, not listening to me. "I also believe we'll need a hat to match. What would you suggest, Miss Newsome?"

I cease arguing and sigh, listening while Mabel and Miss Newsome discuss color, texture, and style. I really don't know why Mabel's going to all this fuss. I don't need a new dress, and I'm not planning on going to that dance her women's group is hosting, even though I implied I might. Why would I put myself through the torture of being in a room full of people, all of whom could stare at me and likely will? And the dancing. Well, who in the world would dance with me?

No one in their right mind, I decide

I remember the day Jacob asked me to dance, staring at me across the room in the hotel ballroom in Land O' Lakes—the day we met.

"You should go talk to him. He's handsome," my friend Kitty French—a young woman as silly and feminine as her name suggests—whispered in my ear, her arm tucked around my elbow in a conspiratorial fashion.

The man with a dark complexion, trim beard, and mustache of umber-brown, met my gaze, our eyes strung together by an unseen cord. Dressed in a charcoal-toned suit, he stood opposite me, across the dancefloor, with a cup of punch cradled in his hand. His full, even lips curled upward in a slow progression, as if he just realized that he'd won a prize. I gulped and had a feeling the prize might be me. I dropped my gaze, smoothed down the deep-red, silk fabric of my skirt, and tucked my lips in, trying to avoid a blush, but the heat on my cheeks told me that I failed.

"Well," Kitty prodded. "His smile is an open invitation, if you ask me."

I fished for an excuse, so I didn't have to be brave. "I can't approach him. That would be improper."

I disliked doing brazen things and being noticed.

"What is this, the 1860s?" Kitty leaned back and gulped down the rest of the contents of the cup she held in her right hand. "If you don't, I will."

She raised one eyebrow in a challenge.

But as it happened, Jacob made his way to me. The band had struck up a slow waltz.

With his dark eyes sparkling, he asked me, "May I have this dance?"

I hesitated. I didn't even know his name. He must have read my thoughts, for he introduced himself, and I stuttered out a reply, giving him my name.

Then, as if on cue, he held out his hands to me, passing his cup off to waitstaff. I nodded and gulped, forcing my drink on Kitty, who pouted.

Jacob's arm pressed around me, and his thick hand held mine firmly. As we twirled around the dancefloor, he asked me all manner of questions, which I answered in a near breathless blur.

To have the attention of a richly dressed, handsome man sent my head spinning. With each step, turn, and twirl, I lost a bit of my heart to him. Little did I know that, years later, he would hand it back to me, broken beyond repair.

My heart aches thinking about our past. "Oh, Jacob…"

"Molly?" Mabel's puzzled brows question me. "Did you say something? I missed that."

She waits for me to answer.

Gazing down, I say, "Oh, nothing. Just thinking about…the hat." I lie, clear my throat, and manage, sweeping away the bittersweet memories. "It will be lovely."

Lifting my eyes, I smile and nod, hoping I reassure Mabel. I don't want her to think of me as an ungrateful friend.

Mabel's smile holds the happy sunshine of a child. "I'm so glad you like it."

She is a gift-giver at heart; nothing seems to provide her with more joy than blessing other people with gifts. That's not my forte. I have always struggled with finding or creating the right gifts for people. Why, I do not know. It's not that I don't care or don't listen. Perhaps it's because I often second-guess myself.

I glance at the clock on the wall, wanting to leave this place. All the beautiful things around me only serve to remind me that I am not. Beautiful, that is.

"Lincoln said to meet him at two," I remind Mabel.

Mabel fiddles with her bag, digging through it. "Oh my, where has the time gone?" She continues looking through her bag. "I appear to have left my cash at home. I'm so sorry."

Wearing two pink blotches on her cheeks, Mabel turns to Miss Newman.

"Not to worry. I will put it on your account. Pay when you

come to pick it up." Miss Newman rips off a piece of paper from a pad. "Your receipt," she says with a flourish and hands the paper to Mabel.

Mabel bats her eyelashes several times, a kindly smile on her lips. "I appreciate this. Thank you so much."

"It is I who thank you for your patronage, ladies. You will not be disappointed," Miss Newsome states with confidence as Mabel gathers up her bag and the hat box, and we head toward the shop door.

We make our exit and begin to walk to where Lincoln said he would meet us. As we amble toward our meeting place, I dig deep inside of myself in a great effort not to sink into sadness, but the memory of Jacob pulls at me. Does he ever still think of me? Most of our years together were good, blessed, but those last six months after the accident he changed. To be fair so did I. And then one day he left. That last straw of my husband leaving me toppled me over into despair. That was the day my mother contacted the asylum. Since, I have thought of Jacob as dead to me.

Mabel's gaze roves over my features, I imagine looking for something to blame for my lapses. "Are you feeling unwell?"

The last thing I need is for Mabel to fuss over me.

"A memory caught me off guard. It's nothing, really," I explain.

Mabel relieves me of her pointed stare and pans her gaze to the planked walkway in front of us. "A good or…bad memory?"

I stride off-kilter next to her; Mabel's legs are longer than mine. "A good one, I suppose. But bittersweet."

Several seconds of the clicking of our heels on the boardwalk fill the space between us.

Mabel gives me a glance out the corner of her eye. "Well, aren't you going to tell me?"

A sigh escapes my lips. "I thought of Jacob and how we met."

Mabel doesn't immediately ask me how. She remains quiet. After a minute, she asks, "Do you miss him?"

Do I? "Yes and no. I miss who he was and…who we were together."

"I'm sorry."

"Thank you." I turn to Mabel. "But in a way, I'm glad he's no longer here to hurt me."

She gulps, concern written in every line of her face. "Was…he a violent man?"

"No. He did turn to drink to drown his sorrows, but it was mostly what he didn't do or say that dug deep."

"How do you mean?"

We are almost back to the auto, where I can see Lincoln waits for us in the shade of a towering oak, so I keep my answer short. I have no wish to divulge my secrets to him.

"Jacob could not see past my scars. The words 'I love you' never left his lips again after…" I swallow back the ending.

Mabel starts to speak. "I'm so…"

I hold up a hand. "No! Don't say it." In a sudden outburst, my voice rises beyond my control, frustration fueling my protest. "I don't need your sympathy, Mabel. It's not why I came here!" Lincoln turns our way and starts to get out of the car, his heavy brows angled down. I rein in my tone. "Can you understand?"

My eyes meet Mabel's, begging her.

"Well, yes, but can't a friend express concern and sorrow for what you've been through? We are friends, aren't we?"

Mabel's voice cracks, and her big eyes plead with me, hurt lurking behind them.

"Of course, we are," I grate out.

I've done too much talking. My throat burns, like a scraped knuckle on a washboard.

Lincoln steps toward us, his gaze shifting from me to Mabel. "Need some help with anything?"

He's likely wondering what's gone on between us.

Mabel turns to him with what I might call a fake smile. "You may carry these for me and stow them in the vehicle."

She hands Lincoln the boxes from the dressmaking shop, but a dull spot reflects in her eye, showing less life than usual. A familiar guilt settles in my gut.

I seem to hurt everyone I love.

We get in the auto, keeping our thoughts to ourselves all the way back to the farm.

The next week

Mabel grins, her eyes shining. "Oh, don't you look fine? I think the cameo pin is just the right touch." She puffs up my sleeve on the right shoulder, like she's fluffing up a pillow. "Now, promise me that you will try and enjoy yourself."

She reaches up and adjusts my hat.

I hardly recognize myself in the mirror. In the end I am glad Miss Newsome created my dress. She's far more skilled with a needle than me. She styled the dress in straight lines with a low, gathered skirt. Panels of lace run vertically on the front and back, while clusters of brown and blue, ribbon roses decorate the wide neckline. The wide hat does make the outfit. I turn my head slowly from side to side. In this light and with the dotted veil angled over the right side of my face, one can hardly notice my deformity.

Mabel lets out a "Squeeee!" and hugs me. "I knew you

would be lovely." She drops her arms. "Now, I need to throw my glad rags on and get ready." She gives me a slight shove toward her bedroom doorway. "Go downstairs and tell Linc that I'll be ready soon."

"Very well." A sudden thought occurs to me. "We won't be early, will we?"

I hate arriving ahead of time for anything. Better to come late and blend in with the crowd.

"No. We should be right on time. Now go!"

Mabel turns me around and pushes me out the doorway, shutting the painted, wooden door behind me. My black pumps clomp on the wooden floor, sounding like little hammers of doom, chiming out a warning. But because I do not want to dash Mabel's hopes for me, I drag myself downstairs and find Lincoln.

An hour later

The atmosphere palpitates with the music of the band, which has embraced a bit of ragtime, and the feel of too many bodies too close together.

I blink my eyes and suck in a quick breath, as Samuel's wide smile meets me. "Care to dance, Mrs. Lund?"

He is handsome, far too good-looking for me.

I swallow down my inner protests despite his blond curls, slicked back with hair tonic, and the burnt-sienna-colored, well-cut suit, draped perfectly over Samuel's trim but strong frame.

"I'm not much of a dancer," I lie.

I was once light on my feet; Jacob always said so.

Samuel holds out his hand to me. "Nonsense. If I can put my clodhoppers on the dance floor, surely you can accompany me."

I glance over at Mabel and catch her eye. A pasted grin on her face and her innocent eyes can't fool me.

She thinks she's so smart. I can't help but agree with what I know she's thinking: *Samuel sees me as more than a friend.*

Samuel pulls me along with him and before I can protest again, he has me in his arms, guiding me to the rhythm of the music, which has tempered to a slower, more intimate beat. "And might I say, you look beautiful in blue."

"Thank you," I say simply, an unfamiliar blush heating my cheeks.

Twirling me around, he clasps me tighter in his arms when I return to him. "The calming hue suits you, and the style is lovely on you."

He surprises me at every turn. I feel the old, easy choreography of dance steps coming back to me and float with the music within his embrace.

"Mr. Woodson, you shouldn't tell falsehoods," I tease him.

To banter with someone of the opposite sex makes me forget that I see myself as less than desirable. Jacob all but told me so, and it's what I think, when I look in the mirror. But the way Samuel's eyes light up, when his gaze falls on me, speaks otherwise. He takes in my whole person and not just the webbing of scars evident to anyone with an eye. He's even been privy to some of my inward scars and hasn't shied away.

"Not at all, Molly. I speak the truth." He stops me, and we both stand still, the space between us non-existent, my chest pressing against his middle. Couples sway by us in a blur. The music blends together as I focus on him. I dare to gaze at him straight-on. Cradling me more fully with one arm, Samuel lets go of my hand and reaches up to brush the side of my scarred face. "If only you could see yourself as I do."

I want to block out everything but his voice, but the sound of giggling makes me turn my head. Not far away, a trio of young ladies titter behind their hands. The one with blonde ringlets hanging over her shoulder turns up her nose and sends a message via her steely blue eyes that I interpret all too well.

Just who do you think you are, you ugly creature?

That's the question I hear in my heart, and it brings tears to my eyes. I break away from Samuel's embrace. "I'm…I'm sorry, but I suddenly don't feel well. I…"

I don't take time to offer any more of an explanation for my departure. Fighting a dizzy sensation, I turn and weave my way through the crowd, hoping he won't follow me. I chance a glance backward. He stands where I left him with a dumbfounded expression scoring lines on his face. I flip my head back and slip out the exit.

The cool evening air washes over me. I take a couple of slow, deep breaths, working to quiet the cries of "*Imposter! Monster! Hideous beast!*" Usually, I quell such rantings. Dr. Howington from the asylum taught me to, but every now and then they best me. I lean my head back against the board siding of the town hall, a tiredness making my limbs drip with heaviness, and I slide down to the ground, not caring that my new dress crumples down around me into the frosty grass. Tired and fed-up with the attempt to fit back into society, I reprimand myself for coming, for listening to Mabel, and most of all for believing a man could be attracted to me. I give in to tears for a minute, but then wipe my eyes with the hem of my dress and sniff.

Pull yourself together!

I stand and walk to the Ford, hoping soon Mabel will wonder where I am and come looking for me. After yanking open the door of the auto, I hunker down in the backseat and cover myself with an old blanket rolled up on the floor. Determined to wait out the dance, I close my eyes and picture my garden—my place of peace—back at the asylum. It was the best medicine Dr. Howington provided.

He smiled kindly and wiped his damp brow with a white handkerchief, the July heat making us sweat. "Our gardener left last week, and I thought working out in the open air might uplift your soul. I find the activity of work, being in nature, does as much good as manufactured medicine and procedures."

He stuffed his handkerchief back into his pocket. My eyes focused past him on the garden plot before us, which spilled over with neat rows of vegetables of every kind. A few marigolds, cosmos, cornflowers, and hollyhocks capped the end of the plot.

I gained the courage to ask, "Could I plant more flowers?"

Seeing those red hollyhocks made me homesick. I remembered the flowers Mother had grown around the house in Land O' Lakes: clusters of lily of the valley, day lilies, peonies, irises, dahlias, and hollyhocks.

"I don't see why not." Dr. Howington reached into his suit coat and pulled out a pair of gloves. He handed them to me. "You may get started right away."

The canvas gloves rested in my palm and appeared too large for my hands, but I put them on.

He chuckled. "Well, not exactly a perfect fit, but they'll do the trick for now until I can get you a more suitable pair." One thick, salt-and-pepper eyebrow rose. "You will be supervised by Nurse Sandry for a week or two." He shielded his eyes from the sun as he gazed up at the sky. "I think morning garden work might be best from now on."

I offered him a shy smile. "Agreed."

He smiled back. "It's good to see you happy, even just a little." He lowered his arm and sighed. "Now I must tend to Irene, but you may work out here until dinner, if you like. Nurse Sandry should be out shortly for her break. The tools are in the garden shed yonder."

He pointed to a small, brick building on the north side of the garden, nodded once, and walked back to the asylum.

I was left standing alone. The flowers drew me closer. I stepped to the edge of the tilled earth, pulled off a glove, and fingered one red petal. Its silky texture felt like Mother's hair, when I would brush it for her. I took after her with my thick, dark head of hair. Her smiling face and smooth voice floated in my memory. I missed her.

"I may have the rough hands of a laundress, but my hair will always be queenly." She had smiled, her thin lips stretching modestly. "Every woman has at least one true beauty." She had touched my cheek. "As you will come to discover."

I tucked the memories of Mother away and let go of the petal. I used to think the beauty she spoke of was my face. I had perfect, romantic features before the accident: smooth, clear skin, rosy cheeks, a tapered, oval shape, bright, flashing eyes, a modest forehead, and perfectly paired brows. My fingers roved over the scars. Not anymore, I don't.

The flowers would be my beauty…

And they had been and would continue to be so, along with the faith in God I renewed.

A metallic creak and a voice break into my memories, Mabel appearing. "There you are. What happened? Do you feel unwell? Samuel said…"

I cut her off. "I'm fine, now. A dizzy spell hit me before when I was dancing."

I keep my eyes on my lap.

"You should have come found me right away. Lincoln would have taken you home." She opens the car door fully. "You must be freezing with only that old blanket on."

"No. I'm warm enough." Truthfully, I've barely noticed the chilly temperature. "I didn't want to ruin your time."

Mabel scootches into the car and sits down next to me on the seat. "Things were going so well. Last time I glanced your way, you and Samuel were beaming at each other. What happened?"

She doesn't need to know how I reacted and for what reason. "Like I said, I got dizzy."

A sideways slant angles the corner of her mouth back, and Mabel's eyebrows scrunch together. "Hmm, I don't think that's the whole story."

Lincoln arrives before she can question me further; he has impeccable timing.

He appears not to notice that I've been holed up in the Ford for the last hour. "Homeward bound, ladies?"

"Yes," I crack out, my voice sounding rusty to my own ears.

"Righto. I'm beat. Too much pie and dancin'." He cranks the engine, gets in the car, and slams the door, looking at Mabel in the rearview mirror. "You riding back there?"

"If that isn't a problem," she responds.

Linc grins and puts the Ford in gear. "I guess I musta worked up a sweat."

We lurch forward. I pray Mabel is too tired to question me further, as we bounce toward home.

CHAPTER EIGHT

Samuel

The next morning

Happy to be done with chores, I hurry to the house to wash before supper. But I don't look forward to seeing Molly. I avoided her at lunch. A place of hurt has come to roost in my heart like a broody hen; I can't seem to budge it. Molly's abrupt departure from my embrace at the dance last evening left me guessing how she could be feeling.

Does she care for me?

At times it seems so and at others not. Perhaps I'm letting my own romantic notions get the better of me. Honestly, my regard for her has seemed to sprout from a heart I thought was impenetrable to romance. Molly may simply deem me a friend, nothing more.

I stomp off my boots and ease the porch door shut behind me. Craning my neck, I take a look around to see if Molly is in sight.

Mabel appears out of nowhere, a huge smile on her face. "Samuel! Just the person we need." She wipes her hands on her ever-present apron. "You have a guest, a visitor."

She waits expectantly.

"Wh-who?" I stutter out.

I can't imagine who could have come calling for me. No one I know from home knows where I am. At least, I don't think they do. Sitting on the bench, I yank my boots off and peel off my coat.

Mabel's eyes twinkle in the lamplight as she leans against the door jam. "You'll never guess."

I shake my head and shrug, waiting for her to tell me.

"Your mother. Isn't that nice? I bet you've missed each other. And there's nothing like being with family for the holidays. Thanksgiving will be upon us before we know it."

Her words fade as one thought fills my mind: *Mother is here.* It's been months, but I'm not ready to talk to her yet and definitely not ready to forgive her, or myself for that matter.

"Samuel?" Mabel places a light hand on my shoulder. "I thought you'd be pleased."

Her lovely features wrinkle.

I shake my head, slow and purposeful. "Didn't Linc tell you?"

She lowers her voice and one brow. "Tell me what?"

Swallowing, I say, "Of our...difficulties."

I don't want to reveal too much.

She places one hand over her heart and pats the back of her head with the other. "Of course, he mentioned your father's death and your grief, but..."

We catch each other's gaze in the seconds of uncomfortable silence between us.

My mother's head appears around the corner of the doorframe to the kitchen. "Samuel?"

She's changed. Her once prim but happy smile and flashing, gray eyes only reflect the pain of burying one husband right after another.

I sit up straight and clear my throat, grubbing out, "Mother. I didn't expect to see you."

Forcing myself to look into her eyes, I hold steady. Out the corner of my vision, Mabel slips back into the kitchen without a sound.

Mom sighs. "I gather you didn't." She dabs at her nose with the hankie she's pulled out of her lace-edged, black sleeve and sniffs loudly. She has always known how to cook up a thick amount of theatrics. "How could you go off and leave me all alone? I just don't understand it."

Mother keeps her eyes cast down in martyr mode, playing her usual victim card.

Anger brings me to my feet and my voice rises in volume before I can tamp it down. "How on God's green earth would you expect me to stay?" A stream of ire bursts forth "After giving the farm away to that money-grubbin'…" I slap my hand on my thigh and step closer to her until her face is inches from mine and spit out my accusations. "And to see you preening to him like a peahen before Pa was even cold in the ground."

She looks up then, eyes hard and icy.

"Shush your mouth!" she whispers fiercely and glances toward the kitchen, where I vaguely hear Mabel loudly clinking dishes. "You should know me better than to think I, in any way, acted improper with Alfred. We'd been friends for many years, and he comforted me and supported me when your father took his turn."

Grabbing at her black, lace collar, Mother looks up at me. Her small, thin, drawn face gives me a prick in the ribs.

She is my mother, after all.

Her skinny index finger presses against a shirt button on my chest. "And you with your pointing finger. I might point mine right back at you."

The old guilt rears its head again. I swallow, my ears buzz, and a weariness at the same repeated battle with Mother knocks at my brain.

I brush her finger away and turn. "Mabel's getting supper on the table. Lincoln should come in any time."

We still stand in the entryway, awkward and opposed, and I have no desire to keep bickering with Mother in front of Linc and Mabel, much less Molly. *I wonder where she is.*

Her mouth relaxes and her eyes soften. "Yes, well. I missed you, Samuel. A mother wants to see her son."

"How did you find me?"

"Paul Richardson saw you at a dance and mentioned that he had."

That old schoolmate of mine. Leave it to Paul, gossip itself and worse than an old lady at a quilting bee. "Ah. Well, I didn't see him."

"No. He mentioned that your eyes were fixed…elsewhere."

Great. That's all I need: suspicions about a supposed romance.

Lincoln steps into the house, his gaze down until he sees us. "Supper on yet?" He removes his crusty barn cap and nods at Mother. "Excuse me, Mrs. Woodson…ah, that is, Mrs. Skaggs now; Sam has informed me." He grins and extends his hand, then thinks better of it and wipes it on his side. "It's been some time since I saw you last. I'm sorry for your loss."

Mother nods her head and offers the briefest of smiles.

"Thank you. You're looking well, Lincoln."

Mabel appears around the corner. She looks to Lincoln. "There you are."

It's getting much too tight of quarters for me, and I wedge past Mabel. "We should make our way in and let Lincoln have room to get his barn things off."

I motion with my hand toward the kitchen to Mother.

"Yes, of course," Mother says, stepping by Mabel as well.

I point out the dining room and head to the washroom.

Her voice comes from behind me. "Samuel."

I stop but don't turn. "Yes."

"I…" Her voice cracks. "I don't know how to fix what's broken between us."

The breath I didn't know I held fizzles out of me.

"Ya, me either," I admit, and I go to wash the last remains of barn smell from my hands and arms and pray for God's mercy for the rest of the evening.

I finish quickly with my washing and head back to the dining table, sitting across from Molly. Usually, we just eat in the kitchen, but with Mother here Mabel must have thought more formal setting was required. Molly hasn't looked at me once.

Lincoln passes out a generic comment along with a heaping bowl of mashed potatoes to Mother. "It's mild weather we're having for November."

Mother takes the bowl and dishes out a small portion onto her plate. "'Tis, for sure. And it's a good thing too. Still need some wood cut." She pins me with a glare. Her voice has that sharp, little edge to it. "Had to hire the neighbor boy to come chop some more."

Does she have to play this jabbing game of telling me something without really saying it? I don't take her bait. My eyes and Lincoln's meet. He appears to sense her sharp hints.

Mabel diverts the thread of our conversation. "I do enjoy the warmer temperatures. Although I love the beauty of winter, the cold is less appealing to me than it used to be as a child."

I focus on my food, cutting my pork steak into chunks. Mabel and mother discuss the finer points of indoor activities in the wintertime until Mother—who has ignored Molly up till now—asks, "Mrs. Lund, how did you and Mrs. Nelson meet?"

I watch Molly's eyes flicker up, but she shies the burnt side of her face away from Mother.

Clearing her throat, Molly says, "Mabel's sister, Mrs. Robin Holcomb, and I were friends first. I met Mabel through Robin."

Molly chokes on her last few words and takes a drink of water. I can't help but notice how the liquid quivers in the glass as she raises it. Molly dislikes questions about her background. I know her well enough to know that.

Mother lifts a forkful of canned corn to her mouth and asks, "I see, and where did you meet Mrs. Holcomb?"

She waits for Molly to answer.

"Ah, we…" Molly draws out.

Mabel comes to her rescue. With a bright ring in her tone, she turns to Mother. "They worked together. Robin and her husband live on a fine farm in Wisconsin with his aunt and uncle."

Mother, curling her upper lip back at the corner, examines Molly with a hint of revulsion. "I see."

Molly deserves better than this. She's more than some object for people to look down upon.

I nod and speak up. "Molly is a gifted gardener."

Molly catches my eye. I'm relieved to see her lips curl up in appreciation at my compliment.

"Oh, yes," Mabel adds, smiling with an angelic light on her face. "She has plans for a flowerbed around the south side of the house. I can hardly wait to see the transformation."

"You'll be staying until spring then, Mrs. Lund?"

Mother gives me a look I know all too well, meaning stay away. When I was a child, such cautionary narrowing of her eyes used to stop me in my tracks, but I am a child no longer.

Braving her gaze, I say, "I certainly hope so." Expressing the truth of that statement relaxes my shoulders and a sense of peace and rightness accompanies it. I do want Molly to stay. I wipe my mouth on my napkin and change the subject. "That was divine, Mabel. Molly." I nod at each. "Thank you for supper. Those pork steaks had the best sear. Mighty tasty."

"My ma taught me to have the skillet and fat piping hot and the meat dry before adding it." Mabel forks in her last mouthful, chews, swallows, and says, "I'd say it was time for dessert. Molly, will you help me?"

Rising, I wait for Molly. "Oh, no. Let me." I gesture with my hand. "After you."

Molly stands and pushes back her chair but keeps her eyes down.

Mabel raises her eyes and smiles at me. "Why, thank you, Samuel. How kind."

I smile back. "Of course."

I follow Molly to the kitchen, nervous and expectant at the same time to be alone with her. She collects dessert plates from the built-in hutch, and I eye up the apple cake on the kitchen table, my mouth watering.

"Should I slice it up?" I ask.

"Yes. Thank you."

Her words contain a calm quietness, and she sets the plates down gently next to me. A knife already sits by the cake, but instead of reaching for it, I gently grab her hands. She lifts her eyes, large and sad, to mine.

"I'm sorry about my mother."

She shrugs one shoulder. "I'm used to that sort of thing."

"You shouldn't have to be." I rub the back of her palm with my thumb and get up the courage to ask, "What about the other night at the dance? Did I do something to upset you?"

Shaking her head, she says, "No. It's just that…" We look into each other's eyes, but I can't read what's behind her soft as velvet orbs. "You hardly know me."

She looks down, but I tip her chin up until her eyes meet mine again.

My heart starts to beat harder, and a twinge of something I suspect might be love twists my gut in a knot. "That's not true."

Her eye's search mine. "Isn't it?"

My hands slide up her arms to her shoulders. I brush the underside of her scarred jaw with the back of my knuckles.

She stops me, her hand covering mine. "Don't."

I move and lace my fingers through hers. "Why? Tell me that you don't care."

I demand an answer. She can't shut me out like this.

"I haven't told you everything."

"Neither have I."

Molly drops her gaze at a noise from the dining room. "We better get this dessert to the table before Mabel comes to see what's holding us up."

She disentangles her fingers from mine; I dislike the emptiness.

"Promise to go for a walk with me soon, and we can talk further."

"Very well." She scoots the knife closer to me. "Get to slicing."

"Yes, ma'am."

I do as she bids, and together we dish up the cake. Working beside Molly is easy, right. I think how nice it would be to work alongside her every day. I'm determined to make an effort to find out if it's possible.

Molly's hand brushes mine, and the hairs on my arm stand on end. A desire to sense her touch and have her near me unfurls in my heart. She doesn't move away, and I reach down to place a light kiss on her temple.

CHAPTER NINE

Molly
Thanksgiving Day 1919

I keep my distance. The freezing temperature tells me I should snuggle close, but I don't. Light, lazy flakes float down from the gray clouds overhead, reminding me of a snow globe I saw once at a mercantile. I plucked it from the shelf and swirled it around like a demi-god ordaining a storm, but no imagined power rests in my hand today. The weakness of anxiety blisters me instead.

Samuel leans back on the bench at the top of the farm's bur oak ridge. His arm splays out behind me. I don't want to feel his touch. Not yet. Not until I've told him the truth about my past. The words rise up in me.

"I never fully explained where I met Robin, Mabel's sister," I begin, and my eyes fix straight ahead on the tall grass, dried goldenrod, and empty milkweed pods dusted with a layer of snow. My full stomach, from our plentiful meal, twinges. Pulling my red wool scarf tighter around my neck, I forge ahead into the truth. "We met at an…institution in Menomonie, Wisconsin."

Samuel's kind, patient tone welcomes me to continue. "So I've heard mentioned."

I focus on my fingers, picking at a black button on my coat. "It was an insane asylum, Samuel."

I hold my breath, waiting for his response.

He falters. "I…I see." Seconds pass. "No, I don't," he admits, and he slides closer to me. "Please explain. I'm listening."

He slowly draws circles on my back through my wool coat with the flat of his hand.

His action doesn't make me flinch; instead I release my breath and take another. "I couldn't manage after Lonny's death. And then Jacob…"

"Lonny was your son?"

"That's right. My mother was concerned for me and rightly so." I stop, choke, and cough, then take a deep breath before I continue. I hate the tight, strangled sensation in my neck, but I try to ignore it and explain. "I…wanted to die too. I retreated into myself, and nothing worked to draw me out. She saw no other alternative than to have me committed."

I rub the corded muscle on the side of my neck, trying to relax the tension there. Samuel says nothing but moves closer yet and slides his arm around my shoulder. The warmth of his presence makes me want to turn into his shoulder and sob, but I don't. I've cried enough over the past, and I need to let it go.

Samuel curls his arm farther around me and turns me toward him. "I'm sorry you had to go through something like that, but they treated you and you obviously got better, because here you are with me."

My eyes flick up to his, and I sink into his smile.

"And I'm glad," he says.

I hear no abhorrence in his words. I trust in the firm grip of his arm. "You don't sound shocked."

I allow myself to search his blueish eyes.

"You expected me to be?" he asks.

"Yes."

Samuel sighs. "Grief can do crazy things to a body."

I know his father has died. "You and your father were close?"

My anxiety over my announcement has left, as my concern for Samuel's well-being takes precedence.

"Yes. He was a good man and didn't deserve to go as he did, wasting away into nothing, while Mother…"

Samuel clams up. I watch his jaw muscles clench. I turn to him and place the mittened hand that I've been massaging my neck with on the lapel of his gray, wool coat. The speckled pattern of the tweedy weave reminds me that life isn't black and white but many shades in between the two opposing colors.

From the dinner with his mother, I have gathered significant hurt weighs down their relationship.

"You can tell me what happened, if you want," I gently urge.

"I appreciate that." Samuel reaches for my hand with his free arm; his warmth transfers through the wool of my mitten. "She formed an attachment to a man well before my father passed. They married shortly after my father's death. Too soon after."

He stops talking and stares down at his boots and kicks at the crunchy, dead grass underfoot. I wait for him to continue. I won't rush him, for he's been patient with me.

Continuing, Samuel looks up and over at me. "The farm went to him after they married. It should have been mine. Father would have wanted me to have it."

I sense a bitter ring in his voice.

"You left then?" I ask, sympathizing with his predicament. A son should inherit from his father.

Jacob.

His name rings in my mind, and I think of how he grieved the loss of Lonny. I didn't understand then that Jacob's mourning process might differ from mine. I should tell Samuel more about Jacob, but I wish to hear the details of Samuel's story. Jacob will keep for another time.

"Yes, partly for that reason, but…" Samuel turns away from me. He lets go of my hand and bows his head. "Mother blamed me. You see…" He tips his head back up and turns to focus on me. "I killed him."

I'm stunned by his words. I can't equate Samuel's demeanor and his soft, blue-green eyes like pale cornflowers with those of a murderer. "Surely not?"

I search for the truth in first one of his spheres then the other. I don't see a killer.

He sighs bitterly. "As good as."

He scoots down on the bench and flops his head back on the wood-slatted backrest.

"Tell me what happened," I urge him.

Heaving out a sigh, Samuel says, "I provoked him, and one night we got in a terrible fight. Punches were thrown. And then he collapsed." His face takes on a pale sheen. "An apoplectic fit, the doctor said. He died within an hour of our tussle." He shakes his head. "I don't think Mother will ever forgive me, but I can say the same, I reckon."

I don't know what else to say, so I settle for, "I'm sorry."

He fits his hands together in his lap. "Ya. Thanks."

"But you can't think of yourself as solely responsible for his death. He must have been in poor health to collapse so."

I scoot closer to him and reclaim his hand. He echoes my firm clasp.

Samuel rolls his lips in and glances at me out the corner of his left eye. "I suppose, but I can't help but feel guilty. I'm just a flawed, unforgiving, guilty man."

How does he want me to reply to that? I argue, "No. That's not the person I've been privileged to know." I turn toward him fully and take his other hand. "You've shown me kindness and treated me as beautiful when I'm anything but. You're a good man, Mr. Woodson."

I can't help but smile.

Samuel loosens my hold and lifts his hand to cup my chin, forcing my vision directly to him. "Now who's being detrimental? You *are* beautiful, Molly, inside and out."

He pulls me to him, and I can't resist. I push my presumed-dead husband and my deformity from my mind and center my thoughts on the man who's shown love to me and caresses my scars instead of running from them, like Jacob did.

Our lips touch and touch again, the pressure strong but yielding, and a surge of desire I haven't felt in a long time tingles down my spine. Samuel pulls slightly back in what I presume is an attempt to gauge my ardor. Our breath fogs between us, and his eyes spark passion in me. I reach up behind his neck and urge him forward, back to my waiting lips.

That evening

After each of us has had a second slice of Thanksgiving pumpkin pie and a cup of tea, Samuel and I curl by the fire. The scent of spice and cedar hangs in the air. Lincoln and Mabel have gone to bed. The clock strikes 9:00, and I am sure Samuel is tired. The routine of barn chores begins early at 5:00 in the morning.

"You never did tell me how you left things with your mother."

We sit next to each other on the settee. I purposely position a small pillow between us and rest my arm on the embroidered cover, which reads, in black thread, *A stitch in time saves nine.*

Samuel shrugs and smiles in a ho-hum way. "Not much to say. I told her I wasn't going back, and the next morning I drove her to the train station."

I wish I knew how to encourage him. He appears to be trapped in an unmovable situation, but everything is fragile. Perhaps that's the problem—a broken relationship with his mother. I know about broken relationships. They are difficult to mend but not impossible, at least when the person isn't physically missing or dead. My mind wanders to Jacob again. *If miraculously he were found, would I want to mend things between us?* The question grates at my conscience.

Samuel reaches for my hand. I let him enfold his hand around mine, but I have to remind him, "I'm not sure my husband has died." I let the truth sink in, waiting for him to back away from me, but he doesn't. I remind him further, "I'm still married, Samuel."

The truth hurts and causes a deep place of sadness in me. *Do I still love Jacob?* I don't know. The pain he's caused me has certainly dampened any feeling I held for him.

Samuel nods and speaks with care. "Well, that may be, but where is he, this husband of yours? Why isn't he here caring for you? What kind of man leaves his wife like he left you?"

His voice holds the hurt I often feel when I ask the same questions.

"I wish I knew." My fingers squeeze his. "But I'm so thankful for our friendship."

I smile at him reservedly.

A shadow perches on his brow. "Yes. Friends."

I hear the disappointment in his tone. I've gathered he desires to be more than that to me, as I do to him.

"Maybe we should call it a night." I glance at the clock. "It's getting late."

Samuel releases my hand. "Yes, I suppose."

I rise and move to collect our dishes.

Samuel stops me and takes the plates from me, stacking the cups on top. "Let me do that."

He's so thoughtful, kind, and considerate. A sudden burst of emotion over what could be mine causes me to tear up. I gulp back the emotion and hide my face from him.

"Thank you, you're so kind," I manage to mumble.

"It's because I love you, Molly."

He pivots and walks to the kitchen, his long strides making short work of it. His words truly make my tears fall. I struggle not to sob and grieve for what can never be between us.

CHAPTER TEN

Samuel

Usually, the hayloft is a calming place, but right now, with each fork full of hay I lift and pitch, I remember, anger burning in me again over the whole grubby matter.

"Now that Keren and I are married, you're no longer needed here."

Alfred Skaggs's blunt words opened a festering wound.

I stepped closer to the man who'd swindled me out of the farm and my inheritance. "Now that you have what you want, I can skedaddle, huh? And just who do you think is going to keep this place up for you?"

My gaze rolled over his fancy, navy blue suit. I knew Mr. Skaggs wouldn't get his hands dirty.

He stepped, turned, and toyed with a small China dog poised on the mantle of the fireplace in the sitting room. Mother was collecting the eggs from the chicken coop, and we were alone.

He kept his back to me. "I'll hire someone, of course."

My ears burned. "And you'd replace your wife's son—not to mention the man who's kept this place operating for years—with a stranger who doesn't know jack about the farm?"

Alfred slowly turned, a sickly, satisfied smile on his too-full lips. "In a heartbeat."

The heat in my ears spread to my neck and chest. "And what of my mother? Surely, she can't agree to your scheme."

He puckered his mouth and narrowed his prominent eyes. "Keren will do as I say."

I couldn't help but think he looked like an angry fish in a bowl. But Alfred wasn't the one confined; I was. "How can you be so sure?"

My hands balled into fists at my sides.

"She loves me." His upper lip twitched. "She always has."

Before I knew it, my fist met Alfred's nose. He reeled back into the mantle. Mother's China dog crashed to the floor.

Shooting me an angry glare, Alfred yelled, "How dare you!"

He righted himself and threw a punch my way but missed, as I ducked. We rounded each other, moved at the same time, and grappled with each other's lapels, before I pushed off and landed a blow to his jaw.

"You're gonna regret that, son," Alfred said with intent.

He shook his head and wiped at his nose, flaring his nostrils like a bull ready to charge. And he did. We collided, knocking a tea table over. The shattering glass from the lamp atop it sent my mother rushing into the room. She hurried forward with her coat still on and tried to break us apart.

"Stop this!" she shouted, tugging at my arm. "Samuel! Let go!"

In our tussle, she fell back, thankfully onto the couch.

My hands ringed Alfred's neck, and all I had to do was squeeze. But without force from me, he started turning purple, gasping for breath. I let go and backed off.

"Oh, my dear!" Mother cried. She raised herself from where we'd thrown her and rested her hands on either side of his head. "What…what is it?" she sobbed.

He continued to worsen and floundered. She half caught him, folding to the floor along with him. He clawed at his vest, which had lost two buttons. Slurred, guttural sounds came from his mouth, but I could not decipher his meaning. He looked at Mother and reached for her face but didn't quite make it before his hand fell slack and dropped.

"Alfred! Oh, no! Alfred!" Mother cried, with more passion than I'd seen her give at my father's deathbed.

He went slack in her arms. She bowed her head to his chest and sobbed. I kneeled down, shocked at the turn of events. My hand found her shoulder, but she shrugged it off.

She screamed, "Get out!"

"Mother, I didn't mean to…"

She violently shook her head. "Yes, you did." Her sharp eyes shone with bitter tears. "You didn't want to see me happy."

I shook my head and tried to make her understand. "No. It's not that. The farm. Alfred demanded I leave and said that he had control of it now."

She sniffed and wiped at her cheek with the back of her hand. "You lie. Alfred wouldn't do that."

"He did! He just told me so."

She rocked back and forth, still clutching him to her chest. "We could have been so happy together."

It made me wonder if what Alfred said was correct, that she'd not cared for Father as deeply as she had for him.

With her eyes closed, she uttered, "You...you killed him."

Her words clanged heavy bass notes of guilt into my heart. I kneeled down next to Alfred, despite the glare in her eyes.

I found a pulse at his neck. "He lives."

I lifted my eyes to hers, hoping she'd forgive me, but she only focused on Alfred.

"Get help. Go!" she yelled, and I did.

But it was little use. By the time I returned with the doctor, Alfred had passed.

You killed him. *I left quietly with her words ringing in my ears.*

Maybe Mother was right, and I did kill him.

I shake off the memories and fork more hay down from the mow. Dust motes dance in the air, and I cough. I keep at it but stop, holding the pitchfork mid-swipe, when I hear the sound of creaking wood.

Lincoln's head appears and then his body as he steps from the ladder up and over the edge of the mow. "Thought I'd come see what the holdup is."

He smiles good-naturedly, but I can tell from his serious tone that he's concerned.

I plunge some more hay down the chute to show him I'm working. "Ya, sorry. I'm fillin' up the barrow now."

"Good. I want to get the chores done and head in. Mabel's been feeling poorly."

I pause in my work, stab the hay, and lean on the wooden handle of the pitchfork. "I'm sorry to hear that. I can finish up here and feed the cows, if you like."

Lincoln nods. He swipes his hat off in one slow movement. "Ah...I've been meaning to mention. Well, that is to say...aw, heck." Linc crams his hat back on and sighs. "I hope you know what you're doing, is all."

Something tells me he doesn't mean the hay forking. I send him a squinty glare, waiting for him to explain.

"With Molly, I mean." He rolls in his lips before speaking bluntly. "She's…fragile."

Annoyance at his insinuation of unseemly behavior on my part rankles me. "You think I don't know that?"

He nods. "Molly's been through an awful lot."

Lincoln eyes me. I can see he's pondering something.

"Just spit it out, Linc." I wave my arm in the air. "Say your piece."

What does he think I've set out to do—hurt Molly?

"She needs a friend, but…be careful. Her heart's been broken once already, from what I hear."

A spark of anger flashes in me. "You're not my father, Linc, and I'm way past the age of being reprimanded."

I raise the pitchfork up and thrust it into the hay with vigor.

Lincoln holds up his hands in a form of surrender. "That's not what I'm doing. As a friend, I'm simply warning you to use caution. I didn't mean to make you angry."

I guess he's only trying to help. I take a deep breath and calm down. "I don't need anyone meddling in my life; I had enough of that at home."

"I reckon you must have," he agrees.

I look him in the eye and tell him, "I don't need another Mother, but I do need a friend."

Linc smiles his goofy, slanted grin again. "And you've got one." Stepping back to the ladder, he says, "Think I'll take you up on your offer, if you don't mind."

I relax, ready to smooth over the splinter of tension between us. "Not at all. I hope Mabel gets to feeling better. You think she's got the flu?"

Linc moves down the ladder until his chin is level with the stacks of hay. "Her head's aching, but this morning she complained of stomach upset. No fever, though." He shakes his head. "It's not like her."

"I'm sure she'll be better in no time," I encourage him. An idea hits me. "Have you considered that she…might be…" I shrug, "in the family way?"

Lincoln's face fades of color. "Gosh, hadn't thought of that."

He scratches the side of his head.

I grin, happy for my friend at the idea of him being a father. "It'd be nice to have a little one around here."

A longing for my father washes over me and anger again at what my mother did. But instantly I hear, *Who are you to judge her when you're doing practically the same thing?*

The question from my conscience rocks me and tilts my established world of resentment. For all I know, Molly's husband could still be in the picture somewhere, and if so, I've behaved no better than Alfred, hankering after another man's wife. The only difference I discern: Father was present—albeit in his diminished state—while Mr. Lund remains at large.

"I best go check on her." Lincoln quickly retreats down the ladder and calls up, "Thanks for finishing up!"

I make short work of completing my task of filling the barrow below the chute with hay for the cows. I hang up the pitchfork on the barn wall and step down the ladder to feed the waiting ladies. I don't mind the farm work. It usually keeps my mind off dwelling on the past. Tonight has been an exception.

Walking along in front of the cow's stanchions, I toss in handfuls of sweet-smelling hay. The scent opens up a spot of yearning for something sweet in my life, like Molly.

What does the future hold for me? For Molly?

If I mend fences with Mother, I could go back home, but what would I go home to?

A small meow interrupts my ponderings.

The next day

Molly pets the white and gray, mottled kitten I found in a corner of the barn. "He is such a cute little critter."

The little fella has gray patches on his head and feet. Loud purring results from her attention.

I stroke his silky head. "He's certainly got quite a rattler."

Molly adjusts her arms as she holds him. We sit on a bench in the entryway of the farmhouse. Lincoln conceded to me offering the kitten to Molly and keeping it in the house.

"How many others were there?" she asks.

"Four. The mother cat must have had a litter some weeks ago and we never noticed. She dragged all the others off somewhere else. I saw this guy pawing around by himself."

Molly's brows wedge slightly. "What will Lincoln do with him? Does he keep many cats on the farm?"

I can hear the worry in her voice. "Usually just the one mother cat. They give the kittens away, but I bet Linc would make an exception for this fella."

I pet the kitten's back. The kitten arches in response and rubs against me.

Molly laughs. "I think he likes you." Her eyes flick up to mine. "I can't say that I blame him."

A spot in the pit of my stomach warms. How I wish there were no obstacles to pursuing Molly.

Molly's good eye focuses on me. "I'll ask Mabel if I can heat a dish of milk for him."

It does my heart good to see her so happy with the kitten. Taking care of someone or something does wonders for the soul. Maybe that's what I need—someone to care for. My hand brushes Molly's as I pet the kitten, but she doesn't acknowledge it.

Mabel pokes her head around the corner and asks, "What have we here?"

Her face looks pale, but her smile is the same as always. Lincoln surely found a gem in this sweet woman.

"Found this fella in the barn," I explain.

Mabel scratches the kitten under his chin. "He's cute."

"Mind if I heat some milk for him?" Molly asks.

Continuing to pet the kitten, Mabel says, "Sure, but what happened to Lynxy? She mothers her litters well."

"Is that what you call the mother?" I wonder.

Mabel lifts a shoulder and half smiles. "Yes. I think she looks like a lynx."

"You've seen one?" Molly inquires.

Mabel nods. "Oh yes, back on the farm in Wisconsin, but Lincoln told me that he's seen one here too."

The kitten meows pitifully.

Molly hands off the kitten to me. "My cue to prepare this little one's supper."

I watch her as she walks into the kitchen and try to comfort the kitten by petting him, but he tries to get away and follow Molly.

I point Molly's way and say to Mabel, "He's formed an attachment already."

"This will be good medicine for Molly. I think she misses her gardens."

I watch Molly tinker in the kitchen, getting the kitten his warmed milk, and a question builds in me.

I lower my voice and ask Mabel, "How long was Molly at the asylum?"

I want to know more about Molly's past.

Mabel lifts her eyebrows and shrugs. "As a patient one year, but she lived and worked there for several others. I'm not exactly sure how long. There are still some things she hasn't revealed to me, nor do I expect her to."

Forging ahead, I don't care about propriety. "What about her absent, supposed-dead husband? Did you ever meet him?"

I look directly at Mabel, hoping she'll understand why I've asked.

"No, but from what Molly tells me, they parted poorly."

I nod. "I see. But you have no idea where he is or if he's alive?"

I watch Molly pouring the heated milk in a small dish. My time of asking questions out of her earshot has almost expired.

Mabel shakes her head and pulls back a corner of her mouth in revulsion. "No, and as far as I know, he's not written. Molly wrote his family to ask them if they knew his whereabouts, but they had no clue. This was some while back. My guess is that he's somewhere out west. Apparently, from how Molly described him to me, he's adventurous, among other things."

"You think he's still living, then?"

"Your guess is as good as mine."

Molly approaches us and sets the dish of milk down on the floor. "Here we are."

I let the kitten down, and he pads over to Molly's crouching figure. She wiggles a finger in the milk. He comes closer and begins to lap it up.

Molly smiles up at me, clearly pleased. "Someone's hungry. I think I'll name him Mittens."

She doesn't work to hide her face from me like she once did. That tells me she trusts me, and I'm glad. But I check myself. These feelings I have for her must be brought into submission, or I'll be headed for a place of peril and a different kind of heartbreak entirely.

From the song "Love's Old Sweet Song"
by G. Clifton Bingham

CHAPTER ELEVEN

Molly

Early December

Stitch after stitch comforts me. I love the slip of the yarn through my fingers and the soothing, steady motion of the crochet hook. The warmth of the blanket sprawled across my lap while I stitch lends to the cozy atmosphere of the parlor. A crackling fire burns in the woodstove and the oil lamps flicker. Mabel reads on the settee, and Lincoln snoozes in his chair. It's altogether pleasant. The only element missing is Samuel. He's gone to bed early.

I'm almost finished with a thick, crocheted blanket in blue wool, meant for Samuel as a Christmas gift. I've heard him complain of being cold in the barn loft, so I think a warm throw blanket will be an appropriate gift. He's been such a good friend to me. My heart wants him to be more than that, but I know he can't be. At least not the way things stand. A divorce has crossed my mind, but I'd still have to know where Jacob is. He would have to agree, and there would be legal fees, which I don't have money for. My conscience pricks me as well over the possibility of breaking my vows and promise to him, but Jacob broke his promise to go through life with me. Surely that validates a breach of promise.

Mabel yawns and lays the book that she's been reading down on the end table. "I think I'll prod Lincoln to get up and retire with me."

I tell her, "I'm about to fold this up and head up as well, though I want to write a letter to your sister before I retire."

"I need to write her too." Mabel yawns loudly again. "But it will have to wait until tomorrow. I don't know why I'm so exhausted." She moves and jabs Lincoln. "Time for bed, sleepyhead."

Lincoln awakens in a daze. "What? What time is it?"

"Time for bed." Mabel points the way to the stairs. "Put the lights out as we go. Molly's retiring as well."

With a groan Lincoln rises. "Right."

I get up, too, after neatly folding my work up and tucking the crochet hook through some loops. I follow Mabel upstairs, a lantern at the top of the stairs lighting our way.

"Goodnight," she says before she turns into her and Lincoln's room.

"Goodnight," I echo before entering my room and closing the door behind me.

Using a match on the stand, I light a candle in a holder on the wall and another on the little writing desk in the corner.

Gathering my writing supplies, I think about what I should say in my letter to Robin, Mabel's sister. It's been weeks since I've written. Deciding to read through her last missive, I find it in the cubby hole with the others. I slip it out of the envelope and unfold the fine, linen paper.

November 29th, 1919
Dear Molly,

I hope you are well and enjoying the winter on the farm. The weather is mild here so far. Willis has some trouble navigating the icy patches in the drive with his false leg. He has a harder time maintaining his balance. Overall, he's adjusted to his limitations well, but every now and then, his temper flares, and he rails against the way things are. I don't blame him. Sometimes I'm frustrated too.

Although my mind has not gone back to that grim place within my own thoughts, I still have trouble feeling close to Enid. Willis captures her attention. At every opportunity, she goes to "Da," as she calls him. I believe she prefers him, and her preference resurges the guilt I hold over those months I was separated from her and the unmotherly feeling I once held. I guess I deserve her spurning. But I'll keep trying to win her favor, because she's my daughter and I love her dearly.

How is Mabel faring? Mabel mentioned in her last letter that she had gone through a bout of illness. I'm waiting for another letter from her. She mentioned you have formed a friendship with Lincoln's old schoolmate.

I will pray for your continued health and happiness. When the spring comes, please plant some pink and red hollyhocks, and I will do the same. I will forever remember you by those blooms.

Your faithful friend,
Robin

Her mention of the flowers which link us together brings a smile to my face. Our time working in the garden and flower beds at the asylum blended our hearts together. But it was more than that. Our hands working together plucked the weeds out of not only the dirt but also our minds, where deep-seeded, unhealthy patterns of thinking had taken root.

Robin mourned her presumed inadequacy as a mother, and I mourned Lonny and Jacob too. Although I'd gone through most of my deepest waters before Robin arrived, my journey helped lighten hers and vice versa.

I set Robin's letter aside and pick up my pen to write to her. Smoothing out a piece of writing paper, I begin.

December 8th, 1919

Dear Robin,

I'm sorry to hear that Enid still has not fully warmed to your attention. Given time, I'm sure that will change. Time lessens our pain and troubles. Although my thoughts go to Lonny every day, I've learned to let him go and, with him, the pain.

Willis will learn to manage. He's such a strong man and loves you dearly. How blessed you are.

I think about Jacob more frequently these days. At times memories come to me, and I momentarily miss him. Samuel has taken precedence in my heart, however. If it were not for the impediment of my estranged husband, I would allow myself to surrender to the feelings I shouldn't name. Samuel doesn't notice my scars. He sees me, not what has happened to me. Please pray he and I can remain friends.

Hollyhocks will be the first flower seeds that I plant

in the spring, and I will think of you with each new bloom.

Love,
Molly

The words I've written spell out a hopeless future with Samuel. I don't see any way clear for us to be together. Jacob's shadow always stands in the way. I would like to speak plainly with Samuel about our mutual affection, but it would be forward of me to do so. I must wait for him to broach the subject.

Weariness washes over me, and I put away my writing implements. My bed calls to me. As I prepare to rest, I pray for Robin and her daughter. A request for Mabel's health and protection forms in my mind, then my thoughts lead to Samuel, like most days.

Lord, I don't know how not to love him. He's been kind, generous, thoughtful, and looks past my outward flaws to see my heart—something Jacob could not do.

Yet, I pray for Jacob. How he abandoned me hurt me more than I can express, but I wish him no harm.

Help me find a way through this tangle of wishes, desires, heartaches, and vows. Amen

Lying on my side in bed, I shelter a feather pillow in my arms, wishing it were a living, breathing person instead. But who? Samuel or Jacob? Neither seems possible. I clench the pillow and noiselessly cry into it. Gradually I relax, and I find myself in a field of white clover, alone yet not alone.

The next morning

"My Bonnie lies over the ocean. My Bonnie lies over the sea. My Bonnie lies over the ocean. Oh, bring back my Bonnie to me, to me. Oh, bring back my Bonnie to me…"

Mabel switches to humming the old tune.

Her voice surprises me. I don't think I have ever heard her sing. The tone rings out mellow but true, sweet. It cheers and saddens me at the same time. A tear I do not expect rolls down my cheek. I swipe it away and sniff before she notices.

It's been months and months since I've tried to sing. I can't tolerate the physical discomfort nor the way my voice sounds to my own ears: strangled and weak and nothing like it once was. I hate it. I don't recognize myself, so I choose not to sing anymore. It only makes me sad.

When I first realized after the accident that my voice had changed, it wounded me. Then later, when I sang and all that issued forth were ordinary tones in a strangled pitch, I sobbed. I was no longer a talented singer, potentially on her way to a Chicago opera house. The separation from my identity as a singer felt like my skin being flayed from me while I still breathed.

Over the years the pain has lessened, but once in a while the longing to sing or hearing someone else sing, who is clearly gifted, claws at my heart and brings that filleted separation of music and my vocal cords to me afresh. My eyes roll shut as a wave of music memory and pain crashes against me.

I lean against the wall outside the kitchen and listen to Mabel switch to a new song, a favorite hymn of mine: "Be Thou My Vision." I recall the last time I sang those words. It seems like so long ago now. Jacob praised my haunting rendition. I pictured myself as almost angelic as I sang, like I stood before the very throne of God, offering my song as a prayer.

As I finished, the last notes rippled, like the cyclic rings after someone flings a rock into a body of water. I stood next to the baby grand piano in the large music hall, my hand resting in the curve of the dark, mahogany wood. Looks of both rapture and awe lit up the faces of the people in the audience before me. My heart fluttered with the following applause.

When I retreated backstage, after the encore, Jacob met me with a bouquet of red roses that matched my plaid, taffeta dress, and much praise.

"You did marvelous, my love! Beautifully done but not as beautiful as you are." He enfolded me in his arms, while I cradled the flowers, and kissed me on the cheek, before his lips found mine. In between each kiss—the next lasting longer than the previous— he murmured endearments. "My Wild Irish Rose." Kiss. "You're sweet as honey and more lovely than the finest gems." Kiss. "I love you, talented, gorgeous wife of mine." Kiss.

The passion of singing to my heart's content and full capacity mixed with Jacob's overtures transferred me to a euphoric state of being. I was happy. So happy…

"Molly?"

I didn't hear Samuel come in from outside. He stands before me, worry and concern etched on his face. The fresh, cold air surrounds him, making me shiver. I swipe at my eyes and rub my arms, folding them together tightly around my middle. He unbuttons his jacket and takes off his cap, hanging them both on a hook.

He extends his hand, cupping my elbow, and steps near. "Can I help in any way?"

I can't stop my bottom lip from trembling. "Oh, Samuel…"

I want to tell him more and share the reason for my tears, but the floodgates have opened, and I need the comfort of his arms, which I fall into, crying on his shoulder. He massages the base of my neck until my breathing comes easier, but I don't move. In this spot next to him, I experience the kind of peace I haven't since before the accident.

Jacob with all his fancy words and gestures didn't make me feel as sheltered as Samuel does right now. I lean into him and bring my arms up around his neck. I nestle my nose against his skin below his ear, and the sweet smell of hay and bay rum aftershave greets me. *Oh, to stay here in this moment forever, where nothing can harm me. Nothing can…*

"Oh." Mabel's voice registers. I turn and see her blink, startled. "I heard someone and…well, breakfast is ready." Clearly flustered, her cheeks match the pink of the flowers on her apron. She cranks her head the other way. "Come eat when you're ready," she tells us before she walks away.

What does she think of my free behavior toward Samuel? She pushed me into his arms before, but now I have shocked her. But then she doesn't know how engaged my heart has been over these last weeks. I've bonded with this kind, gentle man.

I push back from Samuel just as Lincoln makes his way in, stomping his boots off.

"We should get to the table," I say to Samuel.

Lincoln disposes of his outerwear then notices us. "Phew. Getting chilly out there. Snow's a comin' today, I'd wager." He doesn't mention our closeness or the fact that I've been crying. Surely, my nose and eyes must be red. "Sure smells good. Mabel must have bacon on."

He overemphasizes his words, being far too cheery.

"Sure does," Samuel agrees.

I nod. "Yes. Excuse me."

I duck my head and curve around Samuel, heading to the washroom to splash some cool water on my face. Mabel looks my way as I pass, but I only return a brief glance before I look away. I don't need questions or judgment. Mabel doesn't know all the details of how badly it hurt to give up my music and clear, strong voice—yet another thing she has that I don't.

I pump water into the waiting basin and mercilessly pat my face with the frigid well water. The cold refreshes me, and I dry my wet skin with a towel. My face reflects more redness than usual when I study it in the mirror. I turn left to right, flashing pretty to ugly. I still can't comprehend how Samuel can find me attractive. My bottom lip droops, and I want to give in to tears again.

What is the matter with me?

I haven't been so emotional since Lonny's death. It's been more than five years, and yet every day I think about him. What would he have been like now? Would he still favor Jacob in looks, minus his hair color, or would he have taken more after me?

The clinking of dishes and scraping of chairs tells me that I should finish my reflections and join the others for supper, but I don't want to. My presence will require a pretense of feigning to be in better spirits, but I'm not. I stop my morose introspection and exit the washroom, prepared to put on a decent act.

Breakfast is a quiet affair. I keep silent for the most part, avoiding Mabel's questioning eyes. After, Mabel and I clean up. Her first query hits when Linc and Samuel have retired to the sitting room.

She scrapes some leftovers into a bowl for King and gets right to the point. "What's going on?"

King waits, drool slipping from his chops onto the mat in the entryway, where he's been trained to stay.

"What do you mean?" I ask, trying to pretend ignorance at her insinuation.

Mabel sighs and shakes her head. "You and Samuel have clearly formed an attachment, and I'm not saying that's necessarily wrong. But what about your husband?" She places the dirty serving dish in the sink and lifts up King's dish, turning fully to me. "I don't mean to pry. You've not told me your whole story, but I'm concerned, that's all."

I glance at Mabel then lower my eyes. "I don't know. Jacob seems like someone from another life."

I'm honest, and I hope she can hear it.

King whines, and Mabel carries his dish to him, placing it on the floor. He dives in, wagging his tail. I wait at the edge of the table, my hands on a stack of dirty plates.

When Mabel walks back to the table, she gently takes the dishes from me, carrying them to the sink. "I'll wash; you dry."

I nod and grab a dishtowel off the drying rack.

Mabel half fills the sink with some cold water from the pump and finishes off with hot water from the kettle. When she's elbow-deep in soap suds, she continues. "Tell me what happened. As much as you can."

Before I can start, King scratches at the door, his cue to go outside.

"Linc!" Mabel shouts. "King's got to go outside. Could you let him out, please, so Molly and I can finish up?"

"Coming," Lincoln calls back.

He walks past to let King out to do his business. Glancing our way, he doesn't say anything. After Linc and King exit into the frosty morning, I fill in the gaps I haven't told Mabel, leaving little out. I tell her of the accident that day in the laundry area of the hotel and how the boiling caustic water burned Lonny so badly that it peeled off some of his skin and infection set in. Consequently, he lost his life. I shared our subsequent grief, Jacob's leaving, and my road to depression.

Gliding the towel over the last dish, I lean on the counter. "So, there you have it, a sad story of disaster, loss, abandonment, and insanity."

She embraces me, wet apron and all, her arms strong around me and bolstering me more than any words could. I hug her back.

"I'm sorry," Mabel whispers in my ear.

Those simple words mean more than any others she can offer. I'm glad she hasn't judged me.

"Thanks," I tell her, grateful again for a friend who listens.

Later in the day

I take a gander around the barn loft and say, "I've not been up here yet."

After supper Samuel and I took a moonlit stroll. I started to get cold, and he suggested I step up to his loft and warm up. It was rather an inappropriate suggestion, but I didn't care and followed him.

Here I am now, in his manly abode. It's simple, clean, and tidy, like Samuel himself.

Samuel moves his one chair closer to the heat for me. "Sit down by the stove."

I plunk down, shivering and rubbing my hands to hurry the heat into my fingers.

He crouches down, opens the door, and stokes the stove, putting more wood in. "This will soon get you warmer."

His enticing, easy smile heats my heart. His eyes smolder green tonight like burning moss, not fully lit but being consumed just the same. My heart flips.

I love this man.

My conscience pricks me. I must remind him. "Samuel, we shouldn't be here…together."

He slides a wooden crate over next to the chair. "We're only two friends taking shelter from the cold together. What's wrong with that?"

That's how his words come out, but I don't think that's what he's saying.

However, I smile and don't argue. "Yes." I brush my hands together again. "I feel much warmer already."

"We've been out in the cold for some time. Of course, it feels as toasty as a witch's oven in here, now." He winks. "But in the middle of January with the north wind blowing…"

He whistles, a low slide down the scale.

I tilt my head and flash a piercing glare out the corner of my eye. "Are you sure I'm not Gretel in this story?"

"Ha, ha." The cackling voice of an old crone comes from Samuel, as he lurches toward me. "I must fatten you up first, my dear." He snatches one of my hands and gropes my fingers. "Far too thin."

A laugh I can't control bubbles out of me. His eyes smile, and he echoes me. After a few seconds of shared joy, our gazes meet—serious and steady. Samuel leans closer and pronounces my name like he hasn't before—full of a tender reverence I can't deny.

"Molly."

A log crackles and snaps in the stove, as the sparks between us begin to blaze. Suddenly, he's kneeling before me, running his hands up my arms. I interrupt his advance.

"Tell me a way for us to legally be together, Samuel, before

God," I plead with him.

His determined, smoldering eyes don't waver from mine. "I've thought good and hard about this. I don't want to give you up, Molly. All we have to do is wait another year and a half. Your husband can be legally declared missing. Dead."

The thought never crossed my mind. "I…I suppose so."

My muscles flex, and I can feel a smile on my face creeping into a full-blown grin. *Is it wrong to wish my husband dead, even if it is only in word?* I won't allow myself to dwell on the question.

With one hand Samuel grasps my chin, I imagine so that I can't look away from his penetrating eyes. "Nothing prevents us from being together but a little time." With a look I can't retreat from he asks, "Mollinda Lund, will you marry me, when you are considered a free woman?"

I feel like I've just been given an answer to the impossible question I sought. "Yes. Many times, yes."

Tears linger in the corners of my eyes and then roll down the hills of my cheeks, as Samuel places his lips on mine.

That you may be sons of your Father in heaven;
For He makes His sun rise on the evil and on the good,
And sends rain on the just and on the unjust.

Matthew 5:45 NKJV

CHAPTER TWELVE

Samuel

Early December

Molly's face is a torrent of red and her words are just as furious. "How can you possibly think you can show up here and expect me to be happy about it?!"

I've not heard Molly shout before. Frankly, I didn't think she had it in her, but then, I don't know this side of her—angry but rightly so. Like a cougar about to pounce, Molly faces the man who abandoned her: Jacob Lund.

I stand by her side in the Nelsons' parlor, unwilling to leave her alone with him, wanting to protect her. Lincoln and Mabel have gone outside to give us privacy. A faint smell of pipe smoke and popped corn lingers in the air, not a bad combination. Mr. Lund has rudely interrupted our cozy Sunday afternoon. Lincoln lounged, puffing on his pipe, Mabel read as usual, and Molly and I popped corn on the stove, Mittens playing around us with a ball of green yarn, until trouble arrived.

Mr. Lund bobs his head in consolatory agreement. "I know." He extends his hand in a sort of surrender. "You have every right to be…riled."

His wary but pleading, dark, acorn-colored eyes flick to hers. Molly sighs and shakes her head.

I would like to punch the man. The muscles in my arm flex, preparing to do so, but I restrain myself. My eyes catch the slant of the western sun through the window. The rays highlight the dust in the air, a glittery, peaceful motion so contradictory to what's happening in this space: a battle of two hearts and minds.

"But you have to understand—I've changed," he tells her.

She shakes her head. "How? Why now, just when…"

Molly's large, helpless eyes meet my gaze.

I want to reach for her, wrap my arm around her waist, hold her tightly, and tell her everything will be fine, but I don't. Can't.

She puffs out a ragged breath. "I thought you were dead, Jacob. When I didn't hear from you, I assumed the worst, as did your family. They…"

Molly's voice catches, and she coughs into her sweater-clad shoulder. It must be a strain on her voice to talk so forcefully.

With a nervous twitter, Jacob folds and unfolds his wool cap in his hands. "Joe knew."

"What? Your cousin knew where you were and didn't tell me or say anything to anyone else? Was I so abhorrent to you that you had to flee in such a way?"

He steps closer to Molly, creases on his smooth brow, and I move to intervene. But Molly places her hand on my arm; I hold back.

"No. Of course not. I couldn't handle it all, to tell you the truth." Jacob sighs and brushes one hand through his hair. "Lonny's death was…too much for me."

I don't know him, but he has the sound of a man who's acting overly dramatic. I don't trust him, and neither should Molly. But I bite my tongue and don't say so.

"If you had stayed, we could have helped each other. I may not have had to go into…" Molly doesn't say the word, but I know she means the asylum. A cough erupts from her again, and she reaches for a nearby, half-full glass of water on the side table, taking a drink before she continues. "Your feelings changed toward me. You can't deny it."

Her eyes harden, and her mouth pinches at the corner that isn't scarred.

Jacob throws up his hands—white and lily-livered in my opinion—still clutching his cap tightly in one. Whatever work he's been accustomed to has not been manual labor. His fingernails are neat and trim with no dirt caught beneath.

He keeps ignoring me entirely and focuses on Molly. "Maybe a little, but everything was so askew. I didn't feel for anything or anybody." He touches her on the shoulder, and she stiffens, the muscles in her neck bulging. "You must understand."

Slow tears fall from her eyes and thicken her tone. "Don't you realize how selfish that was?"

I begin to feel like an interloper and wonder if I should leave them alone. I make a move to go but can't.

He narrows his eyes into almost a squint and hardens his thick lips. "And how you retreated into your mind wasn't?"

Molly doesn't answer but asks in a more controlled voice, "Explain to me why you've come now. It's been over five years."

Finally, Jacob turns contemptuous, smoky eyes on me. "Does *he* have to be here? Can't we speak in private?"

I turn to Molly. "I'll go, if you want?"

She shakes her head. "No." She turns to Jacob. "Samuel, that is, Mr. Woodson, is my friend. We've become…rather close of late."

He furrows his brows and sneers. "How close?"

"You have no right to object to my friends or any associations, for that matter." She shouts, "You weren't here!"

Her voice catches, and she coughs into the crook of her arm.

He drops his gaze and pauses. "Fair enough." Braving a look back up, he tells her, "I've missed you, Mol. I truly have."

His eyes are hollow and boyish, and I almost feel sorry for him. Almost, but not quite.

He reminds Molly, as if she doesn't remember, "And… we're still married."

Molly says what I'm thinking. "I don't know how you could call this a marriage." She visibly takes a deep breath. A weariness has sagged her shoulders. "Maybe it would be best if you go, Jacob, and we can talk about this another time. I'm sure the Nelsons want their house back."

She tips her chin up, firm and determined.

"But I'm here now," he protests.

We all stand in silence for several seconds.

Molly rolls her eyes. "Very well. If you insist." She points to the sofa and armchairs. "Then let's sit."

Molly and I take the chairs, while Jacob perches on the edge of the sofa, looking uncomfortable with this new arrangement.

I have to ask Molly, "Do you still want me here?"

She smiles faintly at me and nods. Addressing Jacob, she asks, "What have you done all this time?"

She smooths the fabric of her dress atop her lap, not looking at him.

Jacob's shoulders rise. "You know, this and that, but that's not important. What matters is I'm here now."

He attempts a half-baked smile.

Molly's eyebrows lower. "And you still haven't told me why."

"So we can be together again as husband and wife." He looks at her then stares at his shoes. "I've had lots of time to think, and I'll admit I wronged you." Impulsively, Jacob leans forward. "Let's remember the good times and put the past behind us. Let's start over."

I roll my eyes. The scoundrel makes redemption sound so easy. My hope of a future with Molly appears thinner and thinner. I want to tell him he can't have her back, that he has lost the privilege of being Molly's husband, but I can't. The words stick in my mouth. I wait to hear how she responds.

"Oh, Jacob…several years ago, I might have welcomed your return, but now…I've changed." Molly has settled back into her usually calm, understated tone. "You have, too, I'm sure. There's no going back to what we once were to each other."

He moves to his knees in front of Molly. "I'm not saying that. No, I understand we can't pick up where we left off, but we can start afresh. Can't we?"

Molly blinks and doesn't say anything.

I decide to step in. "I think it's too late for that." I present a stiff front. "Molly and I have formed an attachment. We wish to be married."

Jacob rises to his feet, and so do I.

He says, "Married? She's already married."

We eye each other like deer about to lock antlers. He's not a large man, but he's muscled. However, I'm sure I could flatten him, if push came to shove.

Molly cuts in with words I've longed for her to tell him. "I want a divorce, Jacob."

"No. No!" He shakes his head and frowns. "I won't agree to that. You're my wife, and I'm taking you back to Land O' Lakes with me."

Molly stands, a stiffness to her backbone. "I will not go back there."

He tips his head sideways as if to gauge her sincerity. "I guess we wouldn't have to. We could start somewhere new. We can decide that later."

Jacob smiles, but he has the look of a snake to me.

Molly doesn't return his smile, and slowly, his fades. "You broke your vow to me, Jacob. I won't go with you, because I…don't trust you."

There's the God's-honest truth. I'm glad she said it. His eyes flicker, and his mouth moves up and down, in what I can only think is uncertainty.

He reaches out and takes Molly's hand in his; she lets him. "I can see how I might have to earn that again. Would you give me a chance to try?"

Molly rolls her lips in, visibly swallows, and looks down. "I…"

I roll my eyes back, again, praying she doesn't say yes.

Lincoln appears out of nowhere and interrupts. I breathe a sigh of relief.

"I'm sorry to interfere, but Mabel's not feeling well. Molly, could you perhaps finish this visit with your…guest at another time?"

"Of course." Molly appears flustered. "I'm so sorry. We didn't mean to inconvenience you. I'll show my guest to the door."

Without waiting for him to reply, Molly grabs her husband's arm, and steers him through the kitchen and into the entryway. From this angle, I can no longer see them.

Lincoln approaches me. His eyes widen. "Phew! What was that all about? The man has been here a long time. Who is he?"

"Molly's husband," I tell him bluntly.

"Oooh." Lincoln draws out his one-word response and arches his brows. "Yikes! Well, I'm going to get Mabel tucked in before the fire with a cup of peppermint tea. She's freezing, and her insides are complaining again. I left her getting changed in our bedroom."

"I'm sorry to hear that Mabel is feeling poorly. Can I help with anything?"

"No, but thanks," Lincoln says, and he heads upstairs.

I step with hesitation toward the door. I want to and don't want to find out what has transpired between Molly and Jacob in these last few minutes. Maybe my ideas of a possible life with Molly will be crushed—yet another thing pulled out from under me. I'm beginning to think "the powers that be" are somehow punishing me for something. What, I don't know. Every future I see for myself gets crushed before it starts.

On impulse, I decide to duck out the back door and head to the loft. I need to think, and my journal calls me.

After I'm tucked up in my chair with a fire started, I let the words come…

Does everything happen for a reason? I don't know. I'd like to think so, but then what about the painful bits? The wars. The deaths. The lost loves. Where is God in all of this? Does He see the pain? Does He care?

I have to believe that He does. Maybe it's not so much about

Him "allowing" events to happen but that our will, our one true power, would be encroached upon if He did interfere. And it's not that He can't, or He wouldn't be all-powerful.

What about Molly? Why did she get burned? Why did her son die? Why did her husband leave her? But most pressing of all: Why has he come back?

It seems all I can pen is questions that I have no answers for, so I guess I'll turn to the one who does...

Dear Heavenly Father,

You know I've not been a devout man. Never went to church all that much, but I'm asking to understand, and if not that, at least to trust You. That there's more purpose to my life than getting shifted by circumstances.

First mother and now Molly, two very different women who've crushed my heart in different ways.

Could You help me repair my family? Could You make a way for Molly and me? It seems wrong to ask You to go against her marriage, but only You have the answers to this very prickly situation.

Please work in our lives what's best.

Amen

With that I tuck my pen and journal away and prepare to nap in my chair, hoping I don't dream of Molly.

Say au re-voir, not goodbye,
For parting brings a bitter sigh.

From the song "Say 'Au Revoir,' But Not Goodbye"
by Harry Kennedy

CHAPTER THIRTEEN

Molly

The same day

"Once, you could hardly look at me." I turn the scarred side of my face to Jacob. My breath fogs in the cold air. "You're telling me that this doesn't bother you anymore?"

I run the back of my fingers over the spidery ridges of my skin. My words are harsh to my own ears. Out the corner of my eye I see his gaze roll over my face. He can't hold back the semblance of a grimace.

I'm right. He still detests my appearance.

I face him and lean against his black Ford, wishing he'd get in and take off, leaving us in peace. "Why do you want me back?"

He's clearly not attracted to me. Can he need female companionship that bad?

He reaches out, touches my shoulder, and slowly slides his hand down my arm. "You're my wife, Mol. Can't a man want to be with his wife?"

I sense his warmth through my coat sleeve. The memory of his past intimate touches flicker in my mind. We did love each other, once. But now?

I settle on the truth in my heart. "I haven't been your wife in many years."

"Our distance didn't erase our vows."

Jacob presses closer and leans in, kissing me on my smooth cheek, his breath hot against my skin. The sensation brings a mixture of pleasure and pain to my nerves. A flash of the image of his bare skin against mine comes to mind. I close my eyes and momentarily relive his caresses, but that was so long ago. *Too long.* I press my hand against his chest.

"I'm not sure I can trust you again," I say, and I search his eyes for any true glimmer of substance, something left of the Jacob I knew and loved.

For a second I see the bond we shared, but he looks away before I can determine if he's safe enough.

He steps back and opens the driver's door. "I'll leave now and give you time to think, but I'll be back tomorrow, to hopefully bring you with me."

A careful smile spreads his lips into a thin, curved line underneath his short, clipped mustache, but no beard shades his face, as when I knew him. Just the mustache. He looks younger without the beard, even after more than five years. I can't deny that he's still the handsome man I remember, although with a few lines around his eyes, most likely creased from our shared sadness over Lonny's death.

How did we allow our grief to divide and undermine us so?

My heart aches for all we bore. It could have been so different. If I could go back in time, I would change so much, but I can't. Time moves forward, and so must we.

He holds my gaze. "I'll see you tomorrow."

He ducks into the Ford and I close the door behind him. After starting the car, he waves from behind the window.

My hand waves back, almost of its own accord, before I tuck it in my pocket and watch him drive away.

I have one day to decide whether I'll go or stay. One day to stand my ground with Samuel or surrender to my past with Jacob.

What am I going to do?

Early the next morning

Samuel and I sit in a mound of hay in the mow, our legs touching.

He asks me, "What about our plans?"

I don't answer right away and watch the morning sunlight sift in through the gaps between the barn boards. It's far too bright for my mood. The thought of leaving my friends and this kind man, whom I've come to care for, pains me.

I try to explain to him. "In order to be true to the kind of person I want to be, I must give Jacob a chance. I couldn't live with myself, much less you, if I didn't. Surely you can see that?" I reach for his hand, but he moves it away. "You must be hurting, but so am I."

He sets his hazel eyes on me, but they do not reflect their usual warmth. "I don't understand how you can trust a man who left you at your lowest point and stayed away for five years. There's got to be more to this."

"So, you're saying that Jacob couldn't possibly care for me anymore, looking like this."

I roll my hand in front of my face. A defensive wound starts to form in my heart. I thought he saw me differently.

"You know that's not what I'm getting at."

A sharp edge points Samuel's words at me, and they prickle like thorns against my heart.

"Do I?" Anger and fear drive my response. "What are *you* after, Samuel? It can't be my ravishing beauty."

I scoot away from him.

"If you have to ask and think that, then you don't know me at all."

He rises, brushing bits of hay off his overalls, the hurt in his voice clear. He avoids eye contact with me. My heart sinks.

I push myself to my feet. "I didn't want to part this way. Can't we be friends and recall each other well?"

"If that's what you wish."

He utters the tightly spoken words in a passionless fashion.

I extend my hand. "I do."

After a few seconds, he takes it, giving it a slight shake and squeeze, but Samuel doesn't smile.

He grips my hand a few more seconds before dropping it. "Goodbye, Molly."

No other farewell remark falls from his lips, as I wish it would. Let him protest, cause a fuss, plead with me, anything but this stoic, final abhorrence of my course of action.

Maybe Samuel doesn't care as much as I thought.

He descends down the ladder. I sit, almost paralyzed with grief and my life-long bane—to perpetually lose those I love.

Oh, Samuel.

Suddenly, I think of the almost finished, crocheted blanket in the living room I have made for him. I won't be able to give it to him now. I can't stop the tears from coming. I sniff and wipe them away with my sleeve, as I hear the rattle of a car entering the drive. Standing, I walk to the mow window and look out to see the black Ford pulling in.

Time to go.

I force myself to walk down the ladder and out to meet Jacob. Lincoln's already hauled my luggage to the drive for me. All that's left to do is say my goodbyes to Lincoln and Mabel. This is not going to be easy.

Mabel's pretty face is scrunched and puffy. "Are you sure this is what you want?" Her red nose and pink-ringed eyes give away her sadness at seeing me leave.

I start to tell her the excuse I keep using; Jacob is my husband.

But Lincoln speaks up. "You send a telegram or a letter if you need anything. There's always a place here for you, Molly."

I see the sincerity in his eyes.

"Thank you. That means so much," I reply.

I look from Lincoln to Mabel, my dear friends. No, they have become more than that to me; they're family.

Jacob leans toward the passenger-side window of the car.

He shouts, "We want to make good time. It's a long trip."

He smiles, but I recognize the impatient twitch at the corner of his eye. When we were together, he was always ready and waiting impatiently for me before we went out, his eye twitching and his foot tapping.

I turn to Jacob and say, "Yes. Coming."

As I swing back, Mabel throws her arms around me. "I'm going to miss you so much!"

She hugs me tightly. I return her embrace, while my eyes water.

I lean back and look at Mabel. "Oh, I almost forgot. Could you tie in the ends of the blanket I was making for Samuel and give it to him for Christmas? It's by your chair. I feel bad about not giving it to him in person."

She wipes away a tear with her finger from the corner of her eye. "Of course. He'll understand, I'm sure."

"Will he?" I whisper the question, but Mabel only offers me a weak, questioning smile. "Oh, I almost forgot; please take care of Mittens for me?" I ask, wishing I could take the kitten with me.

"Yes. Of course." Mabel speaks softly. "He'll be good company for me when I'm missing you."

After I pull back from Mabel, Lincoln steps in and wraps me briefly in his arms.

This is what safety feels like. Lincoln lets go and moves away, and a doubt arises. *Am I doing the right thing?*

"Wait!" Mabel cries and clasps my hand, her eyes wild and happy at the same time. "Lincoln and I want you to be the first to know..."

She looks up at her husband with love.

He hooks his arm around her shoulder and grins. "We're expecting."

I'm too stunned to speak. Of course, I'm happy for them. Who wouldn't be? But a portion of my heart bleeds at the injustice of it all. I shouldn't be jealous, but again I'm fighting the beast.

I smile widely and try to sound believable. "Congratulations."

Mabel touches my arm. "Promise me that you'll come back when the little one is born, if not before."

It's all I can do not to hide from Mabel's searching gaze. I'm afraid if she searches too deeply, she'll find the truth. I wouldn't want that. I'd never want to hurt her.

"I'll try," I promise and pat her arm.

Turning on my heel, I open the car door and quickly climb into the motor car. I wave through the glass as Jacob takes off.

I swivel around and watch them get smaller with each foot forward. I catch a flash of movement by the corner of the barn and recognize Samuel's gray and red, flannel shirt. He was watching. Yet again, the voice of caution speaks. *Turn around! Go back to those whom you know and love.* But I slide back in the seat next to the man I once promised my troth to.

He winks, flashes a white, toothy smile, and presses down harder on the gas, as we speed down the road. "Don't worry, Baby Doll. We'll have plenty of time to get reacquainted on the trip home."

Has he ever called me "Baby Doll" before? I certainly would have remembered such a tacky nickname. Where Jacob picked that up, I can't imagine, but then those absent years of his life remain a mystery to me.

I get comfortable on the seat and try my best to be amiable. "Tell me where you went first after leaving Land O' Lakes."

He nods and starts un-mystifying the missing years.

From the song "In My Merry Oldsmobile"
by Vincent Bryan

CHAPTER FOURTEEN

Molly

The miles pass—surprisingly, not as uncomfortably as I'd imagined—and Jacob proposes finding lodging for the night. I start to panic, wondering what it will be like for him to face the public with me on his arm. But here I am again, being concerned about what people think. It's a continual conundrum. Then a question more frightening makes me cringe.

What about the sleeping arrangements?

The very thought of being nearly naked and next to him in a bed sends a shiver down my spine. And not the good kind. I'll have to be perfectly clear on physical boundaries and hope that he will be a gentleman.

We roll into a quiet, Mississippi river town, Wabasha, Minnesota, and much to my amazement he chooses a large, classy hotel named The Anderson Hotel. Where he's gotten the money to spend on such luxury, I don't know.

As the sky blushes raspberry pink to the west, we park on the road, gather some luggage, and head in. Large, lofty flakes of snow sift down from the clouds above. I pull my cloche-style hat lower on the right side of my face and wrap my scarf tighter around my neck.

"Ready?" Jacob asks.

His lips part in a modest smile, but his eyes tell me he's nervous. I can't name the particular characteristic of his that makes me think so. Maybe the way his gaze shifts from me to the ground, back to me again. Despite his reserve I nod, take his arm, and we walk a few feet and up some stairs to the door of the beautiful, red-brick building, our shoes crunching on the new-fallen snow. He opens the ornate, wooden door with frosted glass panes for me, and we go in.

The smell of something savory meets my nostrils, and my stomach grumbles. It's been hours since I've eaten. I ate only a few bites of the lunch Mabel packed for us. We check in, and the bellboy leads us to our room.

In a matter of minutes, we find ourselves standing in a richly furnished room with a canopy bed covered in merlot-colored velvet. Gold and burgundy striped wallpaper lines the walls up to a grooved, wooden picture rail, on which hangs several framed paintings. Two are landscapes in muted tones and the other is a portrait of a Victorian-garbed woman under a bower of rambling, deep-pink roses. She lifts one bloom to her nose and looks sideways with a beguiling allure, as if to call the observer to a secret tryst.

"Nice place," Jacob comments as he tosses his valise onto a plump, stuffed chair, upholstered in a forest-green, botanical print. A round side table, with a leaded glass lamp atop it, stands next to the chair.

"Certainly is," I agree and then ask, "Can we…ah, that is, you…afford such a place?"

A grin slants his lips, and he laughs. "What? You don't think I'm good for it?"

I wonder again how Jacob has made his money. I look over his appearance and fine suit, which hardly seems rumpled from the long drive. I turn my head before he catches me examining him and focus on the largest piece of furniture in the room—the bed. Jacob's eyes follow mine. He clears his throat.

He tucks his thumbs under his suspenders beneath his open suit jacket. "Ah…want to freshen up before we visit the dining room? I'm famished."

I reach up to take off my hat but then think better of it. "Yes. Where did the boy say the bathrooms were?"

Jacob steps through the doorway and peers both ways down the hall. "Left, I think."

"I'll be back shortly."

I nod and exit the room, still holding my purse. The bathroom appears after a few paces. I duck in, do my business, then wash my face, toweling off with a plush, white towel. After rummaging around in my bag, I find my face powder and apply it, along with a dab of color to my lips, but not enough to make me look painted, just alive and healthy. Well, at least the good side.

What am I doing? I ask myself for the umpteenth time. Being here in a hotel with my long-absent husband seems so surreal. I never would have imagined life would bring me here: reunited with Jacob. Firstly, I'm not sure I want to be with him. I agreed to accompany him only because I made a vow, and I am duty bound to honor it. However, it's Samuel who holds my heart now. I know a part of me will always love Jacob, despite what he's done, but that's all. If more love comes and I fully give my heart to him again, it will be a miracle.

After I freshen up, Jacob meets me in the hall, and we walk to find the dining room. I'm thankful the space is dimly lit. A fire burns in the fireplace against the opposite wall. It adds to the cozy atmosphere. The well-put-together hostess, dressed in black, seats us with a flourish, and a toothy smile. Thankfully, her gaze misses my scars.

I examine the printed menu before me. A list of hearty-sounding meals with a definite Dutch air comprise the selection.

"Mmm, look at this special, a five-course meal." Jacob looks at me and raises his eyebrows as if to ask, *Why not?* The price is not named, likely for good reason. "Are you game for it?"

"Are you that hungry?"

He shrugs and smiles. "Let's live a little."

I don't commit and continue to look over the other offerings. Out the corner of my eye, I see a man walk up to our table.

"Good evening, my name is Roger. I'll be your server," he says. "What may I ask the cook to prepare for you this evening?"

I look up at our waiter, a handsome, young man, with his cleft chin, dark hair, and ready smile. He blinks when his eyes flit to my face but smiles with sincerity, and I like him for it.

"I think the missus and I will take the five-course meal."

Jacob hands the menu to Roger, who grins, as if we've just dumped a handful of coins in his pocket. He's probably thinking about the big tip he'll receive from such an order. Roger holds his hand out for my menu, and I give it to him. I'm too shocked to argue that I'd wanted the harvest pheasant pie.

Jacob holds up an index finger. "And, waiter, two glasses of your finest wine, please."

Roger nods. "Of course, sir. I will be back shortly with your first course."

He turns swiftly and practically dances through the set of swinging doors opposite us, where the kitchen must be.

I start to protest his extravagance. "You shouldn't have…"

Jacob doesn't let me finish. "Nothing is too good for my girl."

He smiles and winks like I'm eighteen again.

"I haven't been 'your girl' for a very long time," I remind him.

He reaches out and pats my hand, resting by my napkin. "I will remedy that and treat you like you deserve to be treated."

This man next to me is a stranger. The Jacob who left me would never have spoken this way or showered me with favors. Maybe before Lonny's death but certainly not since. *Is this some sort of performance?*

I narrow my eyes at him. "And how is that?"

He sighs. "I'm trying to make up for lost time, Mol. For what I didn't do…didn't say."

The tenderness in his voice and eyes melts my reserve a little.

I make sure Jacob is looking at me before I say, "Nothing can change the years of neglect. You should have at least written to me."

However, my point goes uncontested, because Roger arrives with the wine and our first course: a cold carrot and bean salad in some sort of vinaigrette. He also sets down a basket of crusty rolls and a dish of whipped butter.

"Thank you," Jacob tells Roger.

"You're most welcome."

Roger pours our wine and prepares to leave, tucking the large serving tray under his sturdy-looking arm and exiting as quietly as he came.

Jacob wastes no time in picking up a knife, cutting open a roll, and buttering it generously. He takes a large bite.

I suppress an eye roll and follow his lead to calm my begging stomach. We eat in silence for a while.

In hardly any time at all, he wipes his mouth with his napkin and says, "That was good. I wonder what's next."

"Typical," I say, under my breath.

Men. They are forever focused on feeding their gut or their…well, I won't think about that now. Jacob was hungry for something other than what was on his plate, once upon a time. I rub the back of my hand along my scarred jawline. I would hope his youthful carnal appetite will have slowed by now. However hungry he may be for anything, he's not sampling from my menu anytime soon.

Roger comes back and clears our dishes and sets small bowls of a creamed squash soup before us. An exotic, spicy flavor meets my tongue upon my first spoonful of the creamy, delicious soup.

Jacob focuses on me and pauses his consumption. "You're awfully quiet."

I aimlessly stir my soup around. "I'm tired and hungry. It's been a long day."

I return his gaze.

"Yes. It has," he agrees.

We both eat for a few minutes, until he speaks up, laying his spoon down on the table. "Look, I know we can't erase what's happened and…what I've done, but we can move forward from this spot. We can start something…new together."

"Do you really believe that, or is that just wishful thinking?" I ask.

"It depends on how badly we want it, I suppose." Jacob lifts his wine glass. "To new beginnings."

I lift mine as well and offer a slight curve of my lips, but I don't repeat the words. I can't. I'm not sure I want to begin something new with him.

Next, Roger brings out some kind of meat in a gravy sauce over a small mound of mashed potatoes. Jacob and I lift our forks in unison. It tastes like beef to me. I fork in a few mouthfuls and comment on its tenderness. Jacob praises it as well, then we turn quiet again, enjoying our food.

I decide to fill the gap in conversation. "How are your folks? I'm sorry I haven't asked about them."

I always did like Jacob's mother and father, Clementine and Clifford—the sweetest couple I'd ever met. Even their names sound like they fit together perfectly. I looked to them as a good example of what marriage should be, unlike my folks, who bickered constantly. I loved Clemmy and Cliff, and they loved me in return, I'm sure. They always treated me as one of their daughters.

Jacob wipes his mouth with his napkin. "I forgot to mention, but Pa passed on a few months ago."

"What? And no one wrote to me?"

It hurts that Clemmy and Jacob's sisters, Celia and Janice, didn't see fit to inform me of Cliff's death. They knew I was at the asylum, and, in fact, I received numerous letters from all three women while I was there.

"I'm not sure they knew you'd moved to Minnesota."

"I suppose they could have written and sent a letter to the asylum, but surely the staff would have forwarded it to me. I left them the address, and didn't you say that was how you found me, by calling the asylum?"

Jacob clears his throat and looks down at his food. He forks up a chunk of meat and holds it on the tines. "Ah, yes."

He spins his skewered meat around in the gravy and potatoes before eating it.

"How very odd." I push back my dish; my appetite has waned. "I'm very sorry to hear about your father; Clifford was a good man."

"Yes."

He looks down picks at what's left of his beef. Now, Jacob is the one being quiet, but one thing I've learned: That's the way he grieves—in solitude.

I reach for his hand. "I truly am sorry." He wraps his fingers around mine; it's a familiar sensation, and I don't pull away. "How's your mother doing?" I ask him.

Jacob lifts one shoulder. "She's managing."

I recall Clemmy as a capable, unflappable person, but then grief can wreak havoc on the sturdiest of hearts.

Suddenly, I notice Roger waiting.

"The last two courses. May I take your plates?" he asks, and he blinks at us, waiting with trays of food.

"Yes," we say in unison.

The first hint of hope for a renewed bond of some sort between us flickers in my spirit. We hold each other's gaze as Roger does his work. After he leaves, I notice the plate of dainty pastries, fruits, and cheeses. A steaming pot of coffee finishes the spread.

We pick at the desserts and sip our coffee. Our eyes meet a time or two, and I am more at ease with him. I stifle a yawn.

"Time to call it a night." Jacob echoes my yawn. He digs in

his pocket, lays a fat wad of money on the table, and stands, gently patting his middle. "That was one of the best decisions I ever made, aside from marrying you, that is."

I blink and stare up at him. *How is this man the same one that tossed me aside and took a hike to God knows where?*

He extends a hand. "Let me help you up."

I accept his assistance for a few seconds while pushing back my chair and standing.

"Don't we need to wait for the bill?' I wonder.

"I'm sure I covered it sufficiently and then some."

Jacob offers me his elbow, but I lift my eyebrows at him and pass by.

"After you," he says behind me in a slightly sarcastic tone.

When we make it to the room, Jacob unlocks and opens the door. I turn on the lights; the modest chandelier glows above us. It's so convenient to have electricity at the flip of a switch.

Jacob closes us in and shuts the door. I can't help but focus on the bed again.

Nodding toward the bed, he says, "That quilt sure looks thick. I bet if I fold it a few times, it would make a fair mattress."

I breathe a sigh of relief. "Yes. Doesn't it, though. Here, I'll help you get it laid out."

I walk around the bed and tug at the top of the quilt; he does the same. Together we fold it in half then half again and lower it to a bare spot on the floor. I add a pillow from the bed and the rose-colored, quilted throw blanket from the chair.

"I'd say that's a lot better than some beds I've slept in," he says.

His statement sounds like an invitation to ask him to elaborate, but all I want to do is go to sleep. I need to visit the bathroom before I retire, so I excuse myself and do so.

Upon returning to our room, I see that Jacob has lit the lamp on the table and shut the overhead light off. He's on his side on the folded quilt with the throw blanket half over him. The armoire's doors are open, and his shirt, pants, and suit jacket are hung inside.

"I'll face the other way, so you know…" He makes a winding motion with his hand. "You can get undressed."

Gratitude and amusement mix in my thoughts at the scene and circumstance. I'm thankful Jacob is being such a gentleman, but I'm amused at the strange and awkward feelings I have for this man, who once held me close with nothing between us but skin. Those first days as a married couple were blissful, locked up in a small hotel in Upper Michigan. It's sad and hilarious that we're in another hotel, years later, separated by the past and all the proverbial water under the bridge, except it was more like a flood.

"Thank you," I whisper.

Turning my back to him, I remove my dress, shoes, and stockings. My chemise, slip, and drawers I keep on. I fold back the blanket and sheet and get into the bed.

"Goodnight," I whisper again.

"Goodnight," Jacob replies with a wistfulness I don't ever remember hearing in his voice.

He rises enough to turn down the lamp on the table.

I'm exhausted and sleep shouldn't be hard to fall into, but my thoughts churn. Of Jacob and I in years past. Of Samuel and I in the present. But no, I must place Samuel in the past. He will be but a memory after Jacob and I restart this thing called marriage. Again, a glimmer of possibility flickers in the night like one small firefly. But something inside me won't let the firefly flitter around. Pa told me once that fireflies glow the brightest before a storm. That makes me wonder what's coming.

My eyelids feel heavy, but when I close them, it's Samuel's kind eyes and warm smile that I see, not Jacob's shifty orbs and slanted grin.

From the opera *Carmen*
by Georges Bizet

CHAPTER FIFTEEN

Samuel

December 12th, 1919

I got another letter from Mother this week. I sense a softening behind her words. It's like she wants to ask for forgiveness for marrying Alfred so soon after Father's death and leaving me with nothing, but she can't spell it out on paper. Maybe it's time for me to go home.

When I think about her all alone on the farm, I do feel sorry for her. But Mother and I never got along all that well. With just the two of us and no go-between, like father was, we will probably be at each other's throats.

But then Linc and Mabel need me here, what with a young'un on the way come spring. I'm sure Linc would appreciate the help, and we get along fine, as if we were brothers.

In fact, I think of Mabel and Linc as family. With Molly

rounding out the quartet, we would have made a cozy community. I wonder how she's faring with that husband of hers. She deserves better. But I guess she made her choice, and there's not much I can do.

I lay down my pen and read through my journal entry once more before closing the book. Is there really nothing I can do? I tally possible scenarios in my imagination.

What if I go after her and try to reason with her? Na, she's got her mind made up.

What if I challenge Jacob, make him admit to his neglect, and force him to divorce Molly? Na, sounds like something out of a penny novel.

Maybe I could dig some dirt up on Jacob. Something that would change Molly's mind about him. This sounds underhanded but more reasonable. Where to begin? The last place I know that he was: the asylum. I'll head into town later and use the phone to call there. Maybe he said something to one of the nurses and left a hint to where he'd been before that.

I suddenly realize how cold my feet are. Standing on my icy clodhoppers, I move to the wood bin and toss another couple of logs in the stove, before I tuck myself into bed.

I'm tired, but sleep doesn't come. All I can think of is Molly. I picture Jacob's smooth hands touching her in places that only a husband should, but it's wrong. Those hands should be my hands. Molly should be *my* wife.

But she's not, my conscience reminds me.

Curse the law, tradition, and honor! Being a kind, honorable, law-abiding man has gotten me nowhere, except being homeless, divided from family, and mourning rejection from the woman I love.

I'm too angry to sleep, so I think about ways I could beat Jacob into submission, literally and figuratively. With each punch, his image blurs, until we're running. I'm chasing Jacob, but he always outfoxes me and slips from my grasp when I gain on him.

The next morning

I awake, exhausted, to the crowing of the farm's one mangy rooster. Tossing the covers back, I swing my legs out of bed. I hurry through my morning routine of washing and dressing and head to the barn.

After my chores are done, I ask Linc to borrow the car and head into town. The post office has a public phone, so I park nearby and make my way in.

No one is near the phone. Picking up the receiver, I dial the operator.

"How may I assist you?" a female voice asks on the other end.

"Please connect me to the Dunn County Asylum for the Chronic Insane in Menomonie, Wisconsin," I tell her.

"Very good. Hold the line," she responds with a clipped, business-like voice.

I hear some muffled sounds, then, "Hello, Nurse Sandry speaking."

"H…hello." My tongue can't seem to articulate the words that have been parading through my mind. "I'm seeking information about a man called Jacob Lund. He is Molly Lund's husband. I believe she was a…that is to say, she resided there, working as a gardener."

I hope that doesn't sound too odd.

"And who are you, sir?" Nurse Sandry commands in a voice

that sounds used to giving orders and having them obeyed.

"I'm…a friend of Molly's. I believe she may be in some danger."

She sniffs. "Well, I'd know nothing about that, but a man, claiming to be her husband, came last week, asking to see Molly. However, Mrs. Lund left months ago. I can't recall the town, somewhere in Minnesota, but I'd have to check in the office."

"Oh, no. That's not necessary." I hold the receiver tighter and speak up. "I'm only inquiring about Mr. Lund. Did he happen to say where he'd come from?"

Nurse Sandry sighs. "All's I know is it was somewhere out west. The Dakotas. No, Wyoming. Wait." A few seconds of silence string between us. "Colorado! Yes, that was it."

"He didn't happen to say what city?" I ask.

"Now that I don't recall."

I can't disguise the tinge of satisfaction in my tone. "That's all right. You've been most helpful. Thank you, Nurse Sandry."

"Happy to oblige. Molly and I got on well enough." Her voice softens. "If you do see Molly, tell her we…miss her 'round here."

"Will do. Thank you, again!"

I hang up. I have a starting point. But where to look next? An idea hits me—calling the police in Denver. If Jacob is guilty of anything serious, surely the police will be looking for him.

My spirits drop, however, when I realize I may be taking things too far. He may be a criminal in my imagination only. But then again, maybe not.

There's only one way to find out.

I place several coins in the slot by the phone and ask the operator to connect me to the Denver police station.

"Denver Constabulary," a gruff, male voice growls out.

"Ah, yes. Hello. I'm…" Inspiration hits me, and I tell a white lie. "I'm a private detective seeking information about a man named Jacob Lund."

It isn't a bold-faced lie. I am a private individual, detecting and seeking the truth.

"Lund…Lund. Hmm, let's see." I hear some sounds, like he's rifling through some paperwork. "Ah, here it is. I knew the name sounded familiar. It seems he's wanted in connection with a bank robbery."

"Bank robbery?" I squeak out.

I can hardly believe my good fortune. The man has a record. The corners of my mouth draw up of their own will, in what must be a wide grin. *Gotcha!*

"That's right. Why're you askin'?"

"I may know where Mr. Lund is."

The officer's voice lightens. "You don't say. Hold on." I hear him hollering, "Chief! Chief! You got to hear this." Then some mumbling and static.

"This is Chief Constable Harding." Harding's voice holds authority. "So, you got a lead on Mr. Lund, huh?"

"You could say that."

"What're you trackin' him for?" Harding asks.

I'm not sure what to tell him. "You know…the usual, family trouble."

"Well, bank robbing supersedes that. Tell me where we can find him."

"Land O' Lakes, Wisconsin."

I pray I'm doing the right thing, incriminating Molly's husband.

"Way the heck over there?"

I inwardly cringe. "Being as he's out of the state, does that matter?"

"It tends to be tricky, but since there's a bounty on his head, that can be taken care of. We have to get him back to Colorado, and I know just the man, unless you're up for the job?"

As much as I'd like to hogtie Jacob and haul his robbing rump to Colorado, that's better left to someone used to dealing with criminals. My talent with a firearm extends to shooting the odd rodent now and then.

"I think I'll leave that up to the professionals," I tell Harding.

"Fair enough. Thanks for the tip."

"You're welcome. Thank you for the information."

I hang up, but instead of being giddy with happiness that Molly's husband is an outlaw, I'm sad—sorry that this will bring Molly pain. She doesn't need any more of that. Somehow, I have to reach her before things between them go too far.

Even if Jacob is a criminal, Molly will still be married to him.

I shove the truth of that thought away and focus on my next steps.

CHAPTER SIXTEEN

Molly
Land O' Lakes, Wisconsin
December 12th

"It sure is nice to see you again, honey." Clemmy squeezes me around the middle. She's strong for such a thin woman. Leaning back, Clemmy smiles, and all the wrinkles on her high cheekbones crinkle tighter. Her powder-blue eyes are nothing like Jacob's dark, impenetrable spheres. Hers clearly show sympathy and understanding. She places her hand gently over the scars in the hollow of my cheek. "All of us have scars…"

She pauses with her lips parted, like she wants to say more, but she doesn't.

I swipe at a wetness at the corner of my eye. "I've missed you. And I was so sorry to hear about Cliff."

"Yes. He worked too hard all of his life, but he died doing what he loved."

Jacob told me Cliff crumpled over in pain one day at the lumber mill, holding his chest.

Clemmy releases me and walks to the stove, setting the tea kettle on the front grate. "Would you like a cup of tea?"

I cough; my throat is dry as usual. "That sounds lovely."

"Sit yourself down, then."

Clemmy points to a chair at the table in the kitchen of her home, a tidy log cabin that Cliff and she built after selling the small, clapboard house they'd raised Jacob and his sisters in.

She tinkers with setting some teacups and other tea things on the table, decorated with an ecru, crocheted, lace runner and a basket of pine branches, cones, and red, glass Christmas balls.

The pitchy, fresh fragrance of pine means home to me. I miss my folks, but Dad passed some years ago and Mother lives with Annabelle, my older sister, and her family out East. Mother didn't want to stay in Land O' Lakes by herself, and she couldn't very well stay with me, since I was at the asylum. So, she moved out to be with Annabelle. I don't blame her. We write, but I still miss her, Annabelle, too, although we were never very close. Jacob's sisters were more like sisters to me than she ever was.

"How are Celia and Janice and their families?" I ask.

"Oh fine. They'll both be pleased to see you." Clemmy turns to me. "I can't tell you what a surprise it was to have Jacob back with us. I thought…" she sniffs and pulls a hanky out of her apron pocket, dabbing her nose, "that we'd never see him again. We thought he'd died, and came to find out Joe knew all along where he was. Why, I could have knocked Joe into next week for keeping that a secret." Brandishing a fist and shaking her head, Clemmy pivots back to the stove and pours the now boiling water into the teapot. "As it was, Jacob didn't get to see Cliff before he passed."

"I'm sure that must have been painful."

"He's here now, at least." She eyes me. "Both of you, as you should be—together at last. It's all rather miraculous." Her smile wobbles with emotion. "And you'll stay with me, of course. I'm sure Jacob can find work at the mill with Cliff's past connections."

Jacob and I distinctly discussed settling elsewhere. Apparently, he has not told Clemmy such news.

I look down at the table and then up. "I…we wouldn't want to impose."

She smiles sweetly. "Nonsense. It would work out well for all of us."

I can't argue with her, and I wouldn't wish to hurt her feelings. Jacob will have to inform his family of our plans in due time.

"That's most kind," I say, and leave it at that.

She pours tea in my cup then hers. After covering the teapot with a crocheted cozy, she sits across from me. "Tell me how you are. Jacob said you were living with a friend in Minnesota."

She stirs some honey into her tea.

I add a splash of cream to my cup and take a sip, wondering what to reveal. "Yes. The Nelsons. Mabel and her husband, Lincoln, have become very good friends."

I cradle my cup in my hands.

"How nice. I'm glad that you're not still…" Clemmy pauses and scratches a spot above her right eyebrow. "I mean, it's good to see you moving on with your life. After Lonny's death, we weren't so sure you would…recover."

An apologetic smile widens her cheeks, and she raises one dainty shoulder, clad in a thick, forest-green, cable sweater.

"Neither was I," I admit.

Clemmy takes a drink of her tea. "What about your singing?"

Shrugging and trying not to embrace the old pain, I tell Clemmy, "My career ended before it even started. I gave up hope years ago of pursuing opera. My appearance alone would be off-putting, to say nothing of the alteration to my voice."

Her wrinkles deepen between her brows. "How so? You sound fine."

"My strength, range, and ability to have near-perfect pitch have gone. The boiling water burned the outside of me, but the carbolic from the wash cauldron damaged my vocal cords. When the water splashed into my mouth and down my throat, I swallowed some, and it burned, causing scar tissue."

Clemmy shakes her head. "I remember you sounded hoarse afterward, but I didn't realize."

I give her the bad news, grateful that it doesn't ache as badly anymore. "A specialist I saw at the asylum examined me at the staff doctor's request. He told me I would most likely never improve."

"I'm…sorry, Molly." Clemmy picks at the edge of her saucer, as if she could scratch the spattering of yellow, painted roses off the China. "I know how important singing was to you, but not only that—your beautiful voice was a gift to anyone who heard you."

A tear rolls down her cheek and follows the curve of the wrinkles around her mouth.

Seeing her cry makes me tear up as well. "Thank you for saying so. I grieved the loss, but the years have lessened the jagged pain, as they have over missing Lonny."

She sighs. "He was such a bright light."

My chest feels tight as I agree, "Yes, he was."

Clemmy smiles through her tears, reminding me of a bow

of color after a rain shower. "And we must think of him shining in heaven now."

I start to say more, but Jacob opens the door and steps into the cabin, rubbing his gloved hands together. "Only five degrees out. It'll likely dip below zero tonight."

Turning toward Jacob, Clemmy frowns. "I'm beginning to dislike the winter more and more. When your father and I were first married, we loved it, but as you age, winters become less friendly."

Jacob closes the door behind him and takes off his coat, draping it over a chair. "You should move, Ma, come with us. We'll sell this place and go farther south."

"Move?" Clemmy's eyebrows hitch up. "I find out you're alive and well, and you're talking about moving? I thought you'd come home to stay."

Walking up to his mother, Jacob bends down and kisses her on the cheek. "Bless your heart. Of course, that's what you'd think, Ma." He straightens and walks to the round, red tin on the counter. "Molly and I want to start fresh somewhere new."

He pries open the lid and pulls two ginger cookies out, then crams it back on.

"But...but where?" Clemmy asks with a stammer.

"Oh, not too far away." A handsome smile lights Jacob's features, and his eyes plead with his mother. "After all that's happened, you wouldn't begrudge us that, would you?"

He touches Clemmy's shoulder and winks at me, passing by the table to sit in the rocker by the hearth on the north wall of the cabin.

Clemmy asks him bluntly, "What about your father's wishes? The stipulations in his will?"

Stipulations? What in the world is Clemmy talking about?

Jacob swings back to us, holding up a palm. "We discussed that before. It's settled. You said you wouldn't bring it up."

His gaze flicks to me momentarily. All the swagger and cheer gone from his tone, his words are terse and harsher than I feel his mother deserves.

The wrinkles around her mouth deepen. "Yes, but you didn't tell me about this plan of yours."

"That's beside the point. It doesn't change anything, does it?"

"No, but, Jacob…" Clemmy protests.

I want to say something, but I think it best not to get in the middle of it. Right now, at least.

"Let's discuss this later." Jacob smiles widely again and turns to me. "What do you say I finish these cookies, and we head over to Janice's to visit for a bit before it gets dark?"

My neck prickles in discomfort over whatever stands between Jacob and Clemmy, but I agree. "Yes. I was just telling your ma that'd it be nice to see Janice and Celia too."

Jacob smiles wider. "Fine. Grab your coat, gloves, and hat. Button up tight. I'll just fetch a glass of milk to wash these sweets down." Addressing Clemmy, he tells her, "You're welcome to come, too, Ma."

Jacob breaks a cookie in half and sticks it in his mouth, chewing with vigor. He opens the icebox and pours some milk from a pitcher into a glass he's pulled from the kitchen cupboard.

Clemmy's hand shakes as she settles it against her middle and the light in her eyes dims. "No. You two go ahead. I'll think about what to have for supper when you get back."

"We won't be too long."

Jacob makes short work of the other cookie, as I get dressed in my boots and outerwear. He gulps the milk down then gets his coat on too.

I wave to Clemmy, feeling bad about how dispirited we have left her. "We'll be back soon. Thank you for the tea."

She sends a smile tinged with sadness and a small wave back to me. It pains me to see her hurting. I'm determined to ask Jacob about what his mother said. I sense that there's something he's not telling me.

When we're tucked in the Ford and on the road, I bring up their conversation. "What did Clemmy mean about Cliff's will?"

He rolls down his bottom lip. "Oh nothing, really. Pa just wanted me back home to help care for Ma."

He makes it sound simple, but there has to be more to it. Keeping his focus on the road ahead, Jacob doesn't look my way.

"That's all?" I ask.

"Sure." He turns his head and gives me a quick wink before facing forward again. "Ma wants us to stay, but neither of us wants that, do we?"

"No…but now that I'm here with your family, it's not as painful as I thought. I've missed being around family."

Though Mabel and Lincoln have become like family.

He turns his eyes to me for a few seconds, serious and steady. "Why don't we give it a week or so before we decide anything concrete either way?"

Jacob has ascended another notch on my totem of trust. "That sounds wise."

He smiles. "Good."

We drive in silence for a while, until I start asking about Janice and her family. When I left town, Janice and Gerald, her husband, had just had their second child, a boy named Eliot. Now Eliot is almost six years old.

Jacob told me about the third addition to their family, three-year-old Abner, named after Gerald's father. Too bad Lonny couldn't be here to play with his cousins. They would have had such fun together. I know I shouldn't dwell on all the things Lonny has missed out on doing in life, but it's hard not to go there.

On the spur of the moment I ask, "Do you ever think about what our son has missed?"

"Once in a while, I suppose." Jacob pauses; I can tell he's thinking. "I would have liked to take him fishing."

An image of the two of them in bib overalls with a bait bucket in one hand and a pole in the other flashes through my mind. "That would have been nice. He'd be almost eight now."

I try to picture Lonny at that age. It's difficult.

"Really?" Jacob shakes his head, sighing. "I can hardly believe it. The years sure have flown by."

"Have they?" With a bitter ring, I laugh. "It was more like a crawl for me."

I stare out the window as we pass by forests of pine and spruce.

"Those first years were rough," he admits.

I turn to my husband, glad of the fact that we are sharing something real. "That's an understatement."

He winces. "Yes. I suppose."

"I don't think you'll ever know how much I missed you, Jacob."

I say his name tenderly, like I did when we were first married.

To my surprise he slows the car and brings it to a stop alongside the road, placing it in park, letting it idle. Turning to me, Jacob's eyes search mine.

Instead of the shifty, unsure movement I've been used to, he focuses straight on my face. I lower my gaze to his lips, partially obscured by his mustache. He has let it grow too long. *What would it feel like against my lips? Ticklish? Bristly?* It shocks me that I wonder.

We both move at the same time. His hand slides behind my head, and I cradle the sides of his face in my hands. His warm flesh sends tingles up my arms. The familiar pressure of his lips on mine moves me closer. Before I know it, my arms fully embrace him, pulling him tight against me.

Jacob firmly rings my waist with his arm. We kiss tentatively at first but then devour the years with our mouths. My head spins, and I'm short of breath as the memory of past intimacies begs to be unleashed. But something restrains me: an image of Samuel and his kind eyes, begging me to be his.

I push against Jacob's chest and break away from him.

"We…we need to slow this down," I pant out.

"What? Just when we've started making up for lost time?"

Jacob encloses my fingers in his, but I pull them out, scooting closer to the door.

"I need to think."

"We've done too much thinking. This is what we need." He points to his heart then mine. "Us. Together, loving each other. Neither of us has forgotten how to stir one another to passion."

"But it's about more than passion," I argue.

Jacob sniffs and shakes his head. "Fine. We'll forget it ever happened."

His tone holds a bitter edge. Hurt. Without further contact or comment, he pops the car in gear and drives back onto the road, his foot heavy on the accelerator.

But I can't forget. My heart wonders if I want more, to be

close to him. However, my head tells me to be careful. So, here we sit, as separated as before. And then there's Samuel. I can't get him out of my head or heart. I wonder if he still thinks of me.

145

CHAPTER SEVENTEEN

Samuel

A couple of weeks before Christmas

I smile widely at Mabel, hoping what I have to say will be softened by a compliment to her culinary skills. "That sure was a mighty fine supper. Fall-off-the-bone tender, it was."

She blinks her dark eyes, and pink highlights her cheeks. "Why, thank you, Samuel. And here I thought old Roly, the rooster, would be as tough as a mouthful of eggshells."

I pat my middle and puff out my stomach. "Oh, no. You sure do know how to cook. I haven't suffered one mite since moving here."

Although not tipping the scales, I may have added a few pounds to my scrawny hide since indulging in Mabel's hearty meals. She's a far better cook than my mother ever was.

Lincoln tilts his head and narrows one eye my way. "Look

at you, just passin' out the compliments."

He knows me well enough and clearly suspects an ulterior motive.

With more force than necessary, Mabel taps the serving spoon on the edge of the dish holding the mashed potatoes, while pressing her lips tightly together. "Now, don't be criticizing Samuel for doing what you should. It wouldn't hurt you none to send a few sweet words my way about what goes down your gullet."

Lincoln widens his eyes. "You know how I feel."

His eyebrows hunch down. I sense I may have opened the door to a marital spat.

Mabel's facial features wedge tighter; her round cheeks rise and her forehead furrows. Most likely, tears hover on the horizon.

"And how is that, exactly?" she asks.

Clearing my throat, I say, "Ah, I'm sure Linc…" I look his way and hitch one eyebrow up, "meant to say what I did. I just beat him to it, with my debonair style."

I wink at Mabel and crack a goofy grin.

She bats her eyelashes again, smiles back, then starts to giggle. Soon Linc and I join in. The suggestion of me being "debonair" has tickled all of our funny bones.

After a few shared laughs, I turn serious. "I need to ask for a leave of absence."

I study the stray peas left on my plate for a few seconds but then force myself to look up, first at Mabel then Linc.

Lincoln nods, a sideways grin showing happiness at my proclamation. "Oh? Finally going home, are you?"

I hate to spoil his better judgement of me. "No…I'm going after Molly."

Mabel gasps. "I knew it! Oh, Samuel…"

She starts crying in earnest, but I can't tell if she's happy or sad.

Linc reaches over and pats his wife's hand, not appearing too fazed by her outburst, and asks me, "Are you sure that's wise? What can you do? The man's her husband."

Mabel sniffs and dabs at her eyes with her napkin, looking my way. "But she loves you."

Lincoln makes a point I know all too well. "Love aside. It's the law we have to consider."

"And that's what I'm doing, considering the law. Did you know Jacob is a…wanted man?"

I let the last words hit home.

Linc cocks his head and takes his hand from atop Mabel's. "What?"

Mabel perks up. "He's done something illegal?"

I roll out what I've heard. "If you call bank robbing illegal."

I can't hold back the slight smile of satisfaction on my face.

Linc leans toward me across the table, the jean fabric of his overalls tight against the wood. "But how do you know this?"

I tell both of them about how I called the Denver police station and the news I received in return.

Mabel slams her palm down on the table. "I knew it!" The dishes rattle in response. "The low-down, dirty…"

Linc waves his hand in the air toward his wife in a shushing motion. "And just what do you propose to do?"

"Tell her the truth, of course. I want to get to them before the bounty hunter."

Linc scratches the side of his head. "Bounty hunter? What is this, the Wild West?"

Mabel reaches out her hand to me. "You'll be careful?"

I pat the top of her hand and try to reassure her. "I won't be in any danger, but I need Molly to know the truth about *her husband*." I say Jacob's role with disdain. "And I need to tell her how I…feel." I swallow and look at them both directly in turn. "I know this is a bad time, with Christmas coming and the little one."

Linc tucks in his lips and nods. "We'll manage. You must do what your conscience tells you."

"What your heart's telling you to do," Mabel adds with a smile.

"Thank you both. I appreciate your understanding."

Mabel folds her hands together over her plate and asks, "But how will you get there?"

"I'll take the train most of the way and hitch a ride after that. Whatever it takes."

"I'll drive you to town tomorrow morning," Lincoln states, matter-of-factly. Linc's a true friend, and I count my association with him one of the most blessed of my life.

"I'd appreciate that," I say.

He yawns. "I'm off to read before the fire, unless you need help with cleaning up."

Linc stands, scooting his chair back. He bends and places a brief kiss on Mabel's cheek, the tension between them gone.

Mabel stands as well and starts to collect the leftovers in the serving dishes. "I'll be fine. Go rest."

I get up as well and gather our plates and silverware. I need to ask her womanly opinion. "How do you think Molly will react to my going to find her?"

I set the used silverware atop the stack of plates and walk them to the sink.

She transfers the leftover food to one dish, covers it with a tea towel, and puts it in the icebox. "I'm not sure, but I know she cares for you, and she'll want to know the truth."

"Thanks. I guess I best go pack for tomorrow. Good night."

I tip my head to Mabel as I walk out.

She speaks tenderly behind me. "Goodnight, Samuel. I'll be praying your journey goes well."

I acknowledge her words with a nod and another "Thank you," then I grab my coat, leave the house, and head up to the loft. I need to clear my head. It feels muddled. Writing should help.

After I get settled in my room, with a fire blazing, I sit and start writing.

December 12th, 1919

I've decided to go after Molly, but I'm not sure if it's the right thing to do. Is there one way that's the "right" way? Does such a thing exist, or are there simply ways, no option better than another, just different? I don't know.

In my heart of hearts, I want Molly to be safe. I can say her safety drives me to make a move, and it does. But my desires also play a primary role. I miss her. I want her here with me.

Still, what way exists for us to legally be together? Molly could leave Jacob to face his crime, but she'd remain married to him. Nothing will change that. I doubt he'd divorce her. After all, he came for her for some reason. Was it simply to offer a cover for his unlawful dealings? I find it hard to say.

I'll reveal the truth, because Molly deserves to be treated fairly. The results will have to rest in God's hands. He knows our hearts and, surely, He wants what's best for us. I must surrender my future and Molly's to Him.

I set my writing things aside, stoke the fire, turn down the light, and get into bed. Tomorrow will be a long day of travel.

A couple days later

It took me a day and a half to get to Land O' Lakes, but here I stand, a little rumpled and more than second-guessing my decision to come. I paid a man from the train station to drive me in his truck to the address Mabel had tucked in my pocket before I left. Molly had given it to Mabel, in case she needed to be contacted, and I'm glad she did.

Sliding my shoes along the slick, gravel drive, I take care not to fall. I hitch the strap of my leather satchel on my shoulder and move forward toward the small, log home belching out smoke from the chimney. The crisp air smells of pine needles and ash.

As I near the dwelling, I pause. If I go much farther, there will be no turning back. *I've come this far. I have to go through with it! Besides, it's for Molly.*

After my mental encouragement, I cover the remaining distance in less than a minute, clear my throat, and knock on the door. The silence is deafening.

Maybe no one is home. I pan my head in both directions and look around. I don't see a vehicle, but there are tire tracks in the snow. Stepping around to the back of the house, I spy several outbuildings and a small barn in a triangular-shaped clearing. I hear the faint clucking of hens and the lowing of a bovine.

"Can I help you, Mister?"

The voice startles me, and I turn around to face a young man of about fifteen years. No facial hair shades the smooth planes of his face. One dark eye squints at me, as if measuring my character.

"Ah, yes. Does Mr. Jacob Lund and…his wife reside here?"

I detest calling Molly Jacob's wife.

The lad raises a rosy cheek and itches an ear with one finger. "Don't know. I hear tell Jacob came home, all right, but I ain't seen him."

I take in the boy's overalls and boots. "Do you live here?"

"Na. I help Widow Lund with her chores. Mr. Lund died a few months back." He points to the north. "I live that-a-way."

"I see, and you are?"

"Carson De Winter," he tells me, plain and simple.

"Carson." I look back at the log house. "It appears no one is home; do you know when they'll return?"

"Can't rightly say. Could be visitin' other relations."

"And who might that be?"

Carson pulls a hankie out of his back pocket, blows his nose, and stuffs it back where it came from. "They're at Celia's or Janice's, no doubt—Jacob's sisters. I heard the family's been waitin' for Jacob to get back here, so's they can read the will."

I shift the weight of my satchel, because the strap digs into my shoulder. "Oh, are the Lunds a wealthy family?"

"They've never been wanting, but I wouldn't call 'em rich, though Mr. Lund had a good job at the mill. Manager, he was, see?"

"I see." I gaze at the barn. "Is there somewhere I could rest a spell? It's been a long day."

He flicks his head in the direction of the barn. "I 'spect you could take a load off in the barn. Plenty of hay in the mow to keep you warm."

"Right. Thanks."

I follow Carson to the barn, bemoaning the fact that I've gone from one barn to another, and haven't yet done what I've come to do. Putting off telling Molly the truth cranks the grinder of anxiety in my gut.

The lad turns and squints at me again, before we enter the barn. "How do you know the Lunds?"

"Oh, just a friend of the family. I have some…news they need to hear."

I don't lie, but I've certainly stretched the truth.

Carson opens the barn door and gestures for me to precede him into the building. "Make yourself at home then."

"Thanks," I tell him, hoping I won't have long to wait.

The shadows slant tall and lean, the earmark of approaching dusk. I'm sure they'll be home before it turns dark.

Going about his business, Carson leaves me to climb the ladder to the mow, which I do, finding a fluffy clump of hay to recline in. Sitting still causes me to relax. A sleepiness pulls at me.

I'll close my eyes for a few minutes…

Molly waves at me from the back of a train caboose. I stand on the tracks, empty and desolate. I run to try to catch the train. It takes several efforts, and then I finally succeed. When my hand is on the rail and I am about ready to make a jump for the caboose platform, Jacob appears from nowhere.

He sneers and peels my fingers off the rail. I lose my grip and fall backward. Turning onto my side on the wooden ties, I glimpse back at the train. Molly shouts, but I can't hear what she's saying. Jacob reaches around her and muffles her mouth with his hand, dragging her through the door of the car, until they disappear from sight.

A terrible loneliness but also a terrible anger consumes me. I yell, letting my anguish out. "Noooo!"

I hammer the wood beneath me with a fist, causing myself some amount of pain. I try to stop, but I keep pounding…

"What are you doing here?"

My brain registers the words, but I can't equate them with the image of the train and my burst of physical force and pain. My eyes spring open, and I stare up at a man. It takes a second or two to realize that it's Jacob. Lifting myself up on my elbows, I shake the dream away and attempt to explain, but I sense that I should wait to confront him about his lies. I need to speak with Molly first.

"I must have fallen asleep." I brush the hair out of my eyes. "Your neighbor lad, Carson, told me I could rest in the mow. What time is it?"

I sit up then stand, brushing off bits of hay from my clothes.

Jacob points out the obvious. "You didn't answer my question."

In the dim interior of the haymow, I can barely see his dark eyes through the narrow slits of his lids. He holds a lantern up, while one hand rests on his hip in an unmovable stance.

"I…I have something for Molly."

Standing as tall as I can, I look down on Jacob by several inches. He lowers the lantern.

"And what could you have that she needs?" Jacob asks between clenched teeth.

I didn't prepare myself for his opposition, though I knew it would come. "Look, I must have slept all night, and I'm stiff, cold, and hungry." I hate to ask this man for anything, but it's a way to stall him and maybe get to see Molly. I sigh and rake my fingers through my hair. "Could I get warmed up and perchance have some coffee?"

Jacob rolls his eyes and huffs. "Ya, I suppose. You better follow me." He turns and walks toward the mow's ladder but stops and peers over his shoulder at me. "But you'll make it quick. Give Molly whatever you must and then leave. Understood?"

He blocks my way.

"Understood," I tell him.

He nods but doesn't say anything else. After descending from the mow, we make our way out of the barn toward the house.

I try to make some conversation. "This where you're from? Your family home?"

"The area, yes, but I didn't grow up in this house. Ma and Pa built this not too long ago."

"I see. It's a nice place."

I gaze around the neat yard and buildings with the backdrop of wooded property. I can see why he wanted to bring Molly back here.

He suddenly turns on me, grabbing the lapels of my coat in his hands, a snarl on his face. His breath smells of stale coffee. "You're not here to get to know me. I'll wager you're here to steal something or someone. But I have news for you; Molly's not yours to take. She's mine, and I'll get what's coming to me."

I can only hope so. It's ironic that he should mention stealing. I yank his hands from my coat and brush away his presence. He doesn't make another advance. I give him the meanest look I can manage.

"Molly doesn't belong to you," I bark out, and I can't resist. "Have you told her yet what you've done?"

He narrows his eyes and shouts, "What are you getting at?"

I counter him with another inquiry. "What were you doing out West?"

He laughs bitterly. "Trying to make a living like everyone else."

I take a chance and step closer to him, growling out, "That's not what I heard."

To his credit, Jacob doesn't flinch. "Oh? And what is that?"

Just when I'm about to hold him accountable, I hear the house door bang open. Molly stands in the doorway in nothing but a ruffled, white nightgown, socks, and a blue shawl, her dark hair unbound and flowing around her shoulders, like flower petals to a sepal. One white hand clutches the ends of the shawl to her breast.

"Samuel?"

Her voice cracks in the crisp air and causes me to stiffen as I meet her gaze.

I say her name, slow, purposeful, and full of the love I hold for her. I hope she can hear it in my voice. "Molly."

CHAPTER EIGHTEEN

Molly

When I see him standing here in front of me, I know for certain: I still love Samuel. As if my caring for him would pass. I'm deluding myself if I think I can forget him. *How could I forget such kindness?* My heart nearly stops as I speak his name. He returns mine, lovingly. A force of instant connectivity brings us close, though we stand yards apart.

"What…Why…?" I want to ask him why he's come, but I can't get all the words out. His eyes command mine, but I flick my gaze to Jacob. He scowls at me, the second glimpse of unpleasantness I've received from him since coming back home. I ignore his anger. "Come in." I motion for Samuel to come into the cabin. "It's far too chilly to visit outside."

He nods and smiles, gives a cautious look to Jacob, and steps away from him. "Much obliged."

Jacob tails Samuel, the muscles in his jaw working.

I move back into the house and allow Samuel to pass. He

moves by and doesn't touch me, but an electric-like current arcs between us, and I realize he wants me just as much as I desire to be with him. I breathe in when he's all the way past me, realizing I've been holding my breath.

Why did I let Jacob persuade me to leave Bur Oak Ridge?

Oh, yes…because I'm his wife. I'm beginning to hate the word *wife.* It means little or nothing to me. Jacob is fooling himself if he thinks things will ever be like they were before.

"Go get dressed," Jacob tells me, straight-faced, with no tenderness.

It's as if I'm his to command, but I don't buck his orders. I do need to get dressed and turn without comment to do as I'm bid.

After I finish washing and putting on a demure, navy, wool dress, I enter the kitchen, where Samuel sits at the table with a coffee cup in his hand. Clemmy sets the table for breakfast. Bacon sizzles in a cast-iron skillet and another pot of coffee percolates on the stovetop.

Jacob flings a gray scarf around his neck and pulls on his work gloves. "I'm going to go finish my chores, which were so rudely interrupted."

He looks my way before he heads out the door with the same scowl I saw earlier.

Does he blame me for Samuel showing up?

"You sure came a long way, Mr. Woodson. Must be mighty important," Clemmy states, but she doesn't turn from her work of flipping over the bacon strips.

Samuel doesn't elaborate and sips his coffee. "Yes. It is."

I move to stand next to Clemmy, patting the back of my head, checking if my bun is secure. "I take it Jacob introduced you to Sam…ah, Mr. Woodson…while I got dressed?"

She turns to me. "Yes, he did." Clemmy's light eyes don't accuse me of anything, and I'm glad. She's always been the type to hear others out before passing judgement. "Would you set out a loaf of bread, the butter, and some huckleberry jam?"

"Certainly."

I smile at her in my usual faint way and move to the pantry to retrieve the bread and to the icebox for the butter and jam.

Samuel speaks up. "Can I help in any way, Mrs. Lund? It's very kind of you to offer a perfect stranger some breakfast."

I like that he shows consideration and seems honest and true.

Clemmy turns and looks over her shoulder at Samuel. I can see the twinkle in her eye. "Why, of course. It's no trouble. Doesn't the Bible say to entertain strangers for they might be angels in disguise?"

Samuel laughs. "No one has ever mistaken me for an angel before."

He shakes his head, turning serious. I perceive a sort of cloud has dampened his jocularity, but I'm not sure why.

I place the bread and butter on the table, keeping my eyes from Samuel's. I don't trust myself not to fall into his arms. Turning from him, I spy a cut-glass jam dish perching on a shelf with an array of other decorative dishes, and I choose it to put the huckleberry jam in. Walking back to the table, I set it near the bread.

Samuel touches my hand before I let go of the dish. He glances furtively toward Clemmy at the stove. Her back is to us.

"I must speak with you privately," he whispers.

I have no inclination how we could manage that, so I shrug and widen my eyes, hoping he'll get my meaning. But then I have an idea.

With raised volume, I ask, "Oh, Mr. Woodson, would you be so kind as to help me fetch some fresh eggs from the chicken coop? There's one nasty rooster who lives to attack egg-seekers."

Clemmy looks our way, one hand on her hip, the other holding tongs over the pan.

She squints and says, "I have eggs here on the counter that I'll get scrambled up soon, but I suppose a few more would be nice. And Freddie is a feathered devil. Someday he's going to find himself in the stew pot if he keeps up with his contentious ways."

She doesn't appear to suspect anything.

Smiling, I say, "We'll be right back." I grab a small egg basket from a hook on the wall and walk toward the back door of the cabin. "This way. No need for a coat; we'll be quick."

I signal to Samuel. He stands, and together we exit the cabin. I lead him to the chickencoop, looking around to make sure there's no sign of Jacob. I unlatch the door, and we step inside. Most of the hens are nestled in their boxes.

I grab the large stick we leave by the door to ward off Freddie and hand it to Samuel. "Be prepared. Freddie loves a stealthy attack."

He takes it. "He won't get the better of me."

Samuel grins. Impulsively, I reach up and give him a peck on the cheek.

"Maybe a little more to the center and that'd be worth traveling hundreds of miles for."

Samuel grabs me and pulls me to his chest, wrapping his arms around my back. His lips find mine, and we kiss, I'm sure sharing the longing to be together and the frustration of being separated. I forget about the eggs and Freddie. I fully give in to all the thoughts and dreams of Samuel. Although I remember Jacob's familiar lips, their pressure, form, and movement, kissing Samuel touches something different in me, something new that I long to explore and desire more of.

Finally, we pull back from each other. He cradles the back of my head with his large hand, and his eyes hold mine, a light tenderness, not a possessiveness, in them, so unlike Jacob's dark, commanding eyes.

Samuel brushes my cheek with the back of his knuckles and softly says, "Jacob's not the man you think he is."

I lean my head back, putting more space between us. "What do you mean?"

"I'll bet my life on it that he hasn't told you what he's gotten up to out West."

"He didn't share too many details." I change the subject and pull him closer. "Anyway, I don't want to talk about Jacob. What about us?"

Taking the lead this time, I place my lips on his.

He answers my show of affection but pushes back lightly on my shoulders. "Wait. You have to know." He speaks with serious intent in his tone. "It's why I came."

"Well, I can see you have to get this off your chest. Go ahead."

I wait, trying to be patient while his lips form words instead of kisses.

"Jacob's a wanted man in Colorado."

I take a step backward. "Wanted? What for?"

I can't imagine Jacob breaking the law.

"Bank robbery."

The weight of his words shifts me off balance and a dizzy sensation momentarily wafts over me.

"He's one of three that they're seeking."

"Who's they?" I wonder.

"Well, the Colorado police, of course, but out here they have no jurisdiction. A bounty hunter is after Jacob and his plundering gang."

He informs me of the full extent of the situation.

"Jacob belongs to a gang of criminals?" The idea is preposterous to me. The Jacob I know—well, knew—would never be involved in such a thing. "I can't fathom him associating with criminals, much less agreeing to help them rob a bank." I release Samuel and look him steadily in the eye. "You're sure?"

"There's no doubt about it. I talked with the chief of police in Denver myself."

"I don't understand. Why would you have called the police out there?" I ask.

Samuel scratches the back of his head, his face in a slight grimace. "I…didn't trust the man, and after you left, I called the asylum to see if they remembered his visit to seek you out and if they did, if he mentioned where he'd come from. And he had. The nurse there told me about his being in Colorado."

"Nurse Sandry?" I ask. *That old tyrant.*

"Yes." He snaps his fingers. "That reminds me—she told me to say hello."

I'm surprised. "Did she now?" I suppose toward the end of my time there we'd come to tolerate each other and at times became friendly. But mostly, I remember her as a crank. "But what put you on to Jacob being on the outs with the law?"

"Call it intuition. I figured if he had a shady past, the police would have heard of him. I called the Denver police, and sure enough I dug up the truth."

Samuel's lips arc in a satisfied grin. My face heats and my ears ring. I grip the edge of one of the roosting boxes for support.

How could Jacob have fooled me, tricked me into coming with him? How could he have stooped to such a level as to steal?

Samuel reaches out and grabs my elbow. "I'm sorry. I know this is a shock."

"But…what will we do?" Then I think of who Jacob will hurt the most. "This will kill Clemmy."

"She does seem like a fine woman. Too good a mother for that louse."

"She's always been loving to me, treating me with kindness." I shake my head and think of what we're supposed to be doing out here in the coop. "Let's look for some eggs, before Clemmy wonders what's keeping us."

I move to reach under the first hen, and Freddie flies at me out of nowhere.

"Ahh!" I screech, and I cover my face.

The rooster flaps his wings, and sawdust and straw flutter into the air, while the hens cluck and cause a general ruckus.

Samuel threatens Freddie with the stick, but the rooster is too dumb to move away, until Samuel gives him a firm tap. "Here, you! Get back!"

More flapping about happens, and while Freddie is busy avoiding the stick, I grab a few more eggs from unsuspecting hens.

When the eggs are in my basket, I wave to Samuel and shout, "Let's get out of here."

We both leap for the door at once, escaping Freddie's spurs and sharp beak.

"Whew," Samuel sighs, as I latch the door behind us.

We turn to each other and start laughing. He reaches out a hand.

"Hold still," he says. "You've got some feathers in your hair."

Samuel's fingers move with care and a light touch, plucking out several feathers from my hair. Then I notice he has one large, reddish feather dangling at his temple. I point at it and reach to pick it off him.

"Ahem." A crisp voice behind us stops me. Turning, I see Clemmy eyeing us from the back door of the house. "Did you have to wait for those hens to lay the eggs? Breakfast 'ill be getting cold. Hurry up, now."

She waves her hand in a "come here" sort of way, and Samuel and I both move quickly, back to the kitchen.

Clemmy waits with an extended arm, and I string the egg basket on it. She doesn't say anything further, but I surmise a passel of questions wait behind her tranquil but steady eyes.

After an awkward breakfast, Jacob offered to drive Samuel to the train station. Well, no, he didn't offer; Jacob told Samuel he was taking him. Samuel refused, saying he had some other business in town and asked where he could find lodging.

Of course, I pointed out The Gateway. I think Clemmy picked up the adamant dislike radiating from Jacob for Samuel, so she didn't offer any further hospitality.

Samuel and I shared a look before he got in the car with Jacob.

Now, I sit in the rocker and pray. *Lord, please let Samuel get to the hotel in one piece.*

Maybe I should be praying the same for Jacob, but I'm more concerned about what Jacob might do to Samuel on the several-mile drive over to The Gateway.

Will Samuel confront him?

If he does, then Jacob might run, knowing a bounty hunter is after him. No, I bet Samuel will bide his time. He's most likely staying in town because he's concerned for my safety. I don't think Jacob would ever hurt me. In fact, I've received every signal that he desires to make love to me, but love and hatred often run a fine, parallel line.

Despite Jacob's crime, I don't wish to see him hurt. A part of me will always care for him, but now I know for certain something has to change; I can't stay with him, married or not.

He's a different person, and so am I.

CHAPTER NINETEEN

Samuel

I want to tell him, make him own his mistakes, but if I do, he'll run, sure shooting.

No, I must wait. The words I wish I could say stick in my gullet.

"I want to clear the air and make sure you know that Molly and I are committed to making a future together," Jacob calmly states.

He turns his head enough to look at me out the corner of his eye. His hands curve around the steering wheel of his old jalopy at 3 and 9 o'clock as we rumble down the road I was told leads to the hotel.

He wouldn't be so confident if he knew what passed between Molly and I this morning. "I see."

I don't know what else to say. I certainly can't argue with him. If I allow myself to get angry, I might spill too much information.

We're both quiet for a minute or two, then he says, "If you're staying in town, hoping to come between Molly and I, you're wasting your time. You'd be better off going home."

"I'll keep that in mind," I grind out between clenched teeth.

"As long as we understand each other."

Jacob keeps his face front and center, but I can guess his eyes mean business as much as his voice.

If only he knew.

I swallow, clamp my lips together, and clench my hands into fists in an effort to keep my mouth shut.

Patience. He'll get what's coming to him.

We travel the rest of the way in silence. When he stops by the hotel entrance, I hop out before he makes a move.

Before I slam the door shut, I tell him, "Don't bother getting out. I'll grab my bag from the back. Thanks for the lift."

Pushing the front passenger door shut, I open the back door and collect my gear, slam the door, tap the top of the car a few times, offer a kind of salute, and walk away.

Good riddance.

The spin of tires on gravel resounds behind me, but I don't look back. I step forward with a lagging gait, wondering how I'm going to afford who knows how many days at a hotel.

After checking in and resting in my room for a solid hour, I decide to visit the lobby and see if there's a local newspaper to read. I make my way there and seat myself in a dark leather, upholstered chair before a crackling fire in the huge, stone hearth of The Gateway. The vaulted ceiling with its hand-hewn, wooden beams makes for an open and inviting space. I read through the one paper I find on an end table littered with magazines, but I don't register what I read. My ears tune into a conversation at the front desk.

I recognize the voice of the clerk who checked me in. "You're a long way from home, mister."

"I travel all over. I'm used to being away," a deep, rough voice tells the clerk—Jim, I think his name is.

"Colorado's where you hang your hat, though?" Jim asks, and I hear some shuffling of papers and the clicking of metal on metal.

"Yes. It's as good as any state, I suppose. Say, are you familiar with the local families?"

"Sure. I know most folks around here," Jim answers.

I refrain from turning and looking at them and continue holding the paper before me, to listen incognito. *I guess that's called eavesdropping.* I push aside the tinge of guilt rolling in my gut and concentrate on their words.

"Good. Can you tell me where I might find the Lund residence?" the gravelly voiced guy asks.

I assume he must be the bounty hunter after Jacob.

"Clifford and Clemmy's place? Well, it'd just be Clemmy now. Clifford passed," Jim tells him.

"Ever heard of Jacob Lund?"

"Yes. He's their son, but he doesn't live with Clemmy. Although, I heard someone mention that he's back home, with his long-lost wife to boot."

Jim sounds like he enjoys a good bit of gossip. He continues giving the man from Colorado more details. I feel relieved that I won't have to be the one ratting out Jacob.

A couple with heavy outdoor gear on, shouldering cross-country skis, walks past. They talk and laugh loudly. I lose the thread of conversation at the desk. I finally turn in my seat and look back in that direction, but no one's there but Jim. The Colorado man must have slipped out.

Dang!

I should have risked drawing attention to myself before.

Now I've missed my chance to see what the bounty hunter looks like, if indeed that was him. Should I call and warn Molly? But what if Jacob answers? Maybe I can't anyway. I don't recall if Mrs. Lund has a phone.

Then I notice Jim waving at me. I fold up the newspaper, which I haven't read a word of, get up, and hurry over to the desk.

"I have a call for you, Mr. Woodson." Jim holds the black telephone handset out to me. "You'll have to come around the desk to speak into the mouthpiece."

I do as he directs.

"Thanks," I tell him. I speak into the phone and listen through the handpiece, held to my ear. I hear crackling and a cough. "H…hello?"

"Samuel?"

"Molly?"

I say her name loudly. *Good grief!* Jim probably wonders why I'm speaking with Jacob Lund's wife, but maybe Molly didn't give her name. Though he could have recognized her voice. Well, it can't be helped now. I lower my voice and turn my back to the desk, listening.

The anxious tone in Molly's words cannot be missed. "I've been worried. I wanted to make sure you were…safe."

"I'm fine. Don't worry. But boy am I glad you called." I sneak a look at Jim, who appears to be plenty occupied with paperwork. I dip my voice lower, just above a loud whisper. "Remember who I mentioned the other day?"

"Ah." She pauses and must be thinking. "You mean the man after Jacob?"

"That's the one. Listen…expect the…package soon."

I hope Molly will be able to guess what I mean by my cryptic words.

"Package? What? Oh…I see." Her voice switches from understanding to fear. "Oh dear, what should I do?"

"Nothing. Thanks for calling. I'll stop by soon."

More people mill around, and I stand out. Impatience pricks at me; I don't want to be noticed. I should get off the phone.

"I don't want Jacob to get hurt."

I hear her genuine concern. It makes sense; she was married to the man. *Is married.* I keep forgetting that Molly is still not a free woman, and I haven't decided what to do about it or even if there's anything I can do.

"Let's hope it won't come to that. I must go now. See you soon," I tell her.

"When?" Molly scratches out.

Her throat must be bothering her.

"I can't say for sure, but soon. Goodbye."

I hang up the earpiece, not waiting for Molly to respond.

Jim talks with a heavy-set woman in a mink-fur coat and a tall, thin man in a gray, wool coat and black, derby hat.

The woman huffs. "Two nights, young man. Not three."

"Yes, of course. I'm sorry, ma'am."

Poor Jim bends over the desk and makes an amendment to his work. I pity him, dealing with the public day in and out.

I catch Jim's eye. He smiles, and I nod. "Thanks for the use of the phone."

"Any time, Mr. Woodson," Jim says, turning back to the woman and man.

I practically jog back to my room. I jam the brass key into the lock and enter. Digging to the bottom of my bag, I pull out what I packed on a whim: a revolver. It feels cold and foreign in my hands. I've never fired it. When Pa died it was the one thing Mother gave me of his, and I can't think why. I didn't know he owned it.

I've used a rifle and a shotgun plenty of times, but this piece differs from those guns. Yet the concept is the same—point and shoot.

I tuck the revolver in the back of my pants, making sure it is loaded and the safety is on. Now, I need to find a ride back to the Lunds'. What will happen when I get there remains to be seen.

From the song "The Moth and the Flame"
by George Taggart

CHAPTER TWENTY

Molly

I try to keep my hand from shaking as I hang up the earpiece of the phone at Janice's. I braved coming to ask Janice if I could use her phone. Thankfully, she didn't pester me with questions.

A terrible anxiety over Samuel pricked at me, so I had to check on him. But I should spend my worry on Jacob instead. No matter his flaws, he doesn't deserve to be in peril. I imagine a bounty hunter as a predator, and Jacob the prey.

Will the man come armed? Of course, he will. Oh, Lord, please preserve his life. Help him to walk on a straighter path, if he has strayed so far as to care nothing for other people's property.

Janice peeks her head into the kitchen, where I've been talking on the phone. "All finished?"

My hands grip the butcher block countertop behind me, my rump to the cabinets below. The odor of burnt breakfast toast permeates the room and makes me nauseous; I swallow and take a breath.

What do I tell her? Should I warn her about the man coming for her brother?

Janice tilts her head and faces me, standing in the wide doorway of the kitchen, waiting. The shadows of the dim room play in her pin-curled, acorn-brown hair, making it look darker. Her eyes shine like Jacob's, rich as molasses. In facial structure, however, she has more of Clemmy's thin, delicate features. She smiles, but I can gauge the questions behind the uneven lift of her lips. The right side of her mouth hitches higher than the other and this one blatant flaw makes her otherwise even features more ordinary.

I try to keep my tone as even as possible. "Yes. Thank you again for letting me use your phone."

"We put it in just last year, calling it a business expense, but we hardly ever use the thing." Janice reaches up to a shelf on the wall holding teacups and saucers. "Care for a cup of tea or coffee?"

Her hand hovers over a cup. I shouldn't stay. If I do, no doubt I'll end up telling her everything. But I can't be rude.

"That…would be lovely. Thank you."

I do my best to relax and restrain my urge to race from the room and get back in Jacob's car, which I commandeered while he was busy helping Clemmy with chores.

"Good." Janice turns her dark eyes on me, pointedly. "No need to stand on ceremony. We're family, Molly. Have a seat."

She jerks her head toward the table and chairs."

"Thank you."

I walk forward and pull out a chair; it grates with a screech and I cringe.

Janice busies herself getting the tea things ready. "How are you, Molly? Truly, it's been so long since we sat together and had a good jaw."

A tickle in my throat urges me to cough, and I cover my mouth, coughing into my palm.

A frown worries Janice's lips and forehead. She stretches her hand out, as if she can reach across the room. "Can I get you a drink of water?"

"Yes, please," I choke out, and I massage the side of my neck where the muscles have tightened.

She pumps water into a glass over the sink then hands it to me, touching her throat and pointing out a fact instead of asking a question, as I accept the glass. "From the accident."

I nod in affirmation and take a large drink.

"I'm sorry," she says, as she puts the kettle on and sets out the tea things she's collected. "That was such a terrible time, and then to be left with…" her eyes rove over my scars, "with permanent reminders. Well, I don't know how you've managed." She tips her head back and laughs, surprising me. "But then you always were a strong person. Much stronger than my brother." Janice finishes laying out the dishes and some shortbread and sits opposite me at the table. Sighing, she states, "I've been upset with Jacob for taking off out west. He should have stayed. Been a man. Been brave, but instead he left you to pick up the pieces." She looks me directly in the eyes. "Did you hate him for it?"

"I suppose, for a time, but it wore me out and kept me trapped. I forgave Jacob some years ago for all the pain he's caused me."

She shakes her head. "Well, you're a better person than me. I'm still holding a grudge over how he treated you. That brother of mine doesn't rise above his selfishness enough to acknowledge, never mind care about, the needs of others; it's always been Jacob first. Maybe that's what becomes of being the only boy in the family. Pa doted on him too much and admitted that before he passed." She smiles crookedly again, and her eyes soften. "Pa remembered you at the end, wanting to see you provided for. Tricky old devil."

Janice utters a light chuckle.

I'm genuinely puzzled. "I'm not sure what you mean."

"Oop, just a minute."

Janice hops up to quiet the singing teakettle. She lifts it from the stovetop with a tea towel wrapped around the handle and pours hot water into the teapot she prepared, filling it then placing the kettle back on the stove. She hangs up the towel and caps the teapot.

All the while, I'm trying to piece together scenarios of what she could be referring to. *How did Clifford remember me?*

She plops back in her chair. "There. Now, where were we?"

"Cliff remembered me," I tell her.

"Ah, yes. I'm surprised Jacob hasn't informed you yet, but maybe he didn't want you to know." Janice laughs outright and shakes her head. "Knowing Jacob, that's probably it."

"Would you explain? I'm confused."

From a tiny pitcher, Janice adds some milk to each of our teacups. She catches my studying gaze. "Pa loved you like you were his real daughter."

"I know. I could say I loved him like my own father," I add.

Janice sighs, heavily. "I might as well spell it out for you." She pauses, rolling her lips in and out, a nervous habit. "Pa left a stipulation in the will, saying that Jacob would not receive the house and land Pa left him if Jacob divorced you. But more than that, Jacob was to live with you here. If he doesn't, he gets nothing."

A numbness thickens my throat, making me cough again. My head pounds, and my heart sinks. *Jacob never wanted me back. I was only a means to an end. I should have guessed.* My face pricks in embarrassment when I think about how he's tricked me and played me for a fool.

"Molly? Say something." Janice, wide-eyed and concerned, reaches out to me, her hand halfway across the pine table. "You've gone deathly white. Here." She pours a cup of tea and scoots it over to me before pouring one for herself. "A bracing cup of tea always does the trick to help alleviate any number of problems." Janice rolls her eyes and shakes her head. "This one being Jacob."

"I can't tell you how much of a shock it is to realize why Jacob came for me. It's not because he…"

I want to say "loves me," but I can't get the words out. My eyes sting; tears threaten, but I'm too angry to cry. Too betrayed.

Janice places her hands around her teacup and ventures a sip. "I'm sorry. I can see he's hurt you, yet again."

I stare down at my cup, wishing it was whiskey. Although I've never been a drinker. It would be tempting right about now to drown my aching heart in the numbing effect of booze. But no, I must face this. Bring him to account.

On impulse—call it anger—I tell her, bluntly, "Jacob has robbed a bank."

She blinks her wide-open eyes. Leaning forward, placing both hands on the table, she asks, in an incredulous tone, "What…? How do you know this?"

"My friend from Minnesota, Samuel Woodson, informed

me. Apparently, there's a bounty hunter after Jacob."

I feel a sense of satisfaction at Janice's obvious anger. Her ears are tinged red, and her breathing quickens—tell-tale signs.

"The rat! What was he thinking?" Janice pounds a fist on the table, causing the China to jangle. "Where? When?"

I give her the minimal details that Samuel has told me. "Colorado, some months back. I'm not certain."

Janice places her hand on her forehead. Propped up on her elbow, she leans heavily on the table. "Oh, Lord. This is going to give Ma a turn."

"Yes. I'm concerned about her reaction when she finds out. But, Janice, we need to get back before the bounty hunter gets to Clemmy's. Samuel saw him and heard the clerk at the hotel give directions out to her place to the man. Samuel just told me so on the phone."

"Yes! We should." Janice stands. "Come, let's go."

She pulls me with her out of the kitchen—our tea forgotten. We throw on our coats and hats and hurry out to the car.

"I'll drive," she tells me, running to the driver's side.

We get in. Luckily, the car starts with nary a sputter, and Janice barrels down the road. I'm worried we might end up in the ditch, but she's managing well and probably wouldn't slow down even if I told her to.

Fifteen minutes later we stand in the kitchen of Clemmy's log home.

Her face pales as we relay the news. "I…don't understand. How could Jacob be tied to this crime? Surely, he couldn't have…done such a thing." Clemmy's hand quakes as she places her fingers to her temple. A large lump of dough rests on the table. Her hands and apron are splotched with flour. She sinks into a dining chair. Her eyes roll shut. "I tried. I prayed, and now this?" Her eyes snap open, her voice demanding of us, "Where have I fallen negligent?" She turns to Janice, asking her rhetorical question. "Didn't your father and I teach Jacob right from wrong?"

Janice slides into a chair next to her mother. "Ma, you must calm yourself. You and Pa were good parents. The flaw's in Jacob. He's never grown up, come to terms with who he can be. That's not your fault."

"Where is Jacob?" I ask, nervously wondering when all of this will come to a head. First, I need to speak with him.

Clemmy looks at Janice then me, worry and questions wrinkling her forehead deeper than usual. "In the barn, I think. Although, come to think of it, he's been out there an awful long time."

"I'll go check," I volunteer before Janice says anything.

"Are you sure? Don't you want me to go with you?" Janice asks me.

I'm firm. "No, I'll be fine."

"It's not you I'm worried about," Janice says with a smirk, but she nods and rubs her mother's shoulder.

Clemmy is the picture of a woebegone parent, grieving a prodigal child's ways. Her whole demeanor has slumped south.

I turn from them and head out of the cabin to the barn, still wearing my coat and hat from the ride over. Stopping outside the wide, sliding barn door, I pause and listen but hear nothing out of the ordinary. I slide open the door and step inside. Peering all around, I see nothing of Jacob. Then I hear a slosh and a curse. I hurry in the direction the sound came from.

Jacob comes into view, pouring milk from a bucket into a separator. Some milk pools on the floor around his feet.

He glances at me and smiles. "Hi there. I hope your morning has gone better than mine." He sets the bucket down and swipes his forehead with the back of his hand. "I found a rat in the granary, one cow has some kind of inflammation in her bag, and this is the second time I've spilled the milk, pouring." Jacob's smile fades when he realizes that I'm not smiling back. "Cat got your tongue?"

"Why did you come to get me?"

I want to catch him lying. I imagine I look fearsome, because he appears wary.

He shrugs and offers me a wry smile. "Just as I said. I missed you and wanted us to be together again to try to build a life. I…I love you, Mol."

I want to scream and rail at him, but I won't give him the satisfaction of calling me a hysterical female. I keep my voice steady, unwavering in my accusation. "Liar!"

He shakes his head. "What? Don't you believe me? I thought we were past this."

He wipes both hands on the front of his coat and moves closer to me.

"I've been to visit Janice this morning. She told me about Cliff's will."

Jacob's Adam's apple bobs. His face pales. "It's not how it sounds."

I laugh, bitterly. "Ha! And how is that? Because to me, it sounds exactly as it is—you don't love me. You only came for me to get your inheritance."

Just let him try to deny it!

Shaking his head he says, "No. That's not the whole story."

I reach out and fling my hand back to slap him, but he catches my wrist before I make contact with the side of his face.

He pulls me to him, embracing me in an iron grip. "Would a man who doesn't love you do this?"

He clamps his lips on mine, but nothing of my old regard for him remains. His lips taste bitter to me, as burning as his words. I push on his shoulders with my hands and turn my face away, but he hangs on to me.

"Jacob! Don't!" I shout, pushing harder against him, until he releases me.

I wipe my lips with my sleeve.

"Mol, you must believe me. I was heading your way before I knew about Pa's passing. That interrupted my plans, and I came home first before coming to get you. I was informed of Pa's will after my intentions of reuniting with you."

He stretches his arms out to me, but I back away and shake my head.

"I don't believe you."

He shrugs. "Believe me or not; it's the truth."

I narrow my eyes and demand an answer. "What happened in Colorado?"

Jacob squints back and cocks his head. "I'm not sure what you're getting at."

"Why didn't you tell me you're a *wanted* man, Jacob?" I place my hands on my hips. "But then that wouldn't have gone over very well when you were persuading me to leave Bur Oak Ridge, which I should never have done."

"I don't know what you've heard, but it's a pack of lies," he tells me.

"Really? What? Did bank notes just happen to fall into your lap?"

He stands silent, defiant.

"Answer me!" I demand, shouting again, surprising myself with my anger.

Suddenly, Jacob holds out his hand, palm facing me. "Shh, what's that? Listen."

I keep quiet and do as he says, because I know what's coming. Or should I say who? The crunching of gravel and the slight creak of the barn's side door turn both of our heads. I look in that direction but see nothing.

"Probably just the wind." Jacob lowers his hand. "Come on. Let's go into the house, get a cup of coffee, and talk like rational folks."

He herds me toward the door.

"Your mother knows about your heist. Janice and I told her," I tell him, happy in my figurative punch.

"Heist? What are you getting at?"

How dare he feign ignorance!

"Don't pretend to be coy. You know very well what I'm referring to: the bank robbery in Colorado."

"I didn't rob the bank."

Jacob's words are deadpan. Solid with a tinge of truth, but how can I believe him?

"No? Then why is there a bounty hunter after you?"

My eyes meet his, daring him to fabricate some explanation. For the first time in a long time, I recognize fear in his eyes.

"How do you know this?" he asks.

I'm reluctant to divulge my source, Samuel, to him. He'd hate Samuel all the more for it.

"That doesn't matter," I say, and I keep my eyes on the dirt floor, covered in straw.

Jacob grabs my arm, wrenching it slightly. "Doesn't it? You clearly don't trust me."

"Oww," I protest.

I try to pull free, but he holds me fast.

"No. I don't," I admit. "Why should I?"

He leans close and breathes in my ear, sending a creepy tingle down my spine. "Because I'm your husband."

Jacob opens the door, pushing me along. He turns to latch it, but someone grabs him from behind. I break free from Jacob and stumble forward. After righting myself, I turn and see a man holding Jacob's arms behind his back.

The man yammers out, "Jacob Lund, you're under arrest for armed robbery. It's within my power to capture you and return you to Colorado to face a hearing."

He has on a dark brown Stetson and a leather-fringed jacket of the same shade. His bushy mustache hides his upper lip. The craggy wrinkles under his eyes and at the top of his cheeks give him a "no nonsense" authority, as do his steel-blue eyes.

I gulp and step back.

Jacob struggles to break free from the man's hold. "You got it wrong! I didn't rob the bank or wave a gun at anyone. They just…"

But Jacob doesn't get the chance to finish.

"Save it for the judge," the man growls out.

He whips a pair of handcuffs out of his pocket, moving to slap them on Jacob. But Jacob bashes his head backward against the man's, sending him reeling back enough to loosen his grip. Jacob twists out of the man's hands and rushes a few feet forward before I hear a click. I realize what it is…

The man's aiming a revolver at Jacob's back!

I can't help but yell and point. "Jacob! He's got a gun."

I had to warn him. Jacob stops in his tracks and slowly turns, his hands raised.

"Good thing your missus warned ya. I'm not opposed to shooting a dirty rat in the back," the man says, slow and steady, aiming just as much with his eyes as his gun.

"Listen, you don't know me. I'm not who they say I am. I'm innocent; I tell you. If you would just listen," Jacob pleads, trying to reason with the man again.

With a menacing scowl, the man steps closer to Jacob, until the barrel of the rifle spans only a foot from Jacob's chest. "No, you listen. I just have a job to do—get you back to Colorado, and I'm going to do it."

Then a loud noise, like a car door slamming, turns the man's head. Jacob takes the opportunity to rush forward, swatting the weapon out of the bounty hunter's hand. Jacob makes a break for it and runs hell-bent toward his car, parked in the yard by the house.

But out of nowhere a shot's fired. Jacob falls onto the snow-covered grass, holding his shoulder.

I scream; I can't help it. Looking around frantically, I try to determine what's happened. That's when I see Samuel by the corner of the house, holding a smoking handgun, aiming it where Jacob stood a few seconds ago.

From the song "Hearts and Flowers"
by Mary D. Brine

CHAPTER TWENTY-ONE

Samuel

"What have you done?"

Molly screams the words at me and rushes toward Jacob, who writhes on the ground.

What have I done?

I tell myself it was necessary, that Jacob was getting away, but in truth, I could have tried to catch and restrain him.

I lower the gun. The other man, who is exactly what I imagined a bounty hunter to look like, moves to my side.

He smiles under his bushy mustache and extends his hand. "Fast thinking. Lund could have gotten away. The Law'll be pleased when I tow his sorry hide back to Colorado."

I shake his hand, because I'm not sure what else to do. "Will I be…?" I don't know how to ask if I'll be held accountable for shooting Jacob. And what if he dies? *Oh, Lord,* I pray. "I didn't think; I just shot," I muster, my voice sounding shocked to my own ears.

"Aww, looks like a flesh wound to me." He slaps me on the back. "Don't worry yourself none. Right smart shooting."

"Make yourself useful and get a doctor," Molly shouts at us, as she kneels by Jacob.

I nod and move to the car I rented at the hotel but then turn back to Molly. "Where?"

"In town. You can't miss Dr. Wells's sign." Molly's serious gaze bores into me. "Hurry," she demands.

The bounty man tips his hat my way. "Yes, you go. I'll stay in case the critter makes a rapid recovery."

I nod and get in the car, revving it to life. *Please don't let him die. Please don't let him die.* The words keep reverberating in my mind, like a prayer. It's ironic, because in my thoughts I wanted Jacob gone, even dead, but actually being the one to pull the trigger and taking responsibility for his death is another matter entirely.

I step on the clutch and pop the car into gear, pressing on the gas pedal, spewing up gravel in the curves in the road. I make short work of shifting through the gears as I accelerate. I keep steadily on with little traffic along the way. When I reach town, I barely bother slowing down and race to find the doctor's shingle.

A white sign with black lettering, spelling out: David Wells, M.D., catches my eye, and I pull over, jumping out of the car, leaving it running. I enter the building without knocking, shouting for the doctor.

When he appears, I inform him of the situation. He gathers some supplies and his bag, and soon we are off again.

"Gunshot wound, you say?" he asks as I drive.

"That's right," I tell him.

"And the shooter?" he questions, turning to me.

"Let's not worry about that. Let's just get there, and hopefully you can patch him up."

Dr. Wells nods. "Yes, of course."

He asks a few more details about who is shot, and I oblige with answers but keep it simple.

When we get back to the Lunds', I pull to a stop, not seeing Jacob lying where he had been. *They must have moved him to the house.*

I lead the way, and Dr. Wells and I enter the house. Inside, Jacob is laid out atop the pine table, his face white, but he's still breathing. Molly presses a towel against his shoulder.

"Right, make way," Doctor Wells demands.

He pushes forward toward the table in the Lunds' kitchen, taking charge. Molly steps aside, but Mrs. Lund holds her ground and doesn't release Jacob's hand from where it's pressed in both of hers over her heart. Another car is in the drive still, but I don't see anyone else. The lawman waits outside.

The doctor peels back the blood-soaked towel from the wound on the front side of Jacob's right shoulder. "Let's see what we have."

Thank you, God, that it wasn't the left. If it had been, I might have hit his heart. Jacob moans. His eyes open but roll around, not focusing on anyone.

"Am I gonna die?" Jacob asks in a feeble voice.

"Not if I can help it, young man. I helped bring you into this world, and I'm not going to stand by and watch while you leave it." Doctor Wells, rather well-dressed for a country doctor, sluffs off his navy suit jacket and rolls up his shirt sleeves. "I'm going to give you something for the pain," he tells

Jacob, as he fishes in his medical bag, producing a syringe, which he loads with a clear liquid from a rubber-capped bottle.

He injects Jacob then asks Molly to boil some water. She moves to the stove. I creep back toward the door. There's nothing for me to do here.

"Wait!" Doctor Wells shouts, signaling to me. "You can help. I'll need someone to hold him down, in case the chloroform wears off."

Great. I sigh and move forward to Jacob's side. I'm thankful his eyes flutter shut, so I don't have to look into them.

"I'm going to get this cleaned then extract the bullet." Doctor Wells points toward Jacob's head. "Stand over there and keep your hands at the ready to push down firmly on his forearms if he starts to move." He blinks at me. "Understand?"

"Yes, Doctor," I tell him.

I move where he commands me to. I turn my head to the side as he begins to mop away the blood from the wound with the water and cloth Molly brought him a few seconds ago. I look back when he finishes. Next, the doctor drops some liquid from a bottle onto a gauze pad, which he then holds loosely over Jacob's nose and mouth. After a few seconds, he lifts it away.

A woman with a pale face—I presume one of Jacob's sisters—enters from a back room, carrying more towels and a blanket. She sets them down on a dining chair.

I venture a glance at Molly, but she's busy at the stove again, boiling the instruments of surgery the doctor asked her to. She doesn't look my way. The woman moves to Molly's side. The two whisper. Molly turns and flashes me a sad, sorry look. I'm not sure what it means.

I wonder if Mrs. Lund knows that I'm responsible for

shooting her son. She hasn't said anything to me yet. She's lowered Jacob's hand to his side and lightly caresses the top of his palm. Her eyes close, and her lips move in what I imagine to be silent prayer.

The doctor washes his hands at the sink, then splashes iodine on them. He tips some on Jacob's wound. I sense a tremor through Jacob's muscles, but then he relaxes.

"I need those tools, Molly," Doctor Wells says with urgency.

"Coming."

Molly plucks the tools out of a large pot on the stove with tongs and places them onto a clean towel. Then she rolls the towel up with the tools inside and carries it to Dr. Wells.

He nods. "Thank you."

Without further comment the doctor commences his work. I look away, not so much from squeamishness but because I feel guilty that this is happening in the first place.

It reminds me of the last time I felt this type of guilt. I see Mr. Skaggs, prone on the rug in the parlor back home, me standing over him.

The colors of the room blurred, after Mother shouted at me to get out. I gazed down one last time at her husband, and regret at my anger tightened my gut, making me nauseous.

"What will you do?" I asked.

Her back was to me, as she bent over Mr. Skaggs. My conscience pricked me. If I left, how would she manage alone on the farm and through whatever grieving came?

She turned her head, looking up at me, her face small and pale, the lines on her forehead harsh. "I don't know, Samuel. I can't think right now. How am I supposed to when my husband just died in front of me?"

We held each other's gaze for several seconds, before Mother turned away.

"This never would have happened if you hadn't…" she began but stopped, lowering her head and crying into Mr. Skaggs's shoulder.

Anger rose up in me again. "No! Mr. Skaggs would be alive to return your embrace if he hadn't cut me out like so much spoiled meat."

The blame should have rested with him and his instigation and meddling.

Mother lifted her head. "Spoiled. Yes, that's what you are, Samuel. Only thinking of yourself."

My fists balled up. "How can you say that? I've worked like a dog these last few years, keeping the farm afloat while Dad was ill."

I shook, my heart raw from her accusations.

She whimpered. "I know…but you don't understand what I've lost."

"Ha!" I laughed, bitterly. "And what have I lost, Mother?"

I spat out the word "mother," like I'd bitten into a chokecherry.

She didn't reply but simpered, weaker than I've ever seen her. I could not reconcile this pathetic woman with the strong, almost harsh mother I'd known. Was Mr. Skaggs such a great loss? I was sure she hadn't realized how hard and conniving he could be.

I gave her another chance. "If you want me to stay, I'll stay."

I crammed my hands in my pants pockets and stood on one leg, waiting. She gave an unladylike sniff and wiped her nose down her sleeve but didn't answer.

Just as I'd thought.

"I'll go, and…I'm never coming back," I told her.

With heavy feet, I clomped away and went to pack my clothes and belongings. I heard her sobs start again before the door to the house slammed behind me.

"You can let go now. We're done." Doctor Wells wakes me from my memories with a firm voice. "Surgery went well," he informs us all, before moving to the sink to wash up.

Prying my hands off Jacob slowly, I back up. Molly's nowhere in sight. The woman I don't know comes in from a back room, which I think is Mrs. Lund's bedroom. Mrs. Lund probably needs a rest after all this trouble. I don't recall her moving away from Jacob.

I breathe deeply and move toward the door, but the woman motions for me to stop. I do so with reluctance.

"Let's talk outside," she says.

I nod and accompany her outside into the noon-day sun. We have all forgotten about lunch it seems. I'm not one bit hungry. The woman shuts the door after we exit the house. I grabbed my coat from where I'd thrown it, but she stands coatless beside me, shivering and rubbing her arms. I offer my coat to her, but she shakes her head.

"I'll be fine. I'm Janice—Jacob's sister, as you've likely gathered. You must be Mr. Woodson, Molly's friend." Janice pauses but then continues. "I didn't say anything to my mother about…how Jacob was shot."

She narrows her dark eyes, so similar to Jacob's.

I nod and acknowledge her grace. "I appreciate your discretion."

"Why *did* you shoot him?" she asks.

How do I answer her blunt question? I'm not sure that I know myself.

"He was getting away."

My excuse rings hollow.

"And he deserved to be shot for that?" She shakes her head. "I know my brother isn't perfect, but I can't believe he would rob a bank. He's not a dangerous criminal. He couldn't kill anybody."

"I don't know what he's capable of, but Jacob doesn't need to hurt Molly anymore," I tell her, trying to justify my actions.

When it comes down to it, I believe I acted on instinct, but I don't say that.

"I'm with you there," she confesses. "I don't understand what he's playing at with Molly. He cares about her but…not enough. He never did," she admits.

"Do you think she'll see me before I go?" I ask.

Janice shrugs and shivers more. "You best ask her yourself. I'm going in to say goodbye. I've got to get home and do some chores before the children come home from school. The stove is probably out now too." She sighs. "A woman's work is never done." Turning to me she says, "Maybe you should give Molly a day to think things through. Come back tomorrow."

"I'll do that. Tell her…well, tell her…I'm sorry."

I make eye contact with Janice for a few seconds before she lowers her gaze.

"I will," she promises quietly, and she walks back to the house, opening the door with a creak.

The bounty man appears from behind the bushes by the corner of the house. "Reckon he'll have to recuperate a few days here before I can haul him back to Colorado. Thanks again for taking him down."

He tips his Stetson at me again.

"Don't thank me," I tell him, feeling horrible.

"Well, all the same." He turns toward the house. "I should head in and confer with the doc, now that Mr. Lund is patched up."

He nods again and ambles up to the house, his left leg dragging slightly.

I walk to my rented car, planning what I can say to Molly tomorrow. Nothing I come up with sounds right.

CHAPTER TWENTY-TWO

Molly

The next morning

He caught us at breakfast. Much to my shame, I didn't invite Samuel to partake with Clemmy and I. We were almost finished anyway. Now, Clemmy has gone to feed Jacob—what he can stomach anyway.

Samuel and I face each other by the door of the cabin, keeping our voices low.

Samuel worries his felt hat in his hand, rubbing the brim with his thumb, over and over. "Come back with me to Bur Oak Ridge."

"I can't leave Clemmy and Jacob like this. It'll be days before he's able to travel."

My eyes lower of their own accord. If I'm honest with myself, I'm making an excuse. I wouldn't have to stay. Jacob's sisters and mother are perfectly capable of caring for him, but I need time to sort out to whom my heart belongs, once and for all. And I need time to forgive Samuel for what he's done.

Samuel nods and rolls his lips in, uttering, "Hmm," then nothing more. His silence sparks my curiosity and I look up, meeting the intensity in his eyes. "You don't owe him anything."

His usually calm, clear orbs cloud with something I can't quite name. *Determination, perhaps?*

What Samuel says may be true, but I can't abandon Jacob, suffering as he is. Besides, anger forces stubbornness to the surface of my governing thoughts.

"I think it's you who had no right to take the law into your own hands." I narrow my gaze and firm up my jaw. "Right now, Clemmy could very well be standing next to the coffin of her son, instead of feeding him toast."

His voice softens. "I just wanted to protect you."

I ball my fingers into fists and resist the urge to stomp my foot. "I didn't ask you to."

Samuel reaches for my arm and says, "I thought we decided to put Jacob behind us."

I back away. I can't allow him to touch me, or my resolve to stay may crumble. "I need time to think."

"Yes," he says and searches my face. "I can see you do. He puts his hat on his head and flings his scarf around his neck. "I've only ever wanted to love you, care for you, Molly."

I can sense that, but still, I must listen to my heart, whispering to me to be patient. "I hope you have safe travel back."

My goodbye comes out lacking intimacy. I flash him one last look before I study the tips of my shoes.

"Goodbye, for now, Molly." This time he grabs my arm. "I'm not letting you go."

He squeezes but not enough to hurt, then suddenly releases me, sweeps a quick kiss to my temple, and steps away, pulling open the door and walking out of the house.

A bit of my heart has walked out with him. I sigh, turn, and gather my wits, stuffing my feelings for Samuel down deep in my spirit. At the moment, I have a husband to nurse, however delinquent he may be. I march back to the room Clemmy has settled Jacob in.

She opens the door from the other side just as I'm about to. "Oh, sorry."

She smiles weakly at me, balancing a small tray of dishes in one hand. The lines around her eyes sag, reflecting tiredness.

"How is he?" I whisper.

She moves forward through the doorway, closing the door behind her with one hand, while the other tightly clutches the floral, painted, wooden tray, littered with breakfast dishes and toast crusts, to her middle. Jacob never did like to eat the crusts.

"His wound seems clear of infection, but he's quiet. I've tried asking him about his involvement in this bank robbery, but he keeps me at bay." Her forget-me-not eyes plead with me. "Maybe you could try. He might reveal more to you." Shaking her head, Clemmy squeezes her eyes shut and sniffs. "I can't believe he would do such a thing."

I press my hand against Clemmy's sweater-covered arm. "I'll speak with him. You go rest."

She nods and shuffles toward the kitchen, the dishes on the tray clinking softly.

Filling my lungs with air, I step into the bedroom.

Jacob stares at the footboard of the dark bedstead and doesn't greet me.

No snide remark or joke? It's so unlike him.

I advance to his bedside and perch on the edge of the mattress. *How do I start?* I choose the direct approach.

"Did you do it?" I ask.

My fingers smooth down a few wrinkles in the sheets while I wait for his response.

He visibly swallows, still not making eye contact with me. "No." A sigh escapes his tight lips, and his shoulders slump. I notice a tuft of hair standing up at his crown, making him appear boyish. "Well…not in the way that you think." Jacob turns to me, truth in his wide, dark eyes. He shakes his head. "I didn't take the money, and I most certainly didn't kill anyone. But…I was there. A friend of mine, whom I owed money to, said he'd let me off the hook *if* I'd drive their getaway vehicle."

His forehead furrows, his brows slant down, and his bottom lip droops—the face of remorse. Or is it just regret now he's been caught?

"Some friend," I point out.

"Ya." He takes a deep breath, then grimaces, moaning out, "Owww…"

Despite all that he's done, I hate to see him in pain.

"Take it easy," I tell him, reaching out to touch his shoulder.

He shifts on the bed, situating himself at a different angle. "I forget how much it hurts sometimes, just to breathe." His eyes twinkle a little. "Is Wyatt Earp still waiting to cuff me in chains?"

I smile at his comic association between the Western legend and the man who will be bringing Jacob to the authorities. "Yes, the bounty hunter is still here. He's kept outside most of the time. Although, I doubt he'll pack you up in chains."

"Doc said it'll be a good few days before I'm stable enough

to be transferred. Bounty Man—what in tarnation is his name anyway—shouldn't need to hang around here, making everybody nervous. It's not like I'm gonna take off like this."

Jacob flapped his arm and elbow up and down.

I imagine him with feathers on his bent, bandaged arm in a sling. It tickles my funny bone, and I let a giggle escape.

"What's so comical?" Jacob growls.

I attempt a serious tone, but it doesn't work. "I pictured you as a chicken, trying to flap your way to freedom."

He rolls his eyes. "Sure, you can laugh. You're not a wanted man…errr, woman."

I sober up. "No, I wasn't foolish enough to put myself in the middle of a bank robbery."

"What…do you think they'll do to me?"

Fear wavers in his question.

"Honestly, I don't know."

Does the law hang bank robbers? Surely not. Jacob may have acted foolishly, but he doesn't deserve to pay with his life for it.

We are both silent for a few moments. Then I remember what I had in store for him before Samuel shot him.

I cut to the chase. "Why didn't you tell me about Cliff's will?"

Jacob flashes his eyes at me. What I imagine to be shame tinges his cheeks pink. "Ah…who's been talking?"

"Janice mentioned it."

Sighing, Jacob says, "Leave it to good ol' Jan." Scratching his unshaven jawline with his free hand, he continues, "I didn't know how to tell you."

I let the sarcasm drip from my words. "That's apparent."

"This is our chance. Our fresh start. Don't you see? That's all I wanted. Is that a crime?"

He utters the words with force, demanding an answer. His

remorse and fear are gone, clearly replaced with anger.

His question rolls in my mind. *Is it wrong for Jacob to want a new beginning?*

But I have to know, so I brave the question. "Did you come for me because you love me or because of your inheritance? Was it really only about the money and this place?"

My question hangs in the room like a waiting noose.

Jacob holds my eyes with his, daring me not to turn away. "How could you think that? I came for you because I believed the words Pa wrote."

"Which were?" I ask, and I sit up straight, waiting for him to enlighten me.

"He said we belonged together, that you were and always had been a part of this family."

That warms my heart and eases the ache that's been pricking it. However, I need more.

"But…do *you* love me, Jacob?" I ask him.

He takes his time in responding. "Do you love me?"

We search each other's eyes.

"I don't know," we both answer at the same time.

Finally, Jacob asks with tenderness, "Do we have to right now? We did once, and love can grow again."

He's right, of course. *But there's Samuel. I DO love him. Yet, I love Jacob as well, in a way.* I only offer a shrug. At least I know that it wasn't his intention to use me. That's such a relief. Now I need to tell Jacob my truth.

"I need to be honest with you. I still have…feelings for Samuel."

The declaration sits heavy between us.

He tenses his jaw, rolls his lips in for a few seconds, and eyes me with some sympathy. "I figured."

"Where do we go from here?" I ask.

The familiar choking sensation grips my throat, and I cough.

"That'll likely depend on what the law decides."

For much longer than I expect, we keep our eyes on one another. I move my fingers to his, which curl around mine. Wetness glistens in the corners of his coffee-colored eyes. I feel a tear roll down my cheek.

I sense that we're sharing a common pain, something we haven't done in a long, long time.

Days later

Janice hands her brother a cup of coffee. "Tomorrow's the day, huh?"

Jacob takes the cup.

"I guess so," he utters in a wistful tone.

The three of us sit before the fire, while Celia and Janice's children help Clemmy tack up some cedar boughs and red bows, reminding me that Christmas fast approaches. I imagine Mabel and Lincoln back on the farm, stringing popcorn and cranberries together for the Christmas tree I know Mabel will want to cut down and stand in the parlor.

I turn back to the problem at hand: Jacob leaving with the bounty hunter. The doctor has given permission for Jacob to travel.

"I wish someone could go with you," Janice tells Jacob, but she looks at me.

I suppose it's something a wife should do, look after her husband, but no, I can't. I keep quiet.

Jacob slurps his coffee and turns sad eyes on me over the rim of the cup.

Great. Two people silently plead with me now.

"You'll find representation once you're there, right?"

I hope in pointing this out to be relieved of any responsibility for Jacob.

Jacob clinks the cup back on top of the saucer he balances on his knee. "Don't know how, when I'll be behind bars."

"A lawyer will likely be assigned by the state, but who knows how good he'll be," Janice points out. She crosses her ankles and leans back in the stuffed armchair she's sitting in. "Maybe you could claim that you were coerced. That might make a difference. Get you a lighter sentence."

"Who knows?" Jacob shrugs and sighs. "I wish to God I'd never agreed to drive for Webster."

"That's the name of the man you owed money to?" I ask, trying to recall what Jacob has previously told me.

He nods. "Web's all smiles and jokes until he's got you over a barrel. Then he's a mean son-of-a-gun. I didn't really have much of a choice."

"Hmm, that might work in your favor," Janice says.

Jacob picks up his cup and downs the rest of his coffee in one gulp. "I'm not holding onto hope for that."

"There's always hope," I remind him.

His brows meet in the middle. "Listen to you, with your cheery platitudes." A tinge of sarcasm sharpens Jacob's words to me. "You've changed. A brighter outlook and all that."

"I've learned through the years that you have a choice about what to think of difficult circumstances."

Rather than be annoyed at his insinuation, I'm glad of it, for it's true—I have changed.

He raises his voice and draws the attention of his mother. "And how am I supposed to be happy about this?"

None of us speaks, but then Clemmy pauses in her work, worry present in her motherly tone. "How are you, Jacob? Are you tired? Do you need to rest?"

"No, Ma. I'm fine." He extends his empty cup and saucer to Janice. "Here."

She rises and takes them without comment, adding her own cup to her clutch, walking the dishes to the kitchen.

"Well, if you're sure. Don't tire yourself out." Clemmy tucks away her worried expression and smiles at the children. "We only have a few more to hang. What would you say to cookies and milk when we're done?"

Janice's small brood answers in unison, "Please, Gran."

The children and Clemmy get back to work. That leaves Jacob and I alone again.

"I don't know how I'm going to get through this," he quietly admits.

"One step and one prayer at a time," I say, inwardly cringing at my choice of cliché remark.

But it's true. There's nothing else to do but keep moving forward and ask for help from the One who knows us best.

"Since when did you start praying?" His words are seriously spoken. "I thought your religion left when Lonny died."

"I thought so, too, then things changed." I almost laugh with freedom when I think about what made the difference in my life and led me from a slippery path. "As I tended the vegetables and flowers at the asylum, God tended me. He opened my mind to a different way of perceiving sorrow."

"Hmm," Jacob responds with a slight nod. "God's never been all that close to me."

I shake my head at him. "You have it backward. We are the ones that move. He always remains close to us."

My heart softens toward Jacob once more. I can't believe we are talking about God and real life with real problems. I have a strange desire to sit close to him and cradle his head in my lap, like how we used to sit together, back when we were lovers. Oh, I'm far past that stage now. I can't fathom romantically loving Jacob again, but I care for him deeply. I want to see him finally heal from the loss of our son and for him to step into the freedom I've found in pursuing God. I want to say more. I sense a fountain of stored-up thoughts I've longed to share with Jacob.

But then a knock sounds on the door.

"I'll get it!" Janice shouts from the kitchen.

I watch her appear and open the door. All of us turn that way.

A light, female voice drifts in through the open door. "Hello. I'm so sorry to trouble you. I'm looking for Jacob Lund."

All I can see of the woman speaking is an outline, dressed in gray tweed.

"You'll have to get in line," Janice lets slip. "Sorry, come in."

Janice steps aside, making room for the woman to enter, but she's not alone. A small boy of two or three years of age clings to her skirt.

Jacob shifts up in his seat.

"Good night!" he utters, sounding incredulous, his face ashen. "Petra? What are…? How…?"

Jacob stumbles over his words.

Who is this woman and the boy? By all appearances, Jacob seems to know her well.

"It took some doing, let me tell you," the woman, Petra, says as she steps past Janice and advances into the house. "But we finally found you."

Her thin lips stretch wide in a strange kind of smile that takes up half of her face.

Her mouth is much too large, I silently criticize. I examine the rest of her person in seconds: nicely dressed but not overly expensive attire, medium stature, striking, light gray eyes hooded with fine brows, chestnut-colored hair rolled in a chignon under her mauve, knitted cap, a long, attractive nose with a slight upturn at the tip, and cheeks reflecting the rosy shade of exposure to the winter weather. All together, I'd call her pretty, much prettier than me with my scars, despite her exaggerated mouth.

Jacob leans forward in his seat, his forehead ridging. "But why have…you come?"

"*We* have come to…well, I thought…"

She shrugs and pushes the boy in front of her. He has her face but dark eyes and hair, like…

Oh no. It can't be. He couldn't have!

She pushes the lad forward a mite. "Jefferson, meet your papa."

The little boy looks up at his mother and blinks.

"Oh, my land," Clemmy proclaims.

I watch her nearly fall backward, but Janice's eldest son catches her.

"Steady, Gran," he says and walks her to a chair.

"I…you can't just…" Jacob chokes on his words and ruffles one hand through his hair. "I mean, it's been years since we've seen each other. I came back to find you after…" he glances at me, "but you weren't there."

Janice clears her throat, loudly. "Children, I believe it's time we went home. Say goodbye to Gran." Janice stands behind the chair Clemmy's in and motions to the children, who protest at not having the treat Clemmy promised them but end up obeying her directions to get their coats and boots on. Janice pats her mother on her shoulders. "You get some rest now, Ma."

"Yes, yes," Clemmy replies. "Stop your fussing."

Janice sets stern but loving eyes on Jacob. "I'll be back tomorrow to…say farewell."

He nods. "Thanks. See you tomorrow, Jan. Bye, kids."

Jacob waves as Janice and her brood leave.

"Bye, Mol."

Janice turns one side of her lips up in a quick smile before hurrying the children out and closing the door.

"Bye," I tell her, wishing I could go with her.

None of us moves or speaks for a few moments. I glance at Jacob and then Petra, who are looking at each other.

Clemmy meets my eyes. "Molly, why don't you come help me put the kettle on? We'll make some tea and get out some cookies." She rises shakily from the chair, and I get up and rush to her side, grabbing her elbow. Together we walk to the kitchen. I avoid Jacob's gaze. I want to know what he's thinking, and yet, at the same time, I don't.

Before I lose sight of the parlor, I look back and see that Petra has sat down by Jacob and pulled her little boy into her lap. They look like a family, huddled close together. The idea hurts greatly, a knife to the chest. Oh, it's not so much that Jacob loved someone else—after all, we were apart for years— but the boy…he should be Lonny. It should be me sitting at Jacob's side with *our* son. But no, that is a dream long dead and buried.

I wipe at my damp cheek with my sleeve before I turn to Clemmy and tell her in a shaky voice, "I'll fill the kettle."

She nods and grabs the tray off the side of the cupboard, where it hangs on a hook.

I march to the stove, pick up the blue-spotted, enamel tea kettle, lift the top, and pivot to the sink to fill it with water. When I pump the handle, I watch as the water pours out, gushing in spurts. I think of the one thing that brings me any semblance of happiness—I now have a legitimate reason for filing for divorce; Jacob has obviously had an affair.

But that fact of it leaves me sad as well.

From the song "Meet Me Tonight in Dreamland"
by Beth Slater Whitson

CHAPTER TWENTY-THREE

Samuel

The week before Christmas

In the end with all that has happened, I've decided to go home to Mother, in the hopes of reestablishing a stable link in the sea of my unknown. Despite our past disagreements, something in me cries out to see her, to put the wrongs behind us. I telephoned Lincoln at the train station to not expect me back for a few more days. He understood.

Now, here I sit, across from her at the old, maple kitchen table, a cup of steaming coffee in hand with a slice of carrot cake on a dish before me. The same ruffled, flour-sack valance hangs from the window, and the kitchen still smells of beeswax, musty potatoes, and the spice of apple pie.

Her welcome at my sudden appearance was not unkind. However, we have yet to broach the subject of our distance.

She sets her eyes on me. "So, how are things at the Nelsons'?"

For once Mother's question is open, holding what I discern to be real interest.

"Good, I think. I've been absent recently."

I take a sip of coffee, wondering how to tell her that I shot a man.

The wrinkles at her brow deepen. "Oh? Where is it that you've been?"

She picks at the cake on her plate with a fork, then eats a small bite, waiting, watching me.

"To…help a friend."

One of her eyes narrows in a kind of squint. "What friends do you have away from home or the Nelsons' place?"

She's right, of course, all the people I know and care about are from here or on Bur Oak Ridge. I take a deep breath and enter into divulging my recent escapades.

"Remember Molly, that is to say, Mrs. Lund?"

"I do."

Mercifully she allows me to continue without laying out her opinion of Molly, which I previously insinuated wasn't high.

I meet her eyes, hoping she doesn't judge. "Well, she left the farm…with her husband."

Widening her eyes like an owl, Mother blinks several times but doesn't comment.

"Molly thought he was dead, but he showed up out of the blue. Now she's back in Wisconsin with him and his family, but you see, she didn't know that he…robbed a bank."

"Lord, have mercy." Mother puts her hand to her throat, where a cameo pin rests, a gift my father gave her when he was still well. "The poor woman must be in shock."

"Rather," I agree. "But more than that…I did something stupid."

The concern I've craved from her softens her hard mouth. Her sharp, blue eyes melt. "What could you possibly have done?"

"I shot him."

She gulps out, "Samuel," in a shocked reprimand.

I go on to fill in the details, and she listens without interrupting, which I'm grateful for.

When I'm finished, she asks, "Do you love this woman, Molly?"

No distaste accompanies her query.

"Yes."

A simple, honest truth.

"But how can you be together? Surely, you wouldn't marry a divorced woman."

And there she's pointed out the crux of my problem.

"The way before us certainly seems impossible. Plus, I'm not certain about her feelings. She was shaken after I shot Jacob, her husband."

"Understandably so," Mother admits.

I glance down at the untouched cake on my plate. A shame. Mother's carrot cake is a favorite of mine, but I don't have an appetite.

"Quite," I admit.

Molly does have every right to be upset with me, but I wonder again how she can care for a man who's deceived and abandoned her.

Mother reaches out her hand, palm up, across the table. I slowly tuck my hand in hers. *Have we ever done this—held hands across the table?* I don't think so. It is welcome territory.

"I'm sorry, Samuel. About Mrs. Lund. About the farm…and oh, everything."

Wetness glistens in the corners of her eyes.

I feel a reflexive smile widen my face. "Thanks. Me too."

This is what I'd hoped for.

Mother clears her throat and sniffs. "I have something to tell you as well."

She hesitates, searching my eyes.

"Oh?" I wonder.

"I'm going to sell the farm."

She has dropped a bomb on me, and I don't know what to do with it. The place where I grew up, had many happy memories, the farm Dad worked and loved, sold?

"Why?" I ask, struggling not to give leeway to the rush of memories, along with the sentiment.

Letting go of my hand, she shakes her head and sighs. "I can't keep this place running without you. Besides, there's just too many memories here, both good and bad." She holds my gaze with honesty. "Alfred provided for me in his will."

I guessed as much; although he'd been a greedy man, he must have cared for her. *But what about me? Am I still to be cut out?*

I stare at Mother, searching for answers in her eyes.

"If the farm sells, you can have everything above the expenses," she firmly informs me, without any variance, which tells me that she's thought about this long and hard.

I'm shocked. I never expected to hear such generosity from Mother. "I don't know what to say."

I loosen my necktie, feeling almost faint. Seconds ago, I was inwardly ranting like a child and here she had me in mind all along. I shove the guilt rising in me back down.

She tosses out another surprise. "Unless, of course, you want the old place."

I scratch the back of my neck; a prickly sensation rises there. "I don't know. It all depends on…"

I don't finish. I gather she knows what I mean.

A rare, wide smile stretches Mother's lips, revealing a chip out of one of her middle teeth. She was always vain about that, and perhaps that's why she hardly ever smiles fully.

"There's no need to decide anything quite yet. After the turn of the new year is plenty of time. I can manage until then, but we'll have to see to some change come spring, for sure."

"Yes, of course," I say, nodding and returning her smile.

"It's good to have you home, Son," she says, drinking her coffee and eating the rest of her cake, as if nothing has kept us apart this long, last year.

I take my first bite of cake.

"Mmm, delicious," I tell her.

It tastes like days past, of good times and warm memories.

She flashes her eyes at me, a warmer blue than I remember. "For some reason, yesterday, I was thinking of you and recalled that it was your favorite, and now here you are."

"Yes, here I am."

Blessedly, at least one thing in my life has fallen into place. I give thanks to God above for this unexpected reconciliation with Mother. We're too much alike, so I'm sure there will be times ahead when we won't see eye to eye, but for now the peace is most welcome. Most welcome, indeed.

Bur Oak Ridge
Three days before Christmas

The three of us are in the kitchen. Mabel stands crookedly with one hand on her hip, a frown on her face, and a pinched look in her dark eyes. In her middle, I notice a slight bump under her blue, flowered apron, where the expected addition to their family grows. The smell of sausage, sauerkraut, and fried potatoes clings to the warm air, the remnants of supper.

"So what are you going to do?" she asks me.

I shrug, feeling overburdened by her frustration; I've had plenty of my own. "What can I do?"

A sigh accompanies her exaggerated eye roll. "Well, after all this you can't very well leave Molly with her in-laws, whom she hasn't seen in who knows how long."

"Now, Mabel," Lincoln purrs out, visibly trying to sooth his wife with a smoothing caress down her forearm, covered in a pale gray sweater. "We shouldn't interfere."

She shakes Linc off, turns around without further comment, and continues to clean up the kitchen. Linc eyes me and leans his head toward the sitting room. I get the idea and rise from my seat at the table and follow him. Mabel bangs the cookware and rattles the dishes a little too forcibly.

When we're out of earshot, Linc says, "Sorry. She's been terrible moody. Never seen her like this."

He expels a whoosh of air as he sits in his chair. I choose the couch.

"Is Mabel feeling better? With the stomach upset?" I ask.

Maybe her delicate condition has more to do with her angst, and not my action or inaction.

"Oh, that." Lincoln flicks his hand down, as if swatting a pest. "Didn't last long. Now, she's eating everything in sight." Linc cranes his neck and peers toward the kitchen then looks back at me. "But don't tell her I said so; I'll be sleeping in the barn if she finds out that I'm tattling on her."

"Oh? She's got an appetite, hey?" I tease.

"You could say so. One morning I saw her fixing up an apple

crisp before I went to the barn. By dinner time, it was gone, and I hadn't even gotten one bite."

I cringe. I can't imagine Mabel cramming in a whole dessert by herself.

"Must be cravings," I offer.

"Must be," he agrees.

We sit in silence for a few seconds.

Linc raises one eyebrow at me. "But…what *are* you going to do?"

I meet his gaze. "What happened to 'not interfering?'"

Linc smiles sheepishly. "Weeeell, you gotta do something."

I need to leave the next move up to Molly. "Do I? I feel I've done quite enough."

Linc rolls his marital wisdom out like a sage offering up advice. "One thing I've learned is that women always want you to go after them."

"Is that so? And how have you done so with Mabel?" I jokingly ask, but I do really want to know.

"Sometimes Mabel says she wants to be left alone, but she really needs a hug or for me to listen to what she has to say. I've learned not always to listen to what she says she wants. Or…doesn't want."

"That doesn't make any sense," I point out.

Lincoln nods. "You're telling me."

Genuine curiosity gets the better of me. "How do you know when to do the opposite of what she says?"

"Takes practice. I have to listen for the right tone in Mabel's voice. Sometimes, I still get it wrong," Linc admits, lifting his shoulders.

"Hmm, that sounds tiring."

He winks at me. "Can be, but it's well worth the effort."

"So, you think I should go back to Land 'O Lakes?" I scratch my head. "Molly said she needed time."

"Did she."

Linc says it directly, as an observation, not a question. His forefinger and thumb rest on either side of his chin, while he appears to study me.

I'm too tired to play games and thumb through the possible options. "Hmm, I think I better hit the hay."

I stifle a yawn. It's been a long day. Plus, I need to re-evaluate, in the quiet of my room, if I made the right decision, that is, leaving Molly.

"Samuel." Linc speaks my name with a brotherly familiarity. "It was good to hear about your mother. I'm glad you stopped to see her and that things are better between you two."

"Thanks. Me too." I get up. "Good night."

I nod and give him a sincere smile of gratitude. I leave the sitting room with careful steps, hoping to slip out, but the floorboards creak. Leaving anonymously won't be possible. Mabel turns from the sink, where she rinses what looks like the last dish. She wipes her hands on her apron.

"I didn't mean to lose my temper, earlier." Her eyes are soft and apologetic now. "It's just that you and Molly belong together; I know it. I've been praying for you both."

"Thanks. We surely need it." I offer her a warm smile. "Goodnight. Thank you for supper."

"Sleep well."

I can hear from her tone that there's more she'd like to say, but I'm glad she remains silent.

I nod, move past her, grab my coat, and leave, shutting the door quietly behind me. The thought of going to my lonely loft doesn't appeal to me. I don't want to be alone, but I am.

Please, God. Make a way where there is no way.

The prayer warms my heart as I crunch over the snow-covered yard to the barn. I realize Molly isn't the only woman in the world, but I recognize myself in her. I know who she is. We're alike, well suited to one another, and it's her I desire. I don't want to let her go, but maybe I have to. Maybe Linc is wrong with his philosophy of misplaced need. Maybe Molly is different.

I think hard about how we said goodbye. Was there a wistful longing in her eyes, like I felt in my gut? I think so, but I can't be sure. So, I left. What else could I have done? Anyway, it's no use dwelling on what-ifs.

I enter the barn, climb to the loft, and make ready for bed, all the while wishing Molly were here with me.

CHAPTER TWENTY-FOUR

Molly

Three days before Christmas

I still can't get used to the idea that Jacob has a son—I can't recall his name—with another woman.

Lonny.

With my head in my hands, I wonder if I'll ever stop grieving for my son and let him go.

A knock sounds on my door, and I sit up straight on the edge of the bed in the guest room at Clemmy's, taking a loud sniff and wiping under my nose with the back of my hand.

"Come in," I tell whoever has knocked.

The door creaks open. Janice stands in the doorway with a cup of tea. "I thought you might need a pick-me-up." She moves into the room, the heels on her shoes tapping against the floorboards, and sets the cup and saucer down on the bedside table. "May I?"

214

She points to the straight-back chair in the corner.

I manufacture a smile. "Of course."

She walks to the chair, swipes the seat of her gray, pleated skirt back, and sits. "Gosh, I'm done in, and it's only eleven-thirty in the morning."

It's been hours since Petra and her son left. I didn't speak to Jacob but went straight to my room to lie down after she'd gone. I don't want to talk with him about his past, a past I wasn't a part of.

Janice states the obvious, folding her hands in her lap. "It's been quite an eventful start to the day."

I grip the end of the crazy quilt on the bed and simply nod.

"And…" She grimaces at me. "You had no idea about…?"

She doesn't say the woman's name. I'd like to hate Petra—I don't know her surname—but I can't. Jacob bears the blame, at least according to me.

He had a son with another woman! The words shout in my head, and I want to vocally expel them, but I dampen the urge.

"No. Why would I? After all," I laugh bitterly, "remember that I hadn't heard from Jacob in five years. He certainly wasn't going to write and tell me about his son, after we'd lost ours…"

My voice breaks in the start of a sob, but I squelch it, swallowing down the pain and covering my mouth with my hand.

"I don't think he knew. Well, at least from what Ma told me."

While Petra and her son visited with Jacob, I took a walk. I didn't want to see or overhear them.

It makes the pain a little less if he didn't know. "You think?"

Janice raised one shoulder in a partial shrug. "I can't be sure, but it seems that way."

"And she's going with him to Colorado tomorrow?"

Janice nods. "That's what she said. I just got back from taking her to the hotel."

Then I'm not going with Jacob. It's both a relief and a letdown.

I speak the question in my head out loud. "What am I supposed to do now?"

"I'm not sure. That's up to you, of course, but Ma and I would love it if you stayed here."

A warm smile lifts Janice's lips.

Bur Oak Ridge, with its scenic outlook, cozy farmhouse, my kitten, and Samuel, suddenly comes to mind. As much as I care for Clemmy, Janice, and Celia, and their families, Bur Oak Ridge is more a home to me, especially now that I have no real purpose here. Most likely Jacob will spend time in jail and his…mistress will be there to visit him.

But what about me? Will I be tied to Jacob forever?

I pound my chest with one fist and let a deep, angry groan escape my lips. "Arrrrgh!"

"Go ahead. Cry, rave, whatever you want." Janice flips her hand in the air. "You have every right to be angry. The Lord knows I am."

"I can forgive him for being unfaithful but the boy…it hurts so bad."

Now, I fully give in to my pain and sob. Janice comes to sit next to me and slowly rubs circles on my back. She doesn't reprimand me or chatter but lets me cry.

Finally, the flood recedes. I wipe my eyes and nose with a crumpled hankie and look at her. She has tears in her eyes too.

"Men," she says and generalizes the core of the issue.

But I know that not all men are as fickle and weak as Jacob.

Samuel certainly isn't. I miss him. Seeing his face would bring me a measure of happiness. Have I truly forgiven him for shooting Jacob? Samuel could have killed him.

Yes, I suppose I have. This new chapter in our ill-fated saga has transferred more of the guilt onto Jacob, liar and adulterer that he is. Yet, I can't hate him.

Adulterer. The ugly word brings hope to my heart. It's my way out and a justifiable reason in the courts and the church for divorce. The thought of that word sickens me, for it was not how our life as a couple was supposed to turn out. But the first brick in the facade of our marriage commitment crumbled the day Jacob left. It eroded with his silence, weakened with my depression, and then completely tumbled when he took another woman to his bed.

Janice turns my chin, so I'm looking her way. "Not everything can be fixed. All things have an end sometime."

I know she speaks of Jacob and me.

I hold her accepting gaze. "It wasn't supposed to end like this."

"No, but life rarely goes how we plan it to." Janice stands up and walks to the door, which she left open. "Time to rustle up some lunch. Feel like anything in particular?"

"I'm not very hungry."

She seems not to hear. "Maybe some soup. That's always comforting." She turns to leave the room but pauses. "I do know a good lawyer, if you need one."

"You do?" I venture.

Janice leans against the door jamb. "Yes. A fella I went to school with. He lives in Green Bay now but is home for Christmas here in Land O' Lakes. I could give him a call, if you like."

Gratitude for this woman who is a real sister to me floods my heart. "That might be good. Thanks, Janice…for everything."

"You're welcome, Sis."

She gives me a quick wink and a curve of her lips and walks away. In a few seconds, I hear her opening cabinets in the kitchen, humming *Away in a Manger* to herself.

A seed of hope for the future, a future separate from Jacob, has taken root in my heart. I close my eyes and imagine the possibilities. Samuel occupies a corner of each one. I let my eyes roll open and truly smile for the first time in days.

Later that day

"I'm sorry."

I can't mistake the sincerity in Jacob's tone. We're alone, sitting across from each other in Clemmy's sitting room. Janice took Clemmy to her house this afternoon. I think she wanted to provide Jacob and me with some privacy.

Looking past Jacob out the windows behind him, I see that it has begun to lightly snow, though the sun still shines.

Jacob tries again. "I didn't mean for any of this to happen."

"Yet it did," I point out, catching his eyes for the first time.

What I discern to be a tinge of misery wrinkles his brow and etches lines I don't remember being there a few days ago around his mouth.

"We'd been separated for a long time."

I'm not giving him an inch. "Not by my choice."

"I needed comfort."

My arms remain crossed over my chest. "Apparently."

Why am I so angry with him?

"Good grief! Give me a break. I'm not a saint," he huffs in exasperation.

The hard knot in my heart won't budge. "Ha! No one would confuse you for one."

He sighs. "I'm trying to apologize. It's all I can do. I can't very well go back and change the past."

He's right.

"No." I give in a little and unfold my arms. "But a son, Jacob. A son!" My voice takes on a begging tone. "Can't you see how unfair this is?"

"Hey, this is the first I've heard about him, and it's not like I deliberately set out to hurt you."

He tips his head back on the cushioned headrest of Clemmy's chair, sighs, and pins me with resigned eyes. I relinquish more hurt.

"Ya, I can see that," I agree, and I settle down.

Jacob picks his head up and sits up straighter. "Petra and I were together for only a short while. I went off on a venture with some friends one day. When I returned, she had left. I did try to find her but gave up and then moved on.

"And she truly never told you about the boy?" I ask, needing to know.

"No. I haven't talked to her or seen her in years."

"How did she find you?"

"Saw my name in the paper in Denver and asked at the police station. Someone there told her I'd been rounded up, here in Wisconsin." Jacob shakes his head. "I can't believe she traveled all the way out here."

"What does she want from you?"

"I asked her the same thing. She said she wanted me to know I had a son before something happened to me." Jacob moves to the edge of his seat. "Don't think too badly of her; I never told her I was married."

Heat rises up my neck.

"And you had the gall to badger me about my friendship with Samuel," I spit out.

He raises his voice. "And I'm sorry. How many times do I have to say it?"

I'm glad Clemmy's not here to witness us arguing.

"I talked to a lawyer this afternoon," I toss at him

Sinking back in the chair, he frowns. "What? Really? Already?"

"It's time." Breathing out slowly, I release my pent-up feelings. "It's what's best."

"Maybe." With his thumb, he rubs his upper lip, an action I remember him doing when deep in thought. "Remember how happy we were…once?"

He turns sad, liquid eyes on me.

I can't help but melt somewhat. "Yes, but that was *so* long ago. We can't recreate the past. I think that's what we were trying to do by coming here." I recall his father's will. "I suppose you'll forfeit that stipulation in Cliff's will."

"That'd only be after Ma passes anyway. And it's not solely why I brought you here."

I nod, trying to think the better of him. "I'm glad to hear it."

I get up to get a drink of water. It's getting late. Clemmy and Janice should be back soon.

"Will you see me off tomorrow?" he asks, his voice and eyes hopeful.

I close my eyes momentarily at the tenderness I hear in his words.

I don't commit either way. "Perhaps."

I hear the rumble of a vehicle outside and walk to the window. It's still snowing.

"They're back," I say.

"This is it?" he questions me, clearly disappointed.

I don't know what he hoped for, after all that's transpired.

I stand up straighter and surprise myself with the firmness of my words. "It is."

Car doors slam, and I hear voices. I walk away from Jacob and the future he so carefully planned for us to open the door for Clemmy and Janice.

That evening

Everyone sleeps, well, at least, I think so. Clemmy's bedroom door is shut, and I hear Jacob softly snoring in the other room. I sit before the stove in the sitting room, trying to determine what to do. Should I stay here with Clemmy until the divorce paperwork is drawn up or go back to Bur Oak Ridge?

I'm not keen on traveling all that way by myself, nor do I have the money to do so. And can I get a train ticket and passage so close to Christmas?

No, best stay, my conscience tells me.

I think of last Christmas at the asylum. Wherever I decide to stay, it has to be better than that.

"More gingerbread?" Nurse Sandry asked me, her face not wearing her usual pinched look.

She held a tray with the remains of a gingerbread house the residents made together. I hadn't contributed.

Perhaps she has a heart after all, I told myself.

I passed up her offer. "No. Thank you."

The gingerbread house had lost its roof and a portion of one side. All the gumdrop decorations had been removed and devoured. Old Irene had hoarded most of those. She had a sweet tooth. The remains looked unappetizing.

Sandry moved on. A volunteer woman, Mrs. Clayton, from the local women's group, played Christmas music on the piano. A few residents stood around her, singing with varying degrees of aptitude. Others clustered at two round tables in the dining hall.

Mrs. Clayton waved me over. "Mrs. Lund, do come and join us."

I shook my head and held up my hand.

"Oh, no," I said as loud as I could over the music.

Old Lady Sal eyed me in a mischievous manner and giggled out, "She don't sing. She sounds like a toad." Although Sal was in her eighties, she had the mannerisms of a nine-year-old scamp. "Come croak for us, Molly!" she taunted, yelling above the music.

"Here, here! Enough of that now." Sandry drew up alongside Sal with a snarl on her face. "It's Christmas. Be more charitable."

Mrs. Clayton kept on playing.

Sal made a face behind Sandry's back when the nurse turned her attention to setting the tray down on a round table. The demolished cookie house only had two sides left. I didn't know how it stayed upright.

Mrs. Maynard sat near me in a red dressing gown, wrapping her red yarn ball.

She asked, "Ain't it a beautiful house?" and continued wrapping. She would get the yarn all wrapped up, then she'd unravel it again and start over. I'd never seen her without her ball of yarn. "I had me as nice a house once."

She smiled a gap-toothed grin at me, her gray eyes sunken in her darkened sockets.

I feigned interest. "Did you?"

"You have a home as fine as that?"

Her question made me study the dilapidated cookie structure again. "Not anymore."

"And my husband's a good man. Brings me back red yarn for a

present when he's gone traveling. I love red." She holds up her ball but doesn't miss a beat in wrapping her yarn. "What does your man bring home to you?"

She asked me like we were both happily married and not living in an insane asylum.

"Nothing," I told her.

"'Tis a shame."

She flicked her tongue with a "tsk, tsk" sound and started humming along with the chorus of "Oh, Holy Night."

I commenced counting my losses: no present husband, no home—other than the asylum—no son, no family, no one, really, other than the few friends of any sense that I'd made here.

"You have a Savior, who is Christ the Lord…"

The words in the song popped out at me, and I focused on listening to Mrs. Clayton. The group had finished singing hymns and sang a sweet chorus I'd never heard before, but I held onto those words. "You have a Savior."

I did have someone. The most important person. I dried the dampness that had gathered in the corners of my eyes, thanking God for His presence with me, despite all that I'd lost.

This year I know where Jacob is, I have friends who care about me and family in Clemmy, Janice, and Celia, and I suppose I have a home of sorts as well. But Lonny, of course, remains gone.

I stand, moving along the wall, brushing my hand on the cedar boughs Celia and her children hung up a few days ago. The woodsy, citrus smell rises in the air.

"God, where do I make my home? What should I do? Help me to know. Thank you for always being with me."

I close my whispered prayer with a silent amen. I believe I can rest now and let tomorrow bring what it will.

Reflect upon your present blessings—of which every man has many—not on your past misfortunes, of which all men have some.

Charles Dickens

CHAPTER TWENTY-FIVE

Samuel

Christmas Day

"Ho, ho." Lincoln holds up a new set of trousers against his frame. "Just right. Thanks, Mae. I sure needed another pair."

He smiles at his wife.

It's late afternoon. The Nelsons, myself, and my mother sit in the parlor, enjoying mulled cider, popcorn, and sugar cookies, while we open gifts. A record of Christmas symphony music plays on the phonograph in the dining room.

"You're welcome." Mabel leans over and hands Lincoln another gift, wrapped in brown paper and green string. "That was the practical gift. This is the fun one."

She smiles handsomely, her dark eyes twinkling. Lincoln takes the gift and shakes it.

"Oh?" he asks and hefts it in the air. "Hmm."

"Open it, silly," Mabel encourages Lincoln.

Linc sits down next to her in his chair and unties the string.

Mother watches from the couch with the kitten, Mittens, tucked close to her side on a blanket, and I sit cross-legged on the floor. King lounges nearby.

"Come on!" Mabel demonstrates with an imaginary package. "Give it a rip."

"Hold your horses. I'm getting there."

Lincoln rips off the rest of the paper and reveals a leather roll. He unrolls the leather, which harbors a fine set of woodcarving tools.

He whistles. "Oh, my. Mabel, how did you…where'd you get the money?"

He fingers each tool and lovingly replaces them in the roll.

Mabel sends a wink Linc's way. "A lady never reveals her secrets."

He leans toward her and places a kiss on her cheek. "Your turn." Linc stands up and lifts his index finger in the air. "One momento."

He hurries out of the room and walks to the entryway and out of sight.

"Do you know what he's up to?" Mabel asks me.

I shrug. "Friends never tattle."

"She glares my way with one eye. "Hmmm…"

Mother sits quietly crocheting, lifting her eyes to smile at us once in a while. Mittens batts at the yarn now and then. I'm glad Mabel prodded me to ask Mother here for Christmas.

Soon Linc walks back in the room, holding a large object under a quilt. He places it at Mabel's feet. "Well, go on. Take it off."

Mother lowers her work, clearly interested in Lincoln's Christmas surprise.

Mabel peels back the quilt. "Oh!" A hand flies to her mouth

and tears start brimming from her doe-like eyes. "Oh, Lincoln. How precious."

A beautiful cradle sits before Mabel. I've no doubt Linc made it, though I don't know when. It's a lightly stained, wooden baby bed on a stand. Mabel's gentle touch sets it in a rocking motion.

Mother leans forward, her eyes roving over the cradle. "That is lovely workmanship, Lincoln."

Linc nods, replying, "Thank you kindly, Mrs. Skaggs, for the compliment. I wish I'd have had these chisels when I made it. I could have added some decorative etchings."

Mabel dries her eyes with a hankie she pulls out of her sleeve. She tucks it away again and sniffs loudly. "It's beautiful as it is. Thank you."

"Now for Samuel." Mabel points under the Christmas tree, decorated with popcorn strings, dried fruit, crocheted snowflakes, and candles in colorful tin holders. "The puffy one," she directs me.

I retrieve the package, wondering what can be inside. "You really shouldn't have," I tell her, and I remove the butcher's paper. A thick, blue, crocheted blanket appears under the paper. "Just what I need to keep me warm. Thanks, Mabel."

Mabel smiles at me and says, "It was Molly's idea, and she made most of it. I just finished it for her, after she…well, after she left."

Molly. Here but not here.

"That's nice."

I run my hand over the softness and wish she could be here with us.

Lincoln holds out a small package to me. "Got you something too."

"Gee, thanks," I tell him.

He nods and smiles, settling back in his chair.

I open the small, white box and pull out a silver money clip with the initials S. W. on it in scrolling font. "That's swell. Thanks for thinking of me."

I offer Linc my hand, and we grasp each other's hands in a friendly shake.

"Now you can keep your cash all together, instead of having crumpled bills in your pocket," Lincoln points out.

"Yes, that'll be grand." I pause for a second then announce, "I have something for both of you."

I look at Linc and Mabel. I pluck an envelope etched in gold foil off the tree and hand it to Mabel.

Her nut-brown eyes widen. "What could this be?" She flips it over, breaks the red, wax seal, and begins reading. *"This certificate good for one family portrait at Holland Studios, Pleasant View, 301 Third Street."* Handing the paper to Linc, she says, "That is kind, Samuel. How fun it will be to get a family portrait done after the baby is born. It's very thoughtful, Thank you so much!"

Linc bobs his head at me and grins. "That'll be a treat. Thanks, Sam,"

"Please fetch that green package, Linc," Mabel tells her husband.

Linc reaches under the tree and picks up a package the size of a book but thicker. "This one?"

"Hand that to Mrs. Skaggs," Mabel directs Linc.

He obeys.

Mother takes the gift. "For me?" A pink bloom appears on her cheeks. "You didn't need to go to any fuss. It's nice being here with you on this holiday in your home. Your hospitality is enough."

Mabel looks at Mother and says, "It was no trouble and is only something small to let you know that we are glad you're with us."

Mother smiles. "All the same, thank you." She opens her gift, a fine set of embroidered tea towels with red geraniums. "Geraniums are a favorite flower of mine. How did you know?"

Mabel smiles warmly. "Samuel let it slip one time; I'm a good listener."

Mother caresses the towels, looking more content than I've seen her in a long while. "It's very kind and so well-rendered. Thank you."

"You're welcome," Mabel responds.

I notice the music beginning to lag.

Lincoln gets up to crank the machine. "Oop, better go wind the phonograph; it's wearing down."

King pads after him.

Mabel gets up slowly out of her chair and picks up a plate from the tea table, hovering it under all our faces. "Who's ready for more cookies?"

Linc plucks two from the plate. Mother and I pass.

Mother pulls a package out of her yarn bag and hands it to me. "I thought you might find this handy."

I accept the package with a smile and open it, uncovering a buttery soft, leather-bound journal. "I surely will. I've almost filled mine up."

"You always were scribbling in little books since you could write. Ever thought about submitting your work?" Mother asks, as she pets Molly's kitten.

I shrug, puzzled at her encouragement. Growing up, she was not one to nurture my abilities. "Never crossed my mind. I just jot my thoughts down and some poetry sometimes. Nothing anyone would be interested in reading, surely."

"You never can tell." She looks down at her lap, smoothing over the stitches of her workmanship. "I didn't always say, but I'm proud of the man you've become."

Mother lifts her face, her eyes glistening.

"Thank you. That means a lot," I stammer. She's never told me this before; I would have remembered. Recovering from the shock of her declaration, I say, "I have a gift for you as well."

I stand, making my way to the Christmas tree and pulling another small package from atop several branches. I hand it to her.

She flutters her eyelids; I can see the purple veins in them, her skin, crepe-papery and thin. Mother appears so much older to me now than before Dad died.

"Why, Samuel, how thoughtful." With the greatest of care, she opens the package, wrapped in tissue paper and tied with a red ribbon. "It's lovely!" She pulls out the silk scarf, painted with geraniums, that I bought for her in town at the women's boutique. "You're so thoughtful to remember my preferences. Like your father that way. God rest his soul."

She drapes the scarf around her shoulders.

My heart aches, remembering Dad.

"Do you miss him?" I ask.

I sure do. Dad was a good, kindhearted man. Steady and solid. The person I'd always looked up to.

Running several fingers over the silk, she answers, "Of course. How could I not?"

"I thought with Alfred…"

I don't finish.

"Just because I chose to make a life with Alfred didn't mean that I forgot your father. I'll always love him, but Alfred was there and treated me kindly."

"I'm glad he did."

I want to remind her of the man's threats and conniving ways, but it's better off to leave all that to rest. He's dead, and digging up his past actions won't help her or me any.

Mabel joins us. "I'd say it's time to light the tree."

Talking of the past with Mother is done for now, but I can rest easier, knowing we are on good terms and headed toward a brighter future.

"It's getting dark out." Linc holds out a long, lit matchstick. "Who wants to do the honors?"

"*Arf*," King barks, standing at his master's elbow as usual, looking up with hopeful eyes.

Linc laughs and pets King's head. "Someone with hands?"

"I guess I can."

I take the stick and move to the tree to light each candle. Soon the tree shines with light, to represent The Light of the World, Emmanuel, God with Us. I wave out the stick and it extinguishes with a trail of smoke.

Mabel holds Linc's hand and gazes at the lit tree with awe. "Isn't that beautiful?"

A deep desire to have Molly near me aches inside, almost like the growing pains I had as a kid. *Perhaps I will have to learn to grow, to be separated from Molly? Maybe she won't come back to Bur Oak Ridge.*

My heart sinks momentarily, until Mother starts singing "Silent Night," and the rest of us join in. A flush of warmth and joy resonates in the small parlor as we lift our voices. But when we reach the last stanza, a new voice rings in my ears. I turn, searching in the dim interior for its owner. I suppose we were singing so loud we didn't hear anyone enter. Mabel turns and looks too. I squint, trying to determine who has joined us.

A form approaches in the shadows. The voice draws nearer, sweet but a little raw in parts, just like…

Molly!

231

CHAPTER TWENTY-SIX

Molly

Mabel squeals with glee and reaches out to me as they end the song. "My Christmas wish has come true!"

Linc moves to my side and pats me on the shoulder. "Well, the stray sheep is back among the fold."

Mabel clings to my neck.

I laugh and inch away from Mabel's near chokehold. "Let a woman catch her breath, why don't ya?"

I catch Samuel's eyes. His slow, steady smile filled with the warmth and love I hoped for greets me. My heart won't stop pounding extra hard at my elation at being with those I love this Christmas.

"And…?" Mabel releases me, glances over my shoulder, then studies my face, probably wondering how and why I'm here. The candlelight deepens and darkens the shadows under her eyes, making Mabel appear older. Unshed tears glisten in her eyes. "I thought you'd be in Colorado by now. How is that you're with us instead?" With a hand over her heart, Mabel states, "Don't get me wrong. I'm thrilled that you're here, but…"

Putting a hand on Mabel's arm, Lincoln says, "Now, dear. Let's get a warm-up on the drinks. More hot cider everyone?" He doesn't wait for any answers and motions to Mrs. Woodson, or should I say Mrs. Skaggs? "Come with my wife and me, Mrs. Skaggs. We may need an extra pair of hands."

Mrs. Skaggs blinks. "If you wish." She takes Linc's extended hand, and he helps her up. "Mrs. Lund."

Samuel's mother acknowledges me, in an almost friendly manner, as she moves to pass by me, which surprises me, greatly. I am happy she's here with Samuel for Christmas. It must mean that he's mended fences with her.

I nod and offer a smile. "Merry Christmas."

She smiles and walks past, head held high. "Yes, it is."

Tugging at Mabel's elbow, Linc leads his wife toward the kitchen. "Come along, Mae."

"But I want to talk with Molly and hear how…" Mabel protests.

She turns her head half back.

Linc sends a sideways look toward Samuel but tells Mabel, "Time enough for that later."

"Hmm," Mabel growls out, but she follows Linc, the heels of her shoes clicking briskly on the floor.

When Samuel and I are alone, he steps close to me and places his hands behind my upper arms, cradling my muscles with care. "I don't understand how you're here." He almost whispers the words as he examines my eyes in the flickering light. "But I'm sure glad you are."

I can't look away from the heady glow within his irises, which reflect a deep emerald tonight, instead of their usual hazy blue-green.

I can't resist teasing him. "Well, there are such things as trains."

He chuckles. "Yes, but why are you here and not with…?"

Samuel falls serious and doesn't say Jacob's name. I don't blame him. I want to forget too.

I offer a partial explanation, gazing up at him. "It turns out Jacob didn't need me after all."

One of Samuel's hands moves up to my neck. I lean in closer, echoing his position, continuing to stare up at him with hopeful eyes. His manly scent of woodsmoke and cedar surrounds me, relaxing me, yet arousing me at the same time. I turn my lips up; his eyes flick to them for a moment. The room and the ambient sounds blur as Samuel's lips graze mine.

He expels a question like a soft breath against my cheek, and my skin tingles. "You…forgive me, then?"

I turn my lips to his and ask, teasingly, "What do you think?"

Resisting no longer, my lips greet his, welcoming the man I love with hope resting in my heart.

He responds in turn, drawing me closer, wanting more. "Wait." He suddenly tilts his head back. "What changed? I have to know."

He pulls slightly back from me. But I grab the front of his shirt, drawing him back, my chest resting against him.

"Everything," I utter, my lips lingering inches from his neck.

He tips my head up.

"Tell me more," he softly commands.

I give him the details about Petra and her son—Jacob's son

Samuel huffs out a breath he must have been holding. He pulls me closer in a tight embrace. His breath ruffles the stray hairs at my temple.

"I'm sorry. That must have been difficult to take in," he says.

"It was," I admit. I tilt my head back, looking directly at him. "But," I smile widely, ignoring the tightness on my scarred side, "it's our way out."

"It is?"

I point to my traveling case. "I already have the legal papers to prove it."

A wrinkle forms on Samuel's brow. "What if this woman hadn't come along? Would you have gone with him?"

I nod slowly. "I think I would have, out of duty, at least until his family and I knew what his sentence would be, if found guilty. I owed it to Clemmy and Jacob's sisters, if nothing else. I…" I focus on him with honesty. "I never stopped loving you, Samuel. You were and are my heart's desire."

I want to make sure he understands how engaged my heart is.

Samuel crushes me to his chest. My eyes roll closed in delight as I hear his words.

"And mine, my darling…and mine."

His kisses trace my jawline and my neck; I melt into them, giving even my scars to him, filled with joy at the love of a good man, who cares for me, just as I am.

"Merry Christmas, my love," Samuel says between kisses.

I whisper back an echo. "Merry Christmas."

Ah! Sweet mystery of life
At last I've found thee
Ah! I know at last the secret of it all;
All the longing, seeking, striving, waiting, yearning.

From the song "Ah, Sweet Mystery of Life"
by Nelson Eddy

CHAPTER TWENTY-SEVEN

Samuel

February 1921

The fire burns low in the stove, and the candle on top of the crate next to me flickers in the draft coming from under the loft door. Seated in my chair, I drape the blanket Molly crocheted around my shoulders to block the chill and open the new diary Mother gave me at Christmas. The clean but tangy scent of the blank pages make me smile. I always did like the smell of paper. Deciding to christen it, I pick up a pencil and begin to write.

I can't believe my prayers have been answered, and I have Molly's heart and hand, or soon will have. The divorce is final, and Molly is free. Tomorrow night, I'll ask her to marry me, official-like, under the stars. I am confident she'll still say yes.

I'm not exactly sure what the future will hold for us, but I have a few ideas. I think I'll submit those to God and listen. I've learned to be better at that, and I've come to realize that I need God. I didn't always think that way, but I sure made a mess of things for a while. And I am grateful He helped set my feet on a better path. One that led to Him and to Molly.

Molly. I can hardly remember my life before her. She has become my world, and I look forward to spending every day of my life with her. I'm grateful that Jacob Lund didn't realize what he had in her. Oh, I'm sorry Molly had to go through all the hurt their marriage caused her and all the grief of losing her son, but I am glad it eventually led to me.

I don't even see her scars anymore. In truth, I never really did. The first time I met her, I recognized her heart and, eventually, she mine. It is my prayer that we will always continue to do so. May I be the husband she deserves.

From the song "Blue Skies"
by Ella Fitzgerald

EPILOGUE

Molly

November 1921

Bur Oak Ridge

Mabel holds the baby, wrapped in a baby-blue, crocheted blanket in a puffed, popcorn stitch, and asks, "Well, what does he say?"

We sit together on the back porch, sharing tea and overlooking the fledged-out trees on the hillsides. The bright green of new spring leaves sparkles like distant emeralds in the sun. A waft of plum blossom floats over from somewhere, reminding me that not all sweetness can be tasted. The rhythm of Mabel's rocker on the porch floorboards comforts me, but a twinge of sadness presses on my chest.

I fold Jacob's letter back up and tuck it in my apron pocket.

"That they've split up," I tell her. He's written me a few

times, and I've written back. I go back to stitching the hem of a garment I've sewn for little Charlie, but he fusses in Mabel's arms. I lay down my sewing on a small table and hold out my hands. "Want me to take him?"

Mabel relinquishes my son to me. "I suppose he'll want his mother for a feeding."

I never thought I'd be thinking those words again. *My son.* After Mabel deposits Charlie in my arms, I arrange my blouse for him to suckle. I stroke his butter-soft cheek and marvel again at the gift Samuel and I have been given. We married in March, and now we are thrilled that our family has grown with the addition of Baby Charlie.

"And what of Jacob?" Mabel asks when she sits back in her rocker. "Is he still in prison?"

"For now, but he did write that he may get out early for good behavior."

She shakes her head. "Doesn't seem fair. In my opinion, he's been nothing but bad. He should serve his full sentence. The judge was awfully lenient in his regard."

Mabel huffs and takes a sip of her tea, her hand cradling the delicate teacup.

"I don't wish Jacob any ill will. And I am very sad about him and Petra. He's entitled to a bit of happiness, and so is she."

The tug of Charlie at my breast fills me with peace. A joyful sense I could never manufacture wraps me in a fuzzy warmth. I'll always love and miss my first son, Lonny, but here in my arms lies a new hope. With Charlie's presence, the ghost of Lonny has disappeared. Thank God.

"You're far too kind to that man. After all he's pulled." Mabel huffs. "Anyway, where's his woman gone?"

"Back to her family in northern Minnesota, it seems." I

reposition Charlie and hold him to my shoulder for a burp; he obliges. Sympathy for Petra's circumstances crowds my joy slightly. It must have been difficult for her to move back home with a child whose father languishes in prison. She's likely become the brunt of local gossip.

Mabel's eyes sparkle, and she leans forward, placing her hands on her knees. "Enough talk of Jacob. Let's discuss something far more interesting." She grins. "Guess what?"

I lower Charlie to my other breast. "What?"

"I'm expecting."

I glance to her middle, no hint of enlargement yet. "So soon?"

Bridget, Mabel and Linc's daughter, is less than a year old.

She nods and smiles. A cry sounds from the house.

"Oop, somebody's awake from her nap."

Mabel smiles and scuttles away to free Bridget from her crib.

I close my eyes and lean back, rocking both Charlie and myself on the bench swing. A silent prayer of gratitude rises in my spirit for all the blessings that have come to me in this place of beauty, love, friends, and family. What more could anyone ask for?

I still keep in touch with Clemmy, Janice, and Celia. Samuel said that maybe we could visit come winter. After all, I think of them as family and always will. We might even stop by and see Mabel's sister Robin and her husband and daughter on the way. I relish the thought of seeing my friend again. No one else understands my time in the asylum like Robin does.

Samuel and his mother decided to sell their home farm. She split the funds from the sale with him, and we've used the money to invest in Bur Oak Ridge. Linc and Samuel went to a lawyer to set up a farm partnership, and we live here on the farm with them. Nothing could have made us happier. Samuel and I love it here and feel we made the right choice.

Mrs. Skaggs bought a small house in town, which has little upkeep. She enjoys her life and stays active in the local women's club and volunteers at the library. Many a Sunday, we invite her over for a meal. She and I have warmed to each other, and I no longer sense that she wishes her son had chosen someone more unscathed by trials, both physically and figuratively speaking.

I sigh; my eyes wander over the hillside, the well-kept farm buildings, and the cows dotting the pasture. Tears of thanksgiving well up in my eyes, making everything appear as if I'm looking through the rain, reflecting a rainbow of happiness.

I'll be forever grateful to Mabel for her invitation to us to partake of life with her and Linc here on Bur Oak Ridge, where love found me, scarred though I was, when I least expected it.

The End.

Acknowledgments

I am grateful for the many eyes who have seen and read this work before it has found its way to you. My early readers and those in my Facebook group, Journeying with Jenny, have given me much support, advice, and encouragement along the way.

My family is supportive, as always, of my endeavors in authorship, and I would not be on this path without the continual strength I receive from God.

Thank you, Dear Reader, for choosing to spend your valuable time reading my words.

Many blessings,

Jenny

About Jenny

Jenny lives in Wisconsin with her husband, Ken, and their pet Yorkie, Ruby. She is also a mom and loves being a grandma. She enjoys many creative pursuits but finds writing the most fulfilling.

Spending many years as a librarian in a local public library, Jenny recently switched to using her skills as a floral designer in a retail flower shop. She is now retired from work due to disability. Her education background stems from psychology, music, and cultural missions.

She holds membership in the: Midwest Independent Booksellers Association, Wisconsin Writers Association, Christian Indie Publishing Association, and Independent Book Publishers Association.

Jenny's favorite place to relax is by the western shore of Lake Superior, where her novel series *By the Light of the Moon* is set.

She deems a cup of tea and a good book an essential part of every day. When not writing, Jenny can be found reading, tending to her many houseplants, or piecing quilt blocks at her sewing machine.

Her new historical fiction, four-part series titled *Sheltering Trees* is set in the area Jenny grew up in, where she currently lives, and places along Minnesota's Northern Shore, where she loves to visit. She is currently writing a four-part novella series titled *Botanical Seasons.*

Keep current with Jenny by visiting her website at https://jennyknipfer.com. Ways to connect with Jenny via social media, newsletter, and various book sites can be found on her website.

JENNY BY THE SHORES OF LAKE SUPERIOR

Coming next:

By Broken Birch Bay

A mystery

Dark shadows and white light,
You are a harmonious blend of life.

Ode to a Cluster of Birch Trees, Stanza 1

CHAPTER ONE

May 15th, 1925
Stillwater Prison, Stillwater, Minnesota
In a yard enclosed by wire fencing, I sit on a hard bench, backed by the most graceful cluster of birches I have ever seen; their spring leaves gleam a brilliant green. The trees inspire me to write a poem—something I haven't done in ages—about them, and I may just do that. They look so different to the broken stand of birches by the bay at home. So different to me.

"How?" you might ask.

What's my story? It's one dappled with darkness and light like anyone's. Let me tell you how it happened—who killed who and why.

I'm going to shock you, now…

You're capable of killing. Everyone is. I can hear your thoughts:

"I would never. No! Not me." But you're wrong. You don't know what lengths you'll go to until you must. Never think yourself too good, too righteous, for such a sin. Wasn't it Jesus who said that if you so much as hate a person, you commit murder in your heart?

Then I've done it—murdered someone. More than once. In my heart. But did I in reality? I recall nothing but the stillness of the air and the ringing in my ears—buzzing as if my head were a live hive of bees. Then those two pale faces, witnesses to my act, and that unmoving form, just lying there, splayed out like a bird who's crashed into the window.

I saw a little sparrow, the day before, die that way. One second he flitted and dove. The next he lay on his side, on the concrete step, wings extended slightly, feet curled under, and his beady eye closed. And when do birds ever have their eyes closed?

But those eyes, surprised, spent, drained of that unexplainable light that's present when the spirit still dwells in the body. Only emptiness stared back at me.

That image will haunt me until my dying day.

August 1924
Almost one year prior
Broken Birch Bay, Minnesota

Petra Livingston was named for a dead city, and that's often how she felt. As if life had passed her by, leaving her stuck, locked in the past, its head ever looming over her like ancient ruins.

Crunched up, her knees to her chest, rump firmly planted on the pebbly shore of Lake Superior, she thought back to when the mountains of Colorado captured her heart, along with the dark eyes of a troubled man. Back then, she had told herself that she'd never come back home, to Broken Birch Bay, but that had been a lie or a false hope. Petra watched the rolling waves of Superior, reliving the past and hesitant to move forward with the future.

Can I move forward, or is my life as broken as the stand of birch trees surrounding the bay?

Gazing up at the semi-ring of black and white trunks, Petra studied the trees. The birches looked as if a giant wind had come and snapped off all the tops of the trees, or perhaps they'd been sawed off by a legendary giant lumberjack. Either way, the headless trees reminded Petra of her prior life, a chapter in her existence she'd like to forget. The only good thing that had come from her adventure away from home was Jefferson, her son.

My light and joy every day.

Rather than tell people her son's father was in prison, her folks had doctored up a tale for Petra to stick to. Apparently, her husband, a miner, died of sickness out West, and she came home, a widow with a child to raise on her own. But it wasn't true, at least not the first part.

Petra had come home with a son but had never married, and Jacob had never mined a day in his life. And as far as she knew, he was alive and well and out of prison now. He hadn't come looking for her, nor had Petra expected him to.

We've burned our bridges, and it can stay that way.

"Look at this one, Momma."

Jefferson scrambled over to Petra, his pockets bulging with stones, one large specimen clutched in his hand, his medium-brown hair tousled in the breeze off the Great Lake. He sported a crooked grin on his slightly pudgy, rosy-cheeked, six-year-old face, and a twinkle shone in his dark eyes.

Setting her writing aside, Petra said, "Let's see." She held her thin hand out, and he deposited the cold, wet, sparkling stone in her palm. She examined it, turning it over and over. "Looks like crystal quartz. It's a beauty."

A smile spread her large mouth wider. She was glad that her son scoured the shore of the bay for semi-precious gemstones, just like she had at his age.

He picked the stone out of Petra's hand and held it up to the sunshine. "Maybe Gramps can make a necklace out of this one." The waves rolled and crashed in the background. "Maybe he'll ask me to help."

His eyes widened; he wanted more of his grandpa.

Petra didn't give him too much hope. "Perhaps."

Though her aged father, interested in all things old—thus, her name—enjoyed making jewelry out of stones found along the shore of Superior, he had not asked Jefferson, her sweet but illegitimate child, to assist him. She wasn't sure why.

Maybe he's punishing me by keeping Jefferson from his hobby, his love of the craft.

Dad pitted her against Honey, her sister, in a passive-aggressive way. *"Honey's found a good man with a steady job."*

As siblings, Honey and Petra had had no qualm with each other, except for their teenage spats over things, which now Petra couldn't recall. Still, it hurt—Dad's favor for Honey. When Petra had skipped out on their small backwater town and ways a few years ago, she had left Dad miffed.

Hurt, I suppose, at my getting out from under his fatherly thumb.

Petra's mother, Polly, didn't have a way of holding a grudge like Petra's father, Luke, did. She had welcomed Petra and Jefferson with open arms the day Petra had come back, as if nothing hung between them. A year later, her father still bristled when Petra spoke to him of anything from her time away from home. He'd like to forget, Petra was sure, that she'd left Broken Birch Bay. But Jefferson presented a constant reminder. But though not fully free with Jefferson, Dad loved his grandson. The sparkle in his eyes when he talked with Jefferson told her so.

Jefferson moaned, standing on one foot, at arm's length in front of Petra, with his arms stuck out for balance. "I'm hungry. I wonder if Grandma's made that blackberry pie she said she was gonna make."

He switched to standing on both legs and licked his lips, his eyes glimmering like the dark stripe on a piece of tiger's eye.

Petra had found one of those gemstones once, when she was a girl. Dad had polished it up, hung it as a pendant from a gold chain, and given it back to her. *"For you to remember that we all have light and darkness in us. There's only One who contains no darkness at all. It's Him you must look to. Let Him transform your dark stripes to golden. Only He can."*

He had clasped the pendant around her neck, and it had fallen heavy between her small breasts, a weight she still remembered. She had stroked the glittery, golden striation of the rock's color, wishing to always live in the light.

But the shadows must come.

Petra wondered where the necklace was now. She hadn't seen it in years. But just as Dad had told her, darkness and light dwelled in everyone, and the dividing line between them was shady at best. For a man spouting truth, Dad sat far from perfectly living in the light. His frustration with Petra had transformed into a stumbling block of sorts, making him blind to his own faults.

But then, aren't we all?

Standing, Petra held out her hand to Jefferson, her stomach growling at the thought of Mom's homemade pie. "Let's go see about that pie, shall we?"

Jefferson grinned wider and took her hand, stuffing his rock in his pants pocket with his other hand. Together they advanced on the slight hillside and made off for home. He pulled her along at a clip, propelled by his hunger to get back to her folks she was sure.

However, Petra wasn't eager to return. She tasted freedom and possibilities, here by the lake and the broken birches. Though she was grateful her parents let them stay, she felt it time to establish a home for Jefferson and herself, but how could she, when she was a mother with no real job or income? Petra kept asking herself that question and kept getting no reply.

I'm scared. That's it.

Perhaps. A nameless fear of something loomed in her future, haunting her.

Silly. How can it cling to me when it hasn't happened?

However, the future wasn't like the past, unchangeable and forever a memory. It was a morphing shadow, as if a murder of crows in the sky, dipping this way and that, unpredictable in its destination.

She wondered how many dark and light stripes remained in her life.

What will life bring me? Must I wait for it to deposit what it will, or can I take the lead and forge my own way ahead with my son?

She didn't know. Not yet. But her heart whispered that she would soon.

Made in the USA
Monee, IL
07 July 2026